CRYSTAL

CRYSTAL

HEATHER BURNSIDE

An Aria Book

First published in the UK in 2020 by Head of Zeus Ltd
This paperback edition first published in the UK in 2022 by Head of Zeus Ltd,
part of Bloomsbury Publishing Plc

9 7 5 3 1 2 4 6 8

A CIP catalogue record for this book is available from the British Library.

ISBN (PB): 9781803282923
ISBN (E): 9781789542097

Typeset by Silicon Chips

Printed and bound in Great Britain by
CPI Group (UK) Ltd, Croydon CR0 4YY

Head of Zeus
5–8 Hardwick Street
London EC1R 4RG

www.headofzeus.com

In memory of my dad, Leonard Ross

10.03.1929 – 22.02.2020

I

'I was there when he died,' sobbed Crystal.

'What?' asked Ruby.

'Gilly. I was there when he died.'

Ruby tensed on hearing Crystal's words and watched as Crystal's tears and mucus slid off the end of her nose and dribbled into her pint of lager. 'For fuck's sake!' she hissed and her eyes wandered across the table to Amber, Angie and Sapphire.

Fortunately they were deep in conversation and didn't appear to have heard what Crystal said. But Ruby was taking no chances. The state Crystal was in, she could come out with anything. Ruby might have known it would come to this. Crystal had been inconsolable throughout the funeral and had taken a good measure of brandy to calm her down even before they got to the crematorium.

The funeral had been a wretched affair. Although a few of Gilly's cronies from the Rose and Crown had showed up there was no sign of any family or other friends. Ruby wondered what he had done in his life to make even his own family not wish to attend.

Once they'd arrived at the Rose and Crown for the wake, Crystal's mood didn't improve. As melancholy music played over the pub's speakers, she had downed anything she could get her hands on as well as taking regular trips to the ladies, presumably to load up on coke. But, instead of making her mellow, the drugs and booze seemed to have made her more sombre.

'Come on, we're going,' said Ruby, slamming her drink down on the table and grabbing hold of Crystal's arm.

This caught the attention of the other girls who stared across at Ruby and Crystal. 'I'm taking her home,' said Ruby. 'She's pissed.'

'No, I'm not going,' Crystal drawled.

'You fuckin' are!' said Ruby, tightening her grip. She stood up and pulled Crystal to standing. At almost six foot tall Ruby towered over Crystal who was of average height.

The other girls resumed their conversation, not wishing to get involved. Ruby was known to have a fierce temper and if she said it was time for Crystal to go then they didn't want to challenge her. The feel of Ruby's sharp talons in her arm brought Crystal to her senses and she stood up ready to leave but not before she had tried to down the rest of her pint in one go, spilling most of it over the table.

'Put the fuckin' thing down! We're going,' Ruby repeated.

The girls waited till Ruby had dragged Crystal away from the table before they said their goodbyes.

'You take care, Crystal,' said Sapphire, a young girl with dark hair and a perma-tan.

Amber and Angie muttered their own words of support as Crystal staggered towards the pub exit, supported by Ruby who kept a firm grip on her arm.

'What the fuck are you playing at blabbing off in there?'

demanded Ruby once they were outside. 'Anyone could have fuckin' heard!'

Crystal muttered incoherently and Ruby could tell she was beyond reason. It was obvious she'd have to get her sobered up before she could get any sense out of her. But Crystal's words had grabbed her attention and she was determined to get to the bottom of it.

'Come on, I'll take you to mine. Then we can talk.'

Crystal raised her eyes momentarily before her head lolled again and she allowed herself to be led to Ruby's car.

As soon as they arrived at Ruby's luxury home in Altrincham, she sat Crystal down on a kitchen chair; there was no way she was chancing her throwing up all over the sofa. Then she began plying her with coffee and water to sober her up. It was still an hour before Crystal was in a fit state to hold a conversation.

'Right,' said Ruby. 'I want to know what the fuck's been going on because as far as I was aware Gilly died from a drugs overdose in that rancid flat where he lived. And that's what the fuckin' police think happened too.'

Ruby's concern wasn't for Gilly who had been Crystal's pimp and partner. In Ruby's opinion the man had got what was coming to him. He'd never been any good and Ruby was still confused as to why Crystal had gone back to him after he'd been released from prison for beating her unconscious. Ruby had warned her off him plenty of times but it didn't seem to make any difference; Crystal always went back for more.

But she was worried about Crystal. If she had been with Gilly when he died then it meant she could land herself in a lot of trouble. And, as Crystal's long-time friend, Ruby felt responsible for her and wanted to help her.

They had been through a lot together. Now the madam of her own brothel, as well as a dominatrix, Ruby had come a long way and part of that was down to Crystal's help. Crystal had been the first person Ruby had met in central Manchester's red light district back when they were both just teenagers.

She had had a bad time at Whalley Range and had been glad of Crystal's help at the time when Crystal provided her with a pimp and showed her how things worked in the city centre. They had even lived together at one point in Ruby's former flat in Whalley Range. And when Crystal had suffered the vicious beating from Gilly, Ruby had been the one who had come to her rescue.

Since then Ruby had always felt protective of Crystal. Where Crystal could be weak at times, Ruby was strong and feisty and, although her friend had made daft decisions in the past, Ruby knew that she was basically a sound person and a loyal friend who would always do you a good turn. She also doted on her daughter, Candice, and tried to do the best she could for her.

Now that Crystal was starting to sober up, her tears returned. Ruby felt for her, she really did; it can't have been easy to lose her partner. But it was the choice of partner that bothered Ruby. It was difficult to show empathy when he had treated Crystal so badly over the years. By now Ruby's patience was wearing thin and this latest revelation only added to her stresses. But she knew she'd have to take a softer approach if she was to get anything more from Crystal.

She took Crystal's hands in hers. 'Come on, girl. Out with it,' she said. 'I can't help you if I don't know what's gone on, can I?'

Crystal choked back a sob then spoke. 'I was at the flat. The night he died.' The impact of her words brought another sob and she held back for a moment, trying to recover herself.

'What do you mean? The police found him on his own.'

'I know,' Crystal cried. 'But I was there with him. My mum and dad had Candice for the night so we went back to his. I-I did a runner, Ruby.' She burst into tears again then looked up at Ruby, her face a picture of guilt. 'I shit myself. I didn't expect that to happen. We were just enjoying a few lines like usual. Then we both fell asleep. In the morning I couldn't wake him up and I didn't know what the fuck to do.'

The words were spilling from her now as she worked herself up into a frenzy. Ruby let go of her hands, then put her arms around her and cradled her head in a comforting embrace. 'Eh, eh, it's OK,' she said.

Crystal pulled away till she was facing Ruby, but she wouldn't meet her eyes. 'No, it isn't!' she shrieked. 'I only got to spend a few more months with him. He was so glad to get out of the nick but he didn't get a chance to enjoy his freedom. And now he's fuckin' dead. He didn't deserve to die like that! I should have stayed with him. No one deserves to die on their own.'

'How come the police aren't looking for anyone?' asked Ruby, focusing on damage limitation.

5

'I covered my tracks.' Crystal had now lowered her voice as though she was ashamed to admit it.

'OK,' said Ruby, taking a moment for it to sink in.

'But I can't live with the guilt, Ruby. It's killing me!'

Ruby's hand shot out, lifting Crystal's chin till their eyes met. 'Now you listen to me,' she said. 'Don't do anything fuckin' stupid! What difference will it make if you go fessing up to the coppers now? It won't fuckin' help him.'

'It'll make me feel better. Honestly, Ruby, I don't know how much longer I can live with this guilt.'

'And do you think you'll feel any less guilty if you go blabbin' off to the coppers? And what about Candice and your parents? How the fuck will they feel if you get banged up?'

Once she'd mentioned Crystal's eleven-year-old daughter, Ruby noticed her face cloud with indecision. She let go of Crystal's chin. But she continued to harangue her in the hope she'd see sense. 'Do *not* feel guilty, Crystal. You don't owe him fuck all! I can't even understand why you went back with him anyway.'

She could see Crystal was about to speak but she cut her off, raising her voice. 'Oh, I know, you loved him. Phut! It's time to let go. He was no fuckin' good! You've got to think about yourself now and the people who are still here.'

Crystal nodded and lowered her eyes again. It was several seconds before she spoke, her voice now trembling. 'We've been through a lot together, me and Gilly. Oh, I know you think he was bad news. But he wasn't always like that. He just found it hard to control his temper sometimes. I think it was the drugs. And he wasn't just angry with me; he lost it with other people too. He loved me really, Ruby, in his own daft way. He told me that loads of times. And I know that's why he came back to me.'

Ruby was becoming irritated as she listened to Crystal defending Gilly. 'I know he had a temper but I never fuckin' saw him lose it big time with anyone else,' she snapped. 'You were the one that was always on the receiving end and don't forget that you were the one he beat unconscious as well.'

'No, he didn't just lose it with me,' said Crystal. The guilty expression had returned and Ruby knew there was something more.

'Go on. Who?'

Crystal swallowed and without further encouragement she came out with it. 'He killed a man.'

Ruby sprang back in her seat. 'You're fuckin' joking!'

The words hit her like a thunderbolt. It wasn't only the revelation; it was because it brought home to her that she too was a killer. But, despite prompting Crystal to confide in her, there was no way Ruby was going to share her own secret. Too many people knew already; her partner, Tiffany, and her cousins who had helped her to dispose of the body.

Ruby's mind drifted back to the scene when Kyle, her childhood nemesis, had tried to take advantage of her. Then she thought of her own callous treatment of him and stifled a shudder of revulsion. Although she was ashamed of how far she had gone, she refused to feel guilty for the piece of shit that was Kyle Gallagher. He was another one who deserved everything that happened to him. And, at the end of the day, she had only paid him back for what he had done to her.

Not content with scarring her for life as a child, Kyle

had then moved on to her business, a city centre brothel, where he'd collected protection money and manhandled her girls. But when he'd tried to manhandle her it had been a step too far. There was no way she was going to submit herself to him so he'd had to die.

'What happened?' she asked, quickly shifting the focus back to Crystal and blocking her memories but not before she had subconsciously run her finger over her facial scar.

'He didn't mean to,' said Crystal.

Ruby held back her irritation again as Crystal went on to describe how Gilly had made it his mission to punish a client who had abused her. When they'd eventually tracked him down Gilly had driven him to a secluded place, intent on retribution. But the man had retaliated fiercely, forcing Gilly to take desperate action to stop him.

'He did it for me,' Crystal added. 'He felt really bad about it afterwards. He never meant to kill him.' She paused and took a deep breath before adding, 'So we went back and buried the body. It was on the news about the man disappearing. But we just kept quiet. Gilly didn't want anyone to know.'

'So you kept it secret for him?' asked Ruby. 'As well as helping him to bury the fuckin' body!'

'Yes,' Crystal whispered before finding renewed vigour as she continued. 'But, like I said, he did it for me so it was the least I could do.'

Ruby shook her head but Crystal wasn't finished yet. 'I feel really bad about that too. Now that I've lost Gilly I realise what that man's family must have felt like. I think I should tell the coppers everything.'

'What, and take the rap for what Gilly did? Are you off your fuckin' head? You keep schtum about the fuckin' lot,

Crystal.' Ruby looked at her friend who had now bowed her head low and was sobbing again. 'Are you listening?'

'Yes,' Crystal mumbled.

Ruby felt a pang of sympathy again as she looked at her distraught friend but she refused to submit to it. 'Crystal, it's really important that you listen to what I'm saying. Nothing you do will bring either of them back. They both beat and abused you so you don't owe them or their families anything. You need to put this out of your mind and concentrate on the people that really matter. I want you to promise me that you'll keep your mouth shut and get on with your life.'

Crystal remained silent for a while till Ruby prompted her again. 'Well, what's it to be? Are you going to keep it quiet?'

Crystal raised her head and looked at Ruby. She looked a state; her eyes were red-rimmed and she had track marks on her cheeks where her tears had run, carrying black smudges of eye makeup with them. The tip of her nose was moist with mucus, her lipstick was caked and her hair had slipped out of the scrunchy that had held it in place. It was now sticking up haphazardly; the former hair tie giving it exaggerated volume. And her pasty, scabby face was a vast contrast to Ruby's with her smooth, chestnut-coloured skin that glowed.

It wasn't unusual to see Crystal looking a state and Ruby put it down to her drink and drug abuse. But at the start of the funeral she had made an effort for once, smartly dressed in a knee-length fitted black dress and a grey tweed jacket, and Ruby had been impressed. Now though she was back to normal with her dress creased and riding up her legs exposing a long ladder in her stockings and a suspender belt with fraying lace.

Slowly Crystal nodded. 'Yes, you're right. I'll keep it quiet. But it's not going to be easy.'

'I know. But you can do it. And whenever you're tempted to spill the beans, just remember, Candice needs you.'

2

Crystal tripped on a broken piece of kerb stone, only just managing to stay upright as she made her way towards a waiting car. It was a few days after Gilly's funeral and she was in her usual spot on Aytoun Street looking for customers. The man scrutinised her as she staggered across the pavement then leant towards the open window of his car, losing her balance and almost tumbling inside.

'You in business?' he asked, his eyes narrowing as he took in her state of intoxication.

'Yeah, what you after?' she drawled.

'Full sex.'

'That'sss twenty-five,' she slurred. 'But I don't do bareback so if that'sss what you're after you can fuck right off. And don't think of roughing me up either 'cos I've got a mate who's well hard. She'll kick fuck out of anyone who harmsss me.' Her words were punctuated by hiccups.

'Forget it,' the man said, winding the window back up so that Crystal had to step back quickly to avoid getting her head wedged inside. Once she was out of the way he started the engine and drove further down the street.

The rapid movement made Crystal stumble again but

this time she landed on the ground, the pavement scraping her hand when she reached out to save herself.

'Bastard!' she shouted as she remained seated on the pavement, rubbing her hand and scowling at passers-by who slowed down to take in the amusing sight.

As well as being drunk she was high on cocaine, her intoxication rendering her oblivious to the spectacle she presented. As so often happened with Crystal, her skirt had ridden up her thighs displaying her skimpy underwear. One of her shoes had shot off as she landed, her coarse red hair was untidy and her lipstick was smudged.

Crystal's inebriated brain was slow to react and as she thought about getting herself up off the pavement she sensed someone hovering above. She looked up to see Ron the pimp towering over her.

'What the fuck do you want?' she asked.

'Not you, anyway. Look at the fuckin' state of you! What's wrong? Can't you cut it now your boyfriend's snuffed it?'

'Don't you fuckin' dare!' she began.

But Ron cut her off. 'You won't do any fuckin' business in that state. You'd be better off calling it a day. But come and see me tomorrow, sober, and I might take you on with me.'

'I've told you before, I don't fuckin' need you!'

'Oh yeah? Well, maybe you thought you didn't before your boyfriend died. But you definitely need me now. It's obvious you can't fuckin' hack it without a man behind you.'

'I'm fine!' she yelled, getting up off the pavement and trying to straighten herself up to prove she was stable.

Ron reached out a hand and pushed against her stomach.

Not quite having recovered her balance, Crystal tumbled to the ground again and cursed him as she hit the stone flags.

'Like I say, you can't fuckin' hack it. Go home and get yourself sobered up, Crystal, and we'll talk tomorrow.'

Ron walked away leaving Crystal sprawled in a heap on the ground. But after he had gone a few paces he turned back and shouted, 'Just wait, Crystal. The way you're going on, you'll be fuckin' begging me to take care of you before much longer.'

Eventually Crystal got up off the ground again. Ron was right. She was too pissed to work tonight but she'd needed it to numb the pain. The next car she stopped was a taxi. She couldn't trust herself to find her way home by bus so she tried to act as sober as possible as she gave the driver her address and sat back while he drove.

Ruby couldn't understand why Crystal hadn't been seen out for a while. She'd called in at the Rose and Crown, the rundown pub in the backstreets of Manchester frequented by a lot of the girls, but nobody had seen her for at least two weeks. Judging by the state she'd been in after the funeral Ruby was growing concerned about her and regretted that she had been so busy running her brothel lately that she had neglected to keep an eye on her friend.

As she knocked on the door of Crystal's two-bedroomed terraced house in Longsight she dreaded what she might find. Ruby waited for Crystal to come to the door but when there was no answer she knocked again. There was still no reply. Refusing to be put off, Ruby hammered first on the door and then on the front window.

'Come on, Crystal. I know you're in there,' she shouted. 'Answer the door. I just want to check you're alright.'

The sound of Ruby's venting eventually brought Crystal to the door but as soon as she'd answered it she went back inside, leaving Ruby to shut the door behind her. Although Crystal hadn't lingered at the doorway, Ruby caught a whiff of BO and she cringed. She watched Crystal walk back down the hallway and noticed that she was also unsteady on her feet.

When Ruby walked inside the house, she could detect other odours: booze and a dirty smell as though a bin desperately needed emptying. By the time she reached the living room Crystal was already slumped on the sofa. As Ruby suspected, Crystal had been drinking and, even though it was only early afternoon, there was a bottle of brandy on the coffee table amongst the scattered newspapers, dirty pots and other detritus. Crystal was taking a swig of the brandy from a half-pint glass.

'Wanna drink?' she asked.

Ruby looked at her with distaste. Crystal was wearing a stained lounge suit, which appeared to be several sizes too big. Her hair looked as if it hadn't been brushed for days and her face was devoid of makeup revealing a pasty complexion.

The rest of the living room was in a similar state of apathy with random items dotted about the place: plastic carrier bags, a half-empty box of tissues and a pair of scissors. And the smell was even worse. Ruby could detect a hint of cannabis amongst the alcohol and stale food. In the background the TV was showing a home renovation programme, the stylish pad on screen presenting a vast contrast to the inside of Crystal's home.

'For fuck's sake, Crystal, look at the state of the place!' yelled Ruby, grabbing the TV remote and switching it off.

Crystal shrugged. 'I'll only switch it back on after you've gone.'

'Why haven't you been to fuckin' work?' Ruby persisted. 'Or needn't I ask? Just what the hell has got into you, Crystal? This isn't you!'

Ruby knew that although Crystal didn't have a lot she usually did her best to keep the place tidy, concerned about making it nice for her daughter. But now, she seemed to have stopped caring. This was borne out when Crystal reacted by shrugging her shoulders again.

'What's it to you?' she said. 'Anyway, how do you know whether I've been to work or not?'

'Because I asked around and nobody has seen you. I was fuckin' worried about you, Crystal. And judging by the state of this place I had every reason to be.'

'I'm alright.'

'No you're fuckin' not!' said Ruby, storming over and taking the glass out of Crystal's hand then slamming it on the table. Crystal sat up on the sofa and made as if to grab the glass back but then seemed to think better of it. 'Just what the fuck has got into you? Just because Gilly's died it doesn't mean you have to give up on life. What the fuck did I tell you last time I saw you?'

'You don't own me,' snapped Crystal.

Ruby was stunned for a moment at Crystal's boldness but she soon recovered. 'I fuckin' care about you! That's why I don't like to see you like this. I hope for fuck's sake Candice hasn't seen you in that state.'

'I'll tidy it before she gets home,' Crystal retorted.

But Ruby could tell by the look of guilt that flashed across her face that this was an all too familiar sight lately for Crystal's eleven-year-old daughter. There was no way Crystal would be sober by the time Candice got home from school and it was obvious from looking around Crystal's home that this mess hadn't just accumulated over one day.

'How the hell can you afford to live without working anyway?'

'I manage.' Crystal held up the brandy bottle. 'You don't think I pay for this, do you? Not when I can grab it for free.'

'But what about food? What about bills?'

'It's even easier to nick food than it is to nick booze.'

'And the bills?'

'I'm a bit behind but I'll pay them off.'

'Jesus, Crystal! You've got to stop doing this to yourself.'

'Don't I have a right to fuckin' grieve?' yelled Crystal.

'There's grieving and then there's throwing your fuckin' life away! You need to give up the booze and drugs and get back to fuckin' work, Crystal.'

'Oh, to my high-powered executive role, d'you mean?' Crystal mocked.

'OK, it might not be the best job in the world but it's what you do, and it fuckin' pays well. How else will you provide for your daughter and keep a roof over your heads?'

'It's shit! It's alright for you. I don't see you having to sleep with the clients anymore, having their dirty fuckin' paws all over you and carrying out all their fuckin' sick fantasies.'

'I've done my bit. And how do you think I got out of it? Through my own hard work, that's how.'

'Yeah, after one of your fuckin' rich clients had put the money up for you to open a brothel.'

Ruby was shocked. No matter how many disagreements they'd had in the past, Crystal had never dared to attack her personally, knowing that she only had her best interests at heart.

'Don't you fuckin' dare make this about me, Crystal! I came here today because I'm worried about you but I can see now that I might as well not have fuckin' bothered. If you're determined to wreck your life then why should I fuckin' care? But it's Candice I feel sorry for. If you've got any decency as a mother you'll get back to work. It might be shit but it's the only job you know, and it pays the fuckin' bills!' Ruby shrieked.

'And if you want to come off the game and make a better life for yourself then you're the only one who can fuckin' do it! Victor might have helped me get started but it's my hard work that's grown the business into what it is today whether you like it or not. And I haven't got where I am by slouching around getting pissed every day either!'

Having said her piece, Ruby stomped out of the house. She'd tried her best to make Crystal see sense but if she wasn't willing to listen then there was nothing else she could do.

3

Crystal was sitting at the bar of a four-star hotel in central Manchester waiting to meet a client. She eyed the well-stocked bar as she sipped her brandy and soda while mellow jazz music played in the background. *I could get used to this,* she thought, turning to gaze around the interior of the room. It was a vast expanse of open space in a classical design and the designer had made use of the building's high ceilings with feature lighting to emphasise the plush furnishings and stylish décor.

She'd been back at work for a few days now. Ruby's harsh words had taken her aback at the time but when Crystal reflected on the conversation the following day she knew her friend had been right. Being without Gilly still hurt like hell but she was managing to keep things under control enough to work and look after herself, her daughter and her home, and she wasn't consuming quite as much drink and drugs.

She was meeting a new client, something that normally made her wary, but he had told her a friend had recommended her and passed him her number. This put her at ease to an extent, as did the fact that he was very polite on the phone, and gave her his full name: Justin Foster. He was also paying a lot of money to spend the entire night with her.

The client had asked her to dress classy so that her appearance wouldn't be a giveaway to the hotel staff and clientele. Crystal had therefore obliged, tying up her wanton red hair in a neat bun, toning down her makeup and wearing a flowing maxi dress, which skimmed her curves, rather than clinging to them, and revealed only a hint of cleavage.

Crystal had been thinking of ringing Ruby for a few days to apologise for how she had been last time they had seen each other. The trouble was, although Crystal vaguely remembered having cross words, she had been so drunk that she couldn't remember exactly what she had said. She knew Ruby had given her a dressing-down about lounging around the house getting drunk and she had a feeling that her response had been less than friendly.

But Crystal didn't want to lose their valuable friendship and she knew that Ruby was too proud to ring her so she'd have to make the first move. As she'd arrived fifteen minutes early for the meeting with her client she decided that now was as good a time as any.

'Ruby, it's me,' she began once Ruby had answered the call.

'Oh, right,' was the stony response.

'I-I just want to say I'm sorry for how I was last time you saw me.'

'That's alright. It's up to you how you want to spend your days. Nowt to do with me; you made that clear.'

'Aw, don't be like that, Ruby. I've said I'm sorry. I was pissed.'

'Oh, and that makes it alright, does it?'

Crystal had known Ruby wouldn't make it easy for her; she didn't like to be crossed. It was obvious from her hostile reaction that Crystal had a bit of work to do in making it up to her. But despite her abrasive manner, Crystal knew Ruby was only trying to look out for her. After apologising several times, Crystal decided the best way to get round Ruby was to let her know that she was acting on her advice.

'Anyway, I'm back at work now and I've cut down on the booze and other things.' She whispered the last words, conscious of people around the bar being able to overhear her.

'Good. Glad to hear it.'

Ruby still wasn't conceding much but at least her tone was slightly softer and Crystal was beginning to think that she'd get round her eventually. When she saw a smartly dressed man walk into the bar, Crystal was relieved, as it gave her an excuse to end the awkward phone conversation.

'I'll have to go. I think my client's arrived,' she said, quickly cutting the call and gazing at the man till she caught his eye.

Crystal offered a welcoming smile and the man breezed across to the bar, holding out his hand formally. He was aged around mid-forties, average-looking with dark, intense eyes, and smartly dressed in what appeared to be a high-end suit. He also oozed confidence.

'Crystal?' he asked and when she nodded, he took her hand. 'Pleased to meet you. I'm Justin. Do you fancy another drink here before we carry on the meeting somewhere else?'

'Yes please,' said Crystal, relieved that the man seemed as polite as when she had spoken to him on the phone.

★

It was over an hour later, and Crystal and Justin were now inside one of the hotel's lavish bedrooms. Like the rest of the hotel, the room was classy with tasteful décor, a huge bed and sumptuous furnishings. To one side of the room was a bottle of wine and two glasses with some canapés set out on a walnut dresser.

'Grab a seat,' said Justin, pointing to a cosy-looking sofa.

Crystal didn't hesitate to make herself comfortable, revelling in the luxury of the room, which was a nice change from her own basic bedroom at home. Then she waited while he brought the wine over and sat down beside her.

For a short while they continued the small talk they had begun in the bar area. Justin didn't seem in a rush to get her into bed and Crystal guessed that as he'd booked her for a full night he probably wanted to take his time. He was also treating her more like a girlfriend than a hooker by complimenting her appearance and fussing over her. He didn't give much away about himself, other than to say he was in the fast food industry. Crystal didn't let that bother her as many of her clients preferred not to reveal too much.

But then Crystal noticed that as he continued drinking his manner towards her gradually changed.

'A friend of mine recommended you,' he said, cutting Crystal off just as she was describing another hotel she had recently visited. His tone was almost accusatory as though the recommendation had been a let-down.

'Yes, you said on the phone. Who was it?' Crystal asked.

'You don't need to know that, love,' he snapped. 'Just do the job I'm paying you for and don't ask questions. OK?'

'Yes, of course,' said Crystal. 'You're the client.'

His dark, intense eyes gave a hint of perniciousness. But Crystal was used to dealing with all kinds of clients so for a while she carried on, undeterred, convincing herself that she was getting carried away with her imagination. She smiled, trying to lighten the mood, but it didn't make any difference. From that point onwards the man's attitude became increasingly obnoxious.

'Take your clothes off,' he demanded once they had worked their way through most of the wine.

Crystal obliged; after all, that was what she was here for. As he watched her intently he began removing his own clothes then ordered her to lie back on the bed once she was naked. But he didn't get in bed alongside her straightaway. Instead he took his clothes over to a chair on which he had slung his jacket earlier. He placed them on the seat then took something out of the inside pocket of his jacket, holding onto it with his right hand. Crystal couldn't see what it was at first. It seemed to be some material covering something else but that was all she could discern.

By this time she had drunk several glasses of alcohol on top of the drugs she had taken before leaving home and she was slow to react. When she did see what the man was carrying she sat up. 'Oh no,' she said, spotting the handcuffs. 'I don't do that.'

Justin pushed her back down then shifted his bulk on top of her, pinning her to the bed. 'You'll do as I fuckin' tell you to!' he snarled.

Panic stirred in Crystal and she went to scream but he clamped his other hand over her mouth before she had chance. He let the handcuffs drop to the bed but kept hold of the other item he had been carrying. It was a gag and he swiftly and skilfully tied it around her mouth and secured it at the back of her head.

Next he took the handcuffs and placed them around her wrists, then around the bedposts before locking them in place. By this time Crystal knew she was in for a rough time. She wriggled furiously around on the bed, kicked about and let out a few stifled screams but deep down she knew it was a waste of effort. This man had brought her here to satisfy his depraved desires and there wasn't a thing she could do about it.

For the next hour he abused her body, thrusting savagely till the flesh inside her tore, slapping, punching and biting her. He was having difficulty ejaculating, probably due to the amount of alcohol he had consumed, and he seemed to be taking his frustration out on her. Consumed with terror, Crystal tried to fight him off, twisting her body as she tried to dodge his slaps and punches, but he responded to her struggling by treating her even more viciously.

It was only when she broke down in tears, almost choking on the mucus that clogged her nose and throat, that Justin finally came. He let out a loud grunt, which sounded like it had come from a wounded animal. Then he climbed off her and lay to the side, getting his breath back. As Crystal's arm was fastened across the bed he undid the handcuff and shoved her away so that he would have more space. Crystal yanked at the other handcuff and the man obliged by unfastening that one too and removing the gag.

'We'll leave them off while we're sleeping but don't fuckin' think of going anywhere,' he said. 'I've booked you for the night and I want a repeat in the morning before you get paid.'

Crystal didn't say anything; she was too frightened of making him angry again. Instead she turned on her side and lay there weeping silently into the pillow. She listened to the man breathing heavily and noticed that his breathing seemed to steady eventually. Her plan was to escape from the room once he was asleep. Sod the money! No amount was enough to put up with that sort of treatment. But she was frightened of disturbing him so she stayed still for what seemed like an age.

As she lay there a myriad of thoughts raced through her mind. *How had she fallen for this? She should have known! Was there anything in his demeanour that could have given her a clue? Was her drug and alcohol intake impairing her judgement? And maybe Ron the pimp had been right. Maybe she couldn't hack it anymore without a man behind her.*

After a while, when her sobbing had subsided, she turned tentatively onto her back then glanced across at the man. The evil that was Justin Foster was now fast asleep, his chest rising and falling in slow, rhythmic breaths; the peaceful scene at odds with what had happened earlier. Slowly Crystal got up off the bed, trying to stay as quiet as possible.

As she swung her legs out and raised herself to standing she could feel a burning deep inside her and she stifled a gasp, anxious not to waken him. Her cheekbone was tender from his punches and her breasts were sore where he had sunk his teeth into them. She tiptoed across the room to where her clothes lay draped along the floor, conscious all the time of the pain stabbing at her insides and of the sleeping beast in the room.

Crystal got dressed carefully, her shaking hands making clumsy attempts at the fastenings on her clothes. As she dressed she kept an eye on him in case he stirred, her heart pounding with every twitch he made. When he let out a huge belch she drew in a sharp breath, terrified he'd open his eyes and find her escaping. Crystal's clothes rubbed painfully against her bruised and tender flesh, leaving her angry as well as fearful. What kind of man treated a woman, any woman, in that way? He was no more than a fuckin' animal!

Once she was dressed Crystal started walking steadily towards the door but then a thought stopped her. Why was she walking out empty-handed? She'd more than earnt her pay when all was said and done. Fuck him! She'd help herself and once she was gone there was fuck all he could do about it.

Feeling a mix of fear and fury she stepped towards his jacket and lifted it cautiously from the back of the chair. She took it over to the entranceway then unbolted the door while keeping hold of the jacket. That way she could escape quickly if he woke up and saw what she was doing.

Crystal was surprised to find a large wad of cash stashed in the inside pocket, and, with trembling hands, she quickly slipped it into her handbag. To hell with him! She'd take the lot. It was no better than he deserved after what he'd done to her. She rummaged around in search of other valuables and found a wallet, separate from the large wad of cash.

Driven by anger, she became determined to exact some form of revenge so she also took what bit of cash there was inside the wallet, leaving him with none. Then she turned her attention to the bank cards. There were seven in total, with a couple doubled up in the slots so she grabbed one from the back, hoping that it would be more difficult for him to notice there was one missing, especially with him having so many cards.

But Crystal still wasn't finished. As she stood holding the jacket with the adrenalin pumping fiercely around her body, she decided to check what other treasures it held. There was nothing else of value, just a couple of pieces of paper tucked away inside one of the pockets. One of them had the name Tom Carlton written on it and a four-digit number, 4768, and the other was a list of names. She couldn't work out exactly why he would have either of them in his jacket pocket. But he must have had a good reason, which meant he would miss them. Good!

Driven by a vengeful impulse, she popped them inside her handbag with the cash and credit card. Then she sneaked out of the door, determined to put as much distance as possible between herself and the vile man that was Justin Foster.

4

'Hi, love, have you had a good day?' asked Crystal, approaching her daughter and giving her a hug when she came home from school.

'Yeah, great,' said Candice who was now in the last year of primary school. 'How did you get your bruise?'

Crystal suddenly became aware of the bruise that had developed on her cheek where Justin had thumped her, and she raised her hand to her face. It was the first time Candice had seen it as she'd stayed at her grandparents' the previous night and gone straight to school from there. 'Oh, nothing, I just fell rushing upstairs and banged it,' said Crystal, tutting and nodding her head backwards as if to say, *silly me*.

Candice surveyed her for a few moments before breaking out into a smile. Crystal picked up on her hesitation and guilt gnawed away at her. She was obviously pleased to find her mother sober. Knowing how difficult things had been for both of them over the past few weeks, Crystal was desperately attempting to make it up to Candice. It can't have been easy for her to find her mother drunk and drugged up every day when she came in from school, even though Crystal had had her reasons.

The events of the previous night in that hotel room had

almost driven Crystal back to drink and drugs when she woke up feeling sore and reviled. And the text she had received earlier today had increased that temptation. It was from Justin Foster who had already rung her several times but she'd just ignored his calls. In the text he had threatened to track her down and brutally punish her if she didn't meet him to return the items she had stolen. But, although his spiteful words had struck fear into her, she was determined to keep hold of the items as retribution for what he had done.

After that she'd blocked his number, hoping she would never again encounter him but worried at the same time that he might find a way to get to her through his contact. Crystal wished she knew who it was that had given him her phone number; then perhaps she could persuade him not to tell Justin anything about her or where she hung out.

But she comforted herself with the thought that Justin might deliberately keep quiet because he was afraid of being exposed for the pervert he was. Besides, Crystal only used throwaway phones and she intended to get rid of this latest one once she'd bought a replacement.

She was pleased she had resisted a drink and drugs binge. She'd hidden away the items she had stolen from Justin Foster then tried to put the horrendous experience out of her mind. It was time to pull herself together, and that meant focusing on the good rather than the bad as well as facing up to a life without Gilly. Nothing would bring him back but, as Ruby had rightly said, Candice still needed her.

'We had a maths test today and I aced it,' said Candice, cutting into Crystal's thoughts.

'Good, well done,' said Crystal.

She followed Candice as she walked into the living room and sat down on the sofa. 'Do you want anything to drink, love?' she asked, gazing lovingly at her daughter.

Candice was growing up rapidly and Crystal couldn't help but worry at times what the future would hold for her. She was a likeable, attractive girl with strawberry blonde hair, a raft of freckles dotted across her cheeks and a glowing smile. Although Candice hated her freckles, Crystal thought they made her look cute and innocent rather than streetwise. But, as well as being attractive, she was smart, and Crystal was immensely proud of her.

When Candice turned down the offer of a drink, Crystal plonked herself down beside her, making the most of the time together. 'So, what else have you been up to?' she asked.

'Nothing much. Oh, but we found out something really funny. Do you know Sam Preston?'

'Sam who?'

'Sam Preston. She's a girl in my class.'

'Ah, right.'

'Well, guess what?' Candice continued excitedly. 'We found out today that she fancies Daniel Gutteridge.'

'Oh, OK.'

Candice looked at her mother, bewildered. 'You don't know who he is either, do you?'

Crystal shook her head.

'Aw, Mum. I've told you about him before. He's this horrible boy at our school. He's such an idiot! We couldn't believe she fancies him. It was really funny.'

'Well, it takes all kinds,' said Crystal.

Candice tutted dramatically then turned her attention to her phone, pressing a couple of keys before she seemed to recall something then looked up at her mother. 'Oh, by the way, Mum. What's the name of that nightclub you work in?'

Crystal was taken aback for a moment, temporarily forgetting the lie that she had concocted about what she did for a living. 'Eh? What do you want to know that for?'

'Oh, it's just this thing we were doing at school. All about our parents and what they do for a living. We had to tell the teacher so she could plot the different jobs on a graph, and the types of companies our parents work for. Anyway, I told her I couldn't remember the name of the nightclub where you work but she said that was OK, she'd just put you down as a bar worker in the leisure industry.'

'Oh, that's alright then,' said Crystal, hoping her daughter couldn't sense her discomfort.

Then Candice seemed to get pensive before she said, 'You were the only one on the graph that works behind a bar. Most of my friends' mums work in a shop or office. How come you don't do that?'

'No reason,' said Crystal. 'It just happened, I suppose.'

'Oh. What about my dad? What did he do?'

Crystal could feel herself tense. It was a long time since Candice had asked about her father. She'd seemed satisfied with the story Crystal had told her about them splitting up when she was only little and him no longer being a part of their lives, so this sudden questioning took Crystal by surprise, especially coming so soon after Gilly's death.

Crystal said the first job that came into her head. 'He was a builder.'

'Oh, like Sarah's dad,' said Candice, referring to one of her friends.

She then returned to her phone, seeming happy with the answer Crystal had provided.

Later that night when Candice was in bed, Crystal finally gave in to temptation, taking out the bottle of brandy she had secreted away and pouring herself a generous measure. She reasoned to herself that she was going through exceptional circumstances and as she sipped on the brandy, feeling it warm her insides, she went over the past twenty-four hours in her mind.

Once again she thought about how quickly Candice was growing up and becoming aware of the world about her. She had completely taken Crystal by surprise when she had asked about her occupation and her father's too. But it was only to be expected. As she grew up she was bound to take an increasing interest in the adult world and Crystal wondered for how much longer she would be able to keep her life of prostitution a secret from her daughter.

But what else could she do? Prostitution was the only living she had ever known, and it was the only way to provide for her daughter, especially now Gilly was out of the picture. Since he had come out of prison he had occasionally passed Crystal a wad of notes to treat Candice. It was something he had never done before he went inside and she wondered whether it was to assuage his guilty conscience about the years he had denied Candice was his or the years he had missed out on her upbringing while he was inside.

After sitting there drinking for a while Crystal sensed she was becoming maudlin so she quickly shook off all concerns about her daughter and thoughts of Gilly. But then her mind drifted to the previous night in the hotel room and the abuse she had suffered at the hands of Justin Foster. 'Bastard!' she cursed before taking another large swig of the brandy then thinking about the items she had hidden away.

Somehow her alcohol-fuddled brain connected the guilt feelings over her daughter with the valuables she had stolen. Feeling enthused she went to her hiding place and pulled out the items. She counted the cash for the second time to make sure there really was as much there as she had thought. Seven hundred and twenty pounds! Yes, it was definitely that much.

Then she picked up the credit card. Rather than Justin's name, it showed the name as Tom Carlton. Aah, now the name and number he had written down made sense; it must be the PIN code. The card was obviously fraudulent but it didn't surprise her; a nasty piece of stuff like Justin was probably involved in all sorts of crime and perhaps operated under a number of different aliases. She still didn't know the relevance of the other piece of paper with a list of names on it but she decided to keep hold of it for now anyway.

Crystal wondered whether the card was cancelled or whether she would still be able to use it. Deciding there was only one way to find out, she put the money and the other items back in her hiding place but took the card into the living room and logged onto the Internet on her phone.

Now then, what was it Candice had been asking for? Some skinny jeans. And she might as well look for some new tops for her too. Crystal entered the name of a well-known store in the search engine and began to select items for Candice. But when it came to entering her address on the shopping site a thought occurred to her: assuming the card was stolen then she didn't want it tracing back to her. Damn! She'd have to wait until the following day to hit the shops instead and hope the card hadn't been stopped.

And tomorrow, she'd raid the cash she had stolen too. Why not? Candice had been asking to go on a school trip for a while and it would be nice to be able to say yes for once. She was so buoyed up by the prospect of what she could do with the money that all thoughts of last night were temporarily erased from her mind; her sore, tender flesh now just a persistent nuisance.

Crystal smiled, thinking of how her daughter's pretty face would light up when she told her she could go on the school trip after all. Despite her terrifying ordeal of the previous night she was content that at least some good had come out of it. She just hoped to God that Candice didn't ask her where she'd got the money from, and that Candice and her friends would never discover what she really did for a living.

5

The following day Crystal was in the centre of Manchester as soon as the shops opened. She started with a department store and selected a few items for Candice. Crystal also spotted a few things for herself so she put them in her shopping basket too. If she was going to take the chance with this credit card then she might as well make it worth her while.

Crystal felt nervous as she approached the till. She had never done anything like this before. But then she thought about Justin and what he had put her through and it strengthened her resolve to go through with it. He deserved to be ripped off! As she entered the four-digit code, 4768, into the machine her hands were shaking and she hoped the shop assistant hadn't noticed. Then she waited, subconsciously holding her breath. To her amazement, the card was accepted and she let out a puff of air.

Encouraged by her success she used the card in two other stores before deciding not to push her luck any further. Then she made the trip home, eager to greet Candice with her purchases when she returned from school.

*

A day later Justin Foster was in an upmarket Manchester jewellers' shop near the Royal Exchange. He'd been a bit sharp with his wife the previous day and wanted to make it up to her with a nice surprise. Having returned home from his hotel stay with his pockets several hundred pounds lighter, he had been furious.

Straightaway he'd guessed that the prostitute he had been with had taken his money, especially when she disappeared in the night. He'd tried to ring her using the number his friend had forwarded on to him but his calls and the text he had sent were all ignored. Then the crafty bitch had blocked him.

Apart from the money, his list of contacts had gone missing, which was worrying. He couldn't understand why the little tart would have taken that. It wouldn't mean much to her but for him it was important and he dreaded the thought of it getting into the wrong hands. That was why he'd deliberately not put the contacts on his laptop. If the police lifted him it would be the first thing they'd search, whereas a handwritten list was much easier to dispose of.

He wished he could have got hold of the little slut who had robbed him. But she was long gone so he'd hit out at the next most obvious person: his wife. Now she wasn't speaking to him and he realised he would have to do some grovelling if he wanted to keep her onside. After all, he had a business function coming up in a couple of days and he wanted her with him looking as glamorous and gorgeous as she always did. It was good for his image. He also needed her to keep handling his business affairs. He couldn't be bothered with all that admin shit. He'd rather be out there doing all the wheeling and dealing.

Justin had already tried the two cards he shared with his wife but they were maxed out. That was the problem with sharing credit card accounts with the missus, which was why he kept another card in his own name as well as the fake ones. He was just about to fish out his own card when he noticed that one of the others was missing. Shit! No! A quick check of his jacket pockets told him that the PIN code had also gone, and he was livid.

He abandoned the sale as he was so infuriated at the realisation that it had probably been stolen. Stuff the jewellery! It would have to wait till another day. Justin was more interested in finding out what had happened to the missing card and he had a feeling he knew who had stolen it: the same little bitch who had robbed his cash and his list of contacts.

Justin dashed back to his car, took out the laptop that was stored in the boot ready for his upcoming business meeting, and logged in to the bank account he had opened with a fake ID. He pulled up the missing credit card details on the screen and was raging when he found that several purchases had been made the previous day. A department store and several women's fashion shops. He hadn't shopped at any of them recently and he knew his wife hadn't as she didn't use this card. Unless *she'd* taken it from his wallet. But Danielle wouldn't do that. She knew what would happen if she dared to cross him.

No, it definitely had to be the same little tart who had robbed him in the hotel room, and as Justin thought of how she had conned him, he was furious. Nobody conned him and got away with it and if he ever got his hands on the bitch, he'd make sure she paid for what she'd done.

*

It was several days before Crystal took another night off work. She was relieved that she hadn't come across Justin Foster again and, for most of that time, she had succeeded in blocking him from her memory. Having money to spend had helped take her mind off things but now that the money was almost gone, and after having drunk a good amount of booze, the nightmare of that night was resurfacing. It wasn't the first time a client had abused her but, coming on top of Gilly's death, it made it all the more cutting, and, aside from that, she was really missing Gilly.

As her thoughts mashed together in a drunken jumble she found herself feeling regretful. Just how the hell had she ended up living this lifestyle? A life where clients thought they could treat her in whatever depraved way they liked. Where she obliterated her sorrows through drink and drugs. And where, because of her addictions, she was constantly short of money despite how much she made and the hours she put in to earn that amount.

Crystal cast her mind back to when it had all begun. Although she had now been on the game for more than a dozen years, her life hadn't always been like this. At school she had been a high achiever, excelling in many subjects. She had been particularly adept at ICT, which she had begun studying at A level, as well as Maths and English.

A smile played on her lips as she thought about how Candice took after her with maths. When Crystal was at school the teachers had said she showed promise and had predicted an excellent set of A level results. But then the abuse from one of her mother's many partners had become too much and everything had changed.

For as far back as Crystal could remember her mother had always had a man on the go. The trouble was, very few of them were any good. Her mother was one of those weak-willed women who didn't seem able to survive without a man by her side so, rather than go it alone, she had rushed desperately into a new relationship within weeks each time she finished the previous one.

But the one called Bill was by far the worst. He was ex-forces and a strong disciplinarian, always ready with a punch or a slap if Crystal's mother annoyed him or if Crystal or any of her siblings stepped out of line. In his mind he thought he was keeping them in order but what he was actually doing was terrorising and depriving them.

At seventeen Crystal was eager to explore life outside the home, to go to parties and other nights out like her friends did, but with Bill that was strictly forbidden. Not only was he strict, but he was stingy too. While he was keen to spend all his money on booze and gambling, Crystal and her siblings daren't ask him for anything. Crystal had got round this by working part-time in a shop. It was hard doing her studies as well as working at weekends and after school but at least it enabled her to buy clothes and toiletries for herself.

She had put up with Bill and his cruel ways for almost two years, always wary of upsetting him or putting a step wrong. And for most of that time she'd managed OK. Until the night of the party.

It was her best friend's birthday and a lot of Crystal's friends were staying over for the night. But when Crystal had asked her mother if she could do so as well, Bill had unfortunately overheard the conversation and cut in.

'No, you can't stay overnight!' he said. 'I know what these bleedin' parties are like. Young girls getting pissed out of their heads then wondering why someone takes advantage of them. I want you back in this house by ten o'clock and no bleedin' drinking either. You're only seventeen.'

Crystal didn't bother saying anything; she knew better than to argue with Bill. It would only lead to him giving her a slap. But on the night of the party Crystal defied him, having an alcopop to fit in with her friends, but promising herself it was only the one. Unfortunately, one drink led to another then another and, when her friends pestered her to stay out, Crystal defied Bill and succumbed to peer pressure.

When she returned home the following morning, hungover and full of remorse, Bill was waiting for her. 'What fuckin' time do you call this?' he demanded.

'Sorry. I didn't mean to,' Crystal muttered. 'But all my friends were staying out and I didn't want to be the odd one out.'

'Fuck your friends!' he hollered. 'I thought I told you to be in for ten.'

Then he glared at her as though waiting for a response. Crystal shuffled from one foot to the other, feeling ill at ease under his intense scrutiny. 'I was going to but…'

'There's no fuckin' buts about it!' he shouted. 'I told you to be in by ten and you've defied me.' As he yelled at her she could see the rage within him, his eyes bulging out of his head, which was thrust aggressively forward. 'Come here!' he added.

When Crystal didn't move he strode towards her and grabbed her by the collar. 'Don't think you're fuckin' getting away with this.'

Crystal searched desperately around the room expecting her mother to walk in at any minute. 'Oh, don't think she can help you. She's out at the shops and she wouldn't fuckin' dare anyway. You're gonna be punished. I'll fuckin' teach you not to defy me.'

Before Crystal knew it she was over his knee. He tugged her short skirt up till her bare buttocks were exposed and slapped her repeatedly with his heavy, calloused hands until she was sore. He had hit her so hard that the tenderness remained for days. When Crystal's mother returned from the shops, Crystal said nothing. She knew her mother wouldn't do anything about it; she was too frightened of Bill herself.

Thankfully, her mother had finally got shut of Bill and settled down with a nice guy called Gary who was now Crystal's stepfather. He was the best man her mother had ever spent time with as far as Crystal was concerned. Gary was kind-hearted and thought the world of her mother. He treated her well and was also a protector who would stand no nonsense from anybody.

But although her mother had moved on, Crystal's life was still affected by Bill's treatment. The same day that he had given her a hiding, Crystal packed a few things into a holdall and left the family home, not knowing where she was going to live or how she would survive. After her third night of hanging around Piccadilly train station she met Gilly. He'd seemed so charming and well-spoken and when he offered her a bed for the night, she took it eagerly. It wasn't long before Gilly put her on the game to pay for food and bills, and the drug abuse started soon after. And that had been Crystal's life for the past dozen or so years.

On nights like tonight her wasted opportunities came rushing back to her with startling clarity. This was who she was. A street girl. There just to be exploited, despised, abused. The incident the previous week, as well as Gilly's death and Candice's increasing awareness, had brought Crystal to a low. And, as if matters weren't already bad enough, she was due an attendance at court soon for soliciting. It would probably mean a hefty fine, which she could ill afford.

Crystal hoped she could persuade Ruby to attend court with her. Although they had only just made up, Crystal needed her good friend now more than ever. Ruby was strong and always seemed able to see a way through any bad situation.

But, aside from the court appearance, Crystal had other pressing matters. Concerns over her daughter were increasingly at the forefront of her mind. She wanted Candice to achieve all the things she hadn't been able to and was determined that her daughter would never follow in her footsteps.

But Crystal also knew that it was becoming more and more difficult to keep her lifestyle hidden from Candice. She wondered for how much longer she could keep her occupation a secret. But she couldn't risk telling Candice. It would destroy her and change her view of everything.

All these thoughts made Crystal aware that there was no way she could stay on the game forever. But just how she would survive without the income or what she would do to change things, she didn't know. All she knew was that, one way or another, she had to forge a different future for her daughter.

6

It wasn't Crystal's first visit to Manchester Magistrates' Court; in her profession the prospect of being arrested and fined for soliciting was an occupational hazard. But, at the moment, she could have done without the added stress. There were already enough bad things going on in her life.

As she arrived at the court she was glad to have Ruby by her side. Crystal stopped for a moment, taking in her surroundings and bracing herself for her court appearance. The magistrates' court was in a large, modern, red brick building with an enormous glass panel in the centre. It was situated in Crown Square, an area off Deansgate in the centre of Manchester, which housed all the court buildings, making it appear very formal and official. She looked across at her friend who gave her an encouraging smile.

'Come on, girl,' said Ruby. 'Let's get in there. It'll soon be over with.'

They entered the courtroom, and took up their respective places, Crystal in the dock and Ruby in the public gallery. At first glance Crystal noticed that instead of the usual three magistrates, there was just one man, a district judge. She didn't pay him much attention but instead glanced at her friend, Ruby, drawing comfort from her thumbs-up sign as the arresting police officer entered the witness stand.

Under the guidance of the court legal adviser the witness described the events that had led to her arrest and Crystal listened patiently, willing it to be over. His evidence was indisputable and Crystal already knew she would plead guilty but she couldn't resist another peek at the district judge, a portly middle-aged man. She was curious about his reaction to the policeman's evidence. It was then that she realised, with a shock, that she knew him. He was one of her clients!

As Crystal raised her eyebrows and did a double take, the district judge shifted uncomfortably in his seat and she knew straightaway that he had also recognised her. Despite the gravity of her situation Crystal couldn't help but feel amused at his discomfort.

Eventually she was asked to make her plea and, once she had pleaded guilty, the court adviser passed the proceedings over to the district judge for him to decide on a suitable punishment. The rest of the courtroom watched and waited as he deliberated.

Then the district judge addressed Crystal, still displaying his discomfort as he nervously shuffled papers in front of him and repeatedly cleared his throat. The five-hundred-pound fine that he imposed was harsh and, although Crystal had half expected it, she still felt put out at the thought of having to stump up that much cash. Nevertheless, she was glad to get the proceedings over with and finally leave the courtroom.

When she found Ruby heading towards her down one

of the corridors, Crystal couldn't wait to let off steam. 'Five hundred quid!' she complained. 'That's all I fuckin' need.'

Ruby was just about to respond when she was cut off by the sound of someone approaching from behind and calling Crystal's name. Crystal turned around and was surprised to see the district judge, looking harassed and out of breath.

'Do you mind if I have a word with you in private?' he asked.

'Sure,' she said, shrugging. 'I'll meet you outside in a bit, Ruby.'

As Ruby walked away the judge gazed shiftily around him then led Crystal into a more deserted corridor. Checking that no one could see them, he closed in on her then took something out of his inside jacket pocket. It was a chequebook. Then he also withdrew a pen and she noticed that it was gold-coloured and expensive-looking.

'I need you to keep our arrangement to yourself,' he whispered urgently, pulling open the chequebook and scribbling down the date. 'One thousand pounds?'

Crystal watched as he continued to fill in the details on the cheque. He was a regular client who she was familiar with but as she studied him she saw him in a different light. It wasn't just the rotund middle-aged features and smart suit of officialdom. His human weakness had left him vulnerable, his frailties displayed by his quivering lips and pulsating temple. The irony of his role wasn't lost on her either; it gave him the privilege of passing judgement on people like her when he was one of those men who indulged in the services she offered.

For once in her life Crystal was the one in control. She noticed that his last three words were phrased like a question, and realised there was probably room for negotiation. With all that had happened to her recently, coupled with the current dire state of her finances, she intended to take full advantage. And if he was so eager to part with one thousand pounds then it was probably because that amount of money was nothing to him.

'Oh, I think my silence is worth more than that,' she said.

Despite his nervousness he scowled at her. 'How much?' he snapped.

'Ten thousand would be nearer the mark,' said Crystal, casually.

'Surely you can't be serious?' he hissed.

'Deadly!'

He glanced about him, still jittery, and it was apparent to Crystal that he didn't want anyone to know what he was up to.

'Alright. How about two thousand then?'

'How about eight?' countered Crystal with a confident smile.

'I can stretch to three but that's my limit,' he said with a desperate edge to his voice.

'Seven. And that's *my* limit.'

The man sighed in irritation and checked around him once more. 'Look. I'm being more than generous here. I could always deny it, you know.'

Crystal grinned. 'Yeah, but who would believe you? Don't forget, mud sticks.'

She saw him suck in his breath, his features becoming even tenser, before he said, 'Alright, alright. I can go to five but that really is my absolute limit. I'm going to have difficulty explaining the hefty expenditure to my wife as it is.'

What a fool! thought Crystal. *Fancy admitting he had a wife.* She knew that put her in an even better bargaining position but she also knew that someone could come and spot what they were up to at any second. And she didn't want that because it was bound to send him scurrying away before she'd had chance to get any cash out of him.

'OK,' she said. 'Let's settle on five thousand.'

The judge quickly ripped out the cheque he had been writing, screwed it up and put it in his pocket. Then he wrote out another for five thousand and thrust it in Crystal's hand while glaring at her.

'There!' he said. 'And I don't ever want to set eyes on you again.'

He hurried away before Crystal could respond. But she wasn't bothered. She had a cheque for five thousand pounds in her hand and she knew she could do a lot with that sort of money. She sauntered towards the exit, planning in her head what she was going to spend it on.

There were so many items Crystal could have bought with the five thousand pounds and, as she lay in bed that night, she enjoyed imagining all the things she could do with it. A holiday for her and Candice. New décor and furniture for her home. Or maybe she could treat her parents for being so good to her, often looking after Candice while she was at work.

But then Crystal thought about the vow she had made to change her life before Candice became much older and found out what she did for a living. She wondered how five thousand would enable her to do that. A small business perhaps? But doing what? And how far would five thousand go towards setting up a business?

By the time she got to sleep the prospect of spending the five thousand wasn't quite as exciting. In the face of all the different options available, she wanted to make sure she chose the right one. After all, once the money was gone, it was gone, and she didn't want to regret throwing it away. With her penchant for drugs and alcohol that would have been easy to do and the temptation lay heavily on her.

She hadn't been awake long the next day when an idea came to her. If she was so worried about squandering the money on drink and drugs then why not remove that temptation altogether? She knew deep down that her addictions were the real negative in her life. The reason she was still on the game was because of the drink and drugs, and there was no other way she could think of to earn the vast amounts it took to feed her habit. But what if she could stop taking them? Then she wouldn't need to go on the game.

The more Crystal thought about it, the more it made sense. She knew there were places you could go to get help with withdrawal but she'd never been able to afford it in the past. But that was before she had five thousand pounds. And now that she did have the money, she hoped it would be enough because she knew that booking herself into rehab would be the best thing she could do to change the lives of both herself and her precious daughter, Candice.

7

Crystal woke up in a panic, sweat-drenched and with her heart racing. Her breath was coming in short gasps and as she fought to steady her breathing she felt an impulse to run. She sprang up in bed, cast the duvet aside and swung her legs out. Then, with an urge to keep moving, she began pacing the room. It was the only way she could curb the feelings of anxiety that had besieged her, or at least take her mind off them.

As she strode frantically up and down the room she glanced at the clock. 3.10 a.m. Less than an hour since the last time she had awoken. The insomnia was getting her down and leaving her exhausted. But, despite her exhaustion, she felt a persistent restlessness.

After ten minutes of pacing she was a little calmer. She sat down on the edge of the bed. Then the tremors took over, flooding her body with involuntary movements. She couldn't keep still and knew there was no way she would get back to sleep while she felt like this. She gave it some time for them to dissipate before she lay back on the bed.

Reaching over to the bedside cabinet she grabbed a CD with one of the meditation recordings the rehab centre had recommended, put it into the CD player and pressed play. Maybe that would settle her. But as she tried to concentrate she found she couldn't focus on the words, her mind consumed by the feelings that swamped her body. The constant twitchiness, the sweats and the itching.

Then there were the thoughts that plagued her; visions of dead people. First there was the man Gilly had killed, Tim O'Brien, the last time she had seen him with his throat slit. A guilty feeling overwhelmed her and heightened her anxiety, knowing she was the one who had passed Gilly the knife. Then her mind switched to Gilly himself, and the moment when she had realised he was dead and fled the scene to protect herself.

'Focus,' she told herself. 'Focus!'

Crystal attempted to steady her breathing, following the instructions of the soothing voice on the recording. But as she tried to breathe in deeply, she felt as though her lungs were locked, the tension in her muscles making it difficult to expand her diaphragm. As she fought to inhale, her breathing speeded up till she was gasping for air. Then a strange sensation grabbed her – a stiffness around her jaw that didn't seem right. The muscles tightened even more and Crystal became terrified.

She tried to stretch her jaw but couldn't get rid of that feeling of rigidity. *Shit! What the fuck is happening? What if I'm having a heart attack or a stroke or summat?* Then she felt the pins and needles in her hands and feet. But they weren't the type that would disappear once you rubbed your hands together to get the circulation going again. They were far more aggressive, surging through her hands to the ends of her fingers and making them numb. *Shit! Maybe I am having a heart attack. Maybe this is what it feels like!*

Once again she sprang up off the bed as panic gripped her. 'For fuck's sake!' she yelled, feeling desperate. Then she sank down once more and blubbered like a young child. 'Please, please, take these feelings away. Please!' she yelled once more, relieved when she heard the sound of someone at the door. 'Please, help me!' she cried.

One of the staff from the rehabilitation centre dashed inside. She was a woman in her forties. Large, strong and self-assured, Stacy was the sort of woman who would take no nonsense from anyone. But she was also kind and level-headed, and she had been a godsend to Crystal ever since she had checked herself into rehab.

'Crystal, are you OK?' she asked, dashing over to where Crystal was kneeling on the floor and putting her arms around her.

'Get your fuckin' hands off me!' Crystal yelled, drawing in sharp gasps of air. 'I can't fuckin' breathe!'

Stacy withdrew a paper bag from the bedside cabinet and held it over Crystal's face, which filled Crystal with more panic, feeling as though she was about to suffocate.

'No!' she screamed, trying to wrench Stacy's hands away from her face.

But Stacy held on tight. 'Breathe into the bag, Crystal. Just breathe. It'll help you.'

'I can't fuckin' breathe! You're suffocating me.'

'No I'm not. The bag will help. Just concentrate on breathing as deeply as you can. Don't worry, the feelings will soon go.'

After a few seconds of struggling Crystal did as ordered, her desperation urging her to put her trust in Stacy. As

Crystal felt the pins and needles disappear and her facial muscles return to normal, she looked at Stacy with an expression of gratitude tinged with relief.

'Better?' asked Stacy, smiling kindly.

'A bit,' said Crystal, still aware of her tight muscles and shaky limbs, and feeling slightly embarrassed about her behaviour.

Stacy let go of her. 'You can take the bag away whenever you're ready but it's there when you need it. We keep them for all the patients.'

'What the hell just happened?' asked Crystal, taking the bag away from her face but still holding on to it.

'A panic attack. You were hyperventilating.'

'But I thought I was gonna die. I had pins and needles and my bloody fingers went numb.'

Stacy smiled again. To Crystal it felt as though she was mocking her and she couldn't help but feel a bit foolish. But then Stacy said, 'It's usual with hyperventilation. It's because your body's starved of carbon dioxide.'

'Jesus! That sounds bad.'

Stacy's face lit up in amusement. 'It sounds worse than it is, believe me. It just means that you're breathing out faster than you're breathing in. It happens quite a lot with withdrawal. That's why we have the paper bags in every room.'

'How does that help?' asked Crystal.

'It regulates your breathing. Because your breath goes into the bag, it means you take the carbon dioxide back into your body when you breathe in.'

'Oh,' said Crystal, not really sure what all that meant but just thankful that the paper bag had helped.

'I expect you're experiencing other anxiety symptoms too?' asked Stacy.

Crystal nodded, feeling her lip quiver and afraid to speak in case her voice cracked.

Stacy placed a sympathetic hand on top of Crystal's. 'I know it feels bad,' she said. 'But you're doing really well. Just stick with it and it'll get better soon, I promise.' Then she stood up to leave. 'Keep the bag in your bedside drawer, then you can use it whenever you need to,' she said before walking out of the door.

Crystal wished she felt as confident as Stacy seemed to be about how well she was doing. It was her third day in rehab and she was beginning to regret her decision. Although she hadn't expected rehab to be fun, she had never anticipated that it would be quite as bad as this. And she couldn't help wondering if she would be able to stick it out.

Crystal had only booked in for two weeks and although the staff had warned her at the outset that the first week would be the worst, their words were nothing compared to the reality. Ideally, she should have booked in for at least four weeks and taken medication to help with the withdrawal symptoms but when she'd done her research, she realised that five thousand pounds didn't go a long way when it came to rehab. And, besides, she didn't want to be away from Candice for too long.

She was lucky to find a centre that would let her attend for only two weeks but they had agreed on the condition that she would get further support from an outside organisation once she had checked out of rehab. With a habit as bad as Crystal's two weeks wasn't a lot of time. It meant she would have to go cold turkey because a course of medication would take too long. However, the staff had assured her that they would support her through it during her time in rehab.

So, she'd booked herself in, telling her mum and stepdad, Gary, that the owner of the nightclub where she worked was opening a new branch down south and, as one of their most experienced employees, he needed her help in setting it up. Fortunately they'd bought the idea so now the only problem, apart from the challenges of withdrawal, was explaining to them, on her return, why she'd been uncontactable for two weeks.

She felt bad knowing her parents and Candice would be worried when they couldn't contact her but she had no choice as the rehab centre didn't allow any contact with the outside world. It was part of their conditions and she'd given it a lot of consideration. Apart from the effect on her family, she would miss being able to speak to them too but, although she wasn't happy about the lack of communication, she was determined to get clean. Crystal drew comfort from the knowledge that the sacrifice would be worth it to her family in the long term.

Once Stacy had left her room, Crystal tried to get to sleep again but, once more, sleep evaded her; the anxiety symptoms far more powerful than her state of exhaustion. She was still in despair, wondering for the umpteenth time just how she would get through all this.

But then she thought with regret about the years she had wasted getting artificially high and selling her body. It was a vicious cycle of abuse and degradation while earning the money to pay for her addictions so she could numb herself to the prospect of further abuse and degradation.

And then she thought of her lovely daughter, Candice, and the shame she had felt when she asked her what she did for a living. And that, above everything else, was what spurred her on. She had to see it through. She had no choice. Because, one day, somehow or other, Crystal was going to make her daughter proud of her.

8

It was another eleven long days before Crystal left Flourish Rehabilitation Centre in Derbyshire and stepped into the outside world. The first week had been hell and, although things had improved during the second week, Crystal knew it wasn't over yet. The painful withdrawal symptoms of those early days were behind her but she would still experience cravings for a long time to come, and it would take all her willpower not to give in to them.

On the way to the car park Crystal checked her handbag for the third time that morning. She was seized by a last-minute panic and wanted to make sure she had the contact details for the organisation that would further support her recovery. She knew that ongoing aftercare from them would be invaluable in enabling her to stay on the right path. But she also had to play her role in her own future success and, although it was daunting, she had already surprised herself by how well she had done.

Crystal also double-checked that she had picked up her mobile on the way out. The first thing she decided to do was to ring her mum and let her know she was on her way back.

'Bloody hell, Crystal, we've been worried to death about you!' said her mum.

'I know and I'm so sorry. I'll explain everything when I get there, I promise. I just want to hit the road now and get back to you all as soon as possible.'

Crystal then finished the call and set off for the journey back to Manchester.

During her time inside Flourish Rehabilitation Centre, Crystal had found an inner strength that even she hadn't known she possessed. In that first week the withdrawal symptoms had been so bad that there had been many occasions when she was ready to jack it in and walk away but thoughts of her daughter had kept her going. She couldn't let Candice down.

The second week hadn't been quite as bad, and the withdrawal symptoms weren't as severe. Being in a better frame of mind also meant that she was ready to take part in some of the activities offered by the centre. Figuring she might as well get her money's worth, Crystal opted for as many sessions as she could, including yoga, group therapy, counselling and meditation. She'd found that the activities not only occupied her anxious mind but they also helped her to take a more positive look at life.

As she drove away Crystal gazed around her. The rehabilitation centre was set in beautiful grounds and for the first time she noticed the lush scenery. Verdant hills and valleys stretched out before her. Pastures, bordered by deep green hedgerows and rustic stone walls, were dotted with cows and sheep that grazed contentedly on the sweet grass. And in the distance, a charming wooden bridge curved across a gracefully flowing brook.

All of this splendour had been lost to her on the way in to the centre. But now, with a clear head for the first time in ages, she was developing a new appreciation for the world around her and she opened the car window to let in the fresh aroma of the countryside air. Despite the captivating scenery, though, she longed to put some distance between her and the rehab centre and get back home so she could experience some normality. Before doing so, she needed to call in at her parents' to pick up Candice.

Her desire to see her daughter overrode any cravings she might have for drugs or alcohol. It was almost an hour before she arrived at her parents' home with a ready excuse for her lack of contact.

'Where the bloody hell have you been?' asked her mother, Kath, when she answered the front door. 'We've been worried sick about you. We kept ringing your mobile but it was dead.'

Aged in her early fifties, Kath still looked well for her years, showing only fine lines on her pretty face rather than the deep wrinkles of many of her peers. She had always been slim and was only now starting to gain a bit of excess around her middle. Crystal often marvelled at how she managed to stay looking so good despite all that she had been through.

Despite Kath's words being stern, Crystal knew that they were spoken out of worry and concern. She now had a good relationship with her mother although their initial reconciliation had been awkward. They had never fully discussed what had happened with Bill, but Crystal had always suspected that her mother felt bad about the way he had treated them.

Acknowledging her mother's concern, Crystal said, 'I'm so sorry, the phone reception was really bad where we were.

I tried ringing you loads but it was a waste of time so, in the end, I just switched my phone off.'

Crystal's mother looked suspiciously at her and was just about to say something more when Candice dashed down the hall.

'Mum!' she yelled, flinging her arms around Crystal. 'I thought you weren't coming back.'

Crystal saw the tears in her daughter's eyes and the guilt tore at her heart, knowing how worried her family must have been when she didn't get in touch. But she had done it for the right reasons and hopefully, in time, she would be able to make it up to them.

'I'm so sorry, sweetheart,' she said. 'I wanted to ring you and let you know I was coming home, I really did, but the phone reception there was really bad.'

'Yes, you already said,' her mother pointed out.

Crystal tried to ignore the barbed comment while she took her daughter's chin and gently raised it up till their eyes met. As they did so she felt a powerful surge of emotion. In spite of Crystal's absence, Candice's face was full of unrelenting love and it gave Crystal the strength she would need to get through the challenges that lay ahead.

Her mother soon calmed down; her family's joy at having Crystal back home quickly superseded any worry that had dogged them for the past fortnight. Crystal stayed with her mother and stepfather for over an hour. She felt it was the least she could do when they had been kind enough to take care of Candice for the last two weeks. But really she just wanted to be at home with her daughter.

★

Later that evening when Crystal had put Candice to bed she spent a while relaxing alone. But where in the past she had reached for the booze or drugs, she now switched on the kettle instead. It felt strange to her but it was something she would have to get used to. She would also have to stop getting maudlin whenever she was on her own and try to take a positive approach instead, just like they'd taught her at rehab.

Her spell in the centre had given her plenty of time to think – about her lifestyle, her daughter and her future. Having come this far, Crystal was more determined than ever to stay off the drugs and change her life. But she had another problem. Now that she had spent her money on rehab, there was virtually nothing left. And she still had to find a way to earn a living.

Crystal had already decided what she was going to do. During all those hours in rehab, going over everything in her mind while sleep evaded her, she had come up with a plan. Crystal was going back on the game. But it wouldn't be for long. A few weeks should be enough for her to put her plan in place. And after that, if everything went as well as she hoped it would, she should be set up for life.

9

Crystal walked into the hairdresser's feeling a little apprehensive. She didn't normally feel like this when she visited the salon but she had kept to the same hairstyle for years and now she was going to have a total change. The stylist was a young, trendy, good-looking male who was well groomed and fashionably dressed, which made Crystal feel even more ill at ease.

'What would you like, lovey?' he asked, holding up and examining a coarse, dry lock of her overdyed hair with delicate hands, and staring at it distastefully.

He must have overlooked the fact that she could see his scornful expression in the mirror and Crystal was almost ready to get up and walk out. But she decided against it. She was here now and she wasn't going to let his contemptuous attitude put her off.

'I want it toning down,' she said. The look of virtual relief on the face of the stylist gave her the encouragement she needed to carry on. 'Can you dye it blonde and cut it into a nice bob up to my shoulders? I want it to look more… natural.'

Crystal hesitated before saying the last word, feeling a bit foolish, because she knew that in a way she was modelling herself on someone Gilly had become smitten with many years previously: Maddy. Crystal had never forgotten the classy journalist who she had secretly admired as well as envied.

At the time she had thought she could never be like Maddy but since she had come off the drugs Crystal had begun to view everything differently. Where she had previously been au fait with her appearance, now she detested it because it underlined everything she was. And Crystal didn't want to be that person anymore.

'Well…' said the stylist, gesticulating dramatically as his hands worked their way through Crystal's hair. 'We can certainly give you a bob but I wouldn't recommend going blonde.'

'Why not?' asked Crystal.

'Well, to be honest, I'd have to dye it to death if I was going to switch from red to blonde and it's already damaged. What's your natural colour?'

Crystal cast her mind back to the days before her wanton red hair. It had been a long time. 'It was kind of a brownish blonde.'

'Mousy, do you mean?' asked the stylist, matter-of-factly.

'Yeah, I suppose so.'

'OK. Well, if you want to go natural, why don't you go for a nice mid-brown colour? You don't want to go too bright 'cos that would look tarty but you don't want anything too bland either.' When Crystal hesitated for a moment, he said, 'I tell you what, let me show you some swatches so you can see what I mean.'

The stylist went in search of his swatches, his attitude now switching from contemptuous to enthusiastic at the prospect of transforming Crystal. Once he had returned, he pointed out a few colours to her, commenting on how well they would suit her eyes and colouring. She was beginning to warm to him as his eager approach coupled with his own smart appearance told her she was in the hands of someone who knew what he was doing even if he was painfully direct.

'Course the makeup would have to go too.' Then he paused as if testing how far to push it. 'I mean, that is, if you really want to go for a more natural look.'

'Oh, yes,' said Crystal. 'I'm going for it. That's why I've booked in with the beautician as well.'

'Mands? Ooh, you'll be in good hands there, lovey. She definitely knows her stuff. Between me and Mands we'll have you looking a million dollars in no time.'

Crystal smiled. 'Good,' she said. 'That's what I'm hoping for, a complete transformation.'

'So which colour would you like to go for?'

'Tell you what,' said Crystal. 'I'll let you choose.'

Crystal was now feeling a lot more at ease, knowing that she would soon emerge from the salon looking like a completely different person. And it felt good because for Crystal it represented a significant step in her mission to turn her life around.

Crystal looked in the mirror, a habit she'd got into lately. It was a few days after her salon appointment and she was thrilled with the results. In fact, she felt compelled to keep checking her appearance just to make sure it was really her who was staring back.

The colour the stylist had chosen for her was perfect,

complementing her eyes and skin colour perfectly, and the beautician had been equally helpful. Crystal's makeup was now much more subtle than the heavy makeup she had been used to during her days on the game.

Apart from the salon transformation, Crystal had undergone a transformation of her own. Gone were the sores that had been there permanently during her drug-taking days; her complexion now had a healthy glow instead of being pasty, and her eyes were shining. She'd even put on a bit of weight, which made her face look fuller, and it suited her.

The last few weeks hadn't been easy. She still suffered from constant cravings, and going on the game sober was a whole new experience. Without the mind-numbing effects of drink and drugs she was more aware of the discomfort and degradation.

She'd got through it though. Seeing the improvements in her appearance and being able to tackle her everyday affairs with a clear head had both played their part. But what had helped her more than anything was thinking of a better future for her and Candice. And with every day that passed she was a step nearer to achieving that.

Her time on the game was already behind her. She'd spent the past few weeks building up a stash of money and was amazed how much she'd been able to save now she wasn't squandering it on drugs and drink. Crystal had also treated herself to a laptop; something that would be useful to her in the coming months.

The money she'd saved wouldn't last forever. Ruby had helped her out a bit by letting her do some admin for her massage parlour but it wasn't much. Crystal knew she needed more of a long-term solution, which was why she'd been gathering more than just cash. She walked over to the chest in the corner of her bedroom and pulled out the top drawer. There, in a box underneath her underwear, was everything she needed to carry out the plan she had thought up during her time in rehab.

It was the incident with the judge that had given her the idea but her maltreatment at the hands of the evil Justin Foster had probably prompted it. If the judge was so willing to pay for her silence, then surely a lot of her other clients would be too. And if she could target enough of them, then she should be able to build up a tidy sum of money, which would set her up for the future.

But she didn't want to target just any clients. No, this bunch of losers had been specially selected because they deserved to be targeted. They were the nasties, the perverts, the women haters, and Crystal was going to make sure they paid in more ways than one.

She opened the box with the key that she kept attached to her key ring, and went through its contents. There was a good collection of credit and debit cards, mobile phones, business cards, photographs and even computer sign-on details. Some of these men were so stupid; fancy leaving your computer sign-on details in your suit pocket! It amused her to think that the most patronising ones were generally the most stupid too.

She separated all the objects and information into piles with each pile representing one of her former clients. There were six piles altogether: a businessman, a well-known TV personality, a restaurateur, a doctor, a policeman and another businessman. She looked at each pile. Some were more complete than others but nevertheless she knew she had plenty on each of them. In fact, she probably had enough information to completely destroy her abusers.

Now she just needed to decide who she would target first, and how. It wasn't a difficult decision to make. Although her experience with Justin Foster had been weeks ago, it still plagued her dreams and she often woke up in a sweat reliving it. He had definitely been one of the nastiest clients she had ever dealt with so it was an obvious place to start.

Keeping the items out on the bed, she went over to her laptop and opened the word processor at a fresh page. She drew up a list of the clients she wanted to target initially. Then she carefully placed the items relating to the other clients back in the box but kept out those relating to Justin Foster. Next, she began drawing up a profile template, which she would use for each of the targets. Once she had set out the various headings, she saved a copy under the name 'Justin Foster' then filled in what details she had for him.

Target 1
Name: Justin Foster
Description: Aged around mid-forties, about five foot ten, average-looking, smart dresser, dark hair flecked with grey, and dark, intense eyes
Address: Unknown
Profession: Businessman? In the fast food industry
Personality: Sadistic woman hater, arrogant and aggressive, likes a drink
Phone number: Unknown
Bank details: Yes (in a false name)
Aim: Blackmail and revenge

She looked at the template headings. With regards to his profession, he had said he was in the fast food industry so she'd listed him as a businessman but that depended on whether Justin Foster had been telling the truth. She suspected otherwise so she had therefore added a question mark after the word businessman.

Crystal then took another look at the items she had collected and compared them to the headings. She had a bit to go on even though she didn't yet have any way of getting in touch with him. Although she had kept hold of the credit card she had stolen, she regretted not keeping his phone number when she had changed her throwaway phone; but at the time she hadn't seen any use for it.

With Justin she had even more than was indicated by these headings though; she had the list of names. She decided to insert a further heading, *Information/Items*, where she listed anything else she knew about the target.

For a start, he had been recommended by a friend from what he had told her and that friend had passed him her number, but he hadn't revealed who the friend was. Justin Foster also carried a lot of cash so she noted that down. And the most important item she added under *Information/Items* was a reference to the list of names. She stared at the list and wondered, once again, why he would be carrying such a list. Did it relate to his business? Or to something else?

Deciding there was only one way to find out, she did an Internet search of his name but nothing came up in the results, not for anybody in Manchester anyway. She also tried the name on the credit card but that didn't show much either. Then Crystal scanned the other names on the list, mentally noting a few of them. Dennis Atkinson, Phil Thomas, Roger Purvis. She typed the first two names into an Internet search engine. There were a few of each listed but she couldn't see anything of relevance that might connect them either to each other or to Justin Foster.

Crystal was trying to decide her next move when one of the other names caught her eye: Tommy (Spud). She was sure she'd come across someone called Spud but she couldn't quite place where; nor did she know if his real name was Tommy. There was no way she'd find anything on the Internet without a full name so she decided to ask around. She typed the name under *Other Information* then saved the document and shut down the laptop. *Great,* she thought. She now had a starting point and, hopefully, it would enable her to find out more.

10

Justin Foster tapped on his desk impatiently while he waited for someone to answer his call. Eventually he was rewarded by the sound of a voice on the other end of the line.

'At last!' he said. 'I thought you were never gonna pick up. And where the fuck have you been for the last few days? You been avoiding me, or what?'

'No, boss. I've just been busy, that's all.'

'Right, well I hope that means you've got good news for me at least. Have you found that tart yet?'

'No, I haven't. Not yet.'

'What d'you mean, you haven't? I put you onto her fuckin' weeks ago. What's taking you so long?'

'Well, to be honest, boss, I didn't have a lot to go on, did I? All you gave me was the name, Crystal, and a bit of a description. But no one I spoke to knows a Crystal with red hair.'

'For God's sake!' cursed Justin. 'You'll just have to fuckin' try harder then. I want you to come back to me in the next week with some information about where she is, otherwise you're fired.'

He cut the call before the man could say anything further.

'Fuckin' useless!' he cursed. 'I wish I'd have listened when I was warned what a useless twat Phil Thomas was.'

He just hoped that his threat would make his employee come up with something. Apart from anything, he had to get back his list of names; it was too risky leaving it otherwise. If his employee didn't get back to him with some information then he'd just have to put someone else on the job. But, somehow or other he was going to find the thieving little bitch and, when he did, she'd be sorry she ever crossed him.

Crystal walked into Ruby's Massage Parlour where she had agreed to meet Ruby so they could go out for a drink together.

'You'll have a bit of a wait,' said Tiffany, Ruby's partner who helped her run the massage parlour, which acted as a front for a brothel. 'She's still with a client.'

'No worries,' said Crystal, knowing that Ruby's sessions as a dominatrix could often last a while. 'I'll go and grab a coffee if that's OK.'

'Sure, help yourself. I'd come and join you if it wasn't so bloody busy on the desk.'

Crystal smiled at Tiffany and went through to the waiting area. There was nobody sitting there this evening and she presumed the girls were all busy. She hadn't been there long when she saw Ruby walk past the front desk and lead a man towards the exit.

The man was tall, aged around mid-forties and skinny with a slight stoop. Crystal got up and made her way towards them, waiting for the man to go. As he walked away he patted Ruby on the back and as Crystal drew closer to them she heard him say, 'Don't forget what I told you. It's to stay strictly confidential and let me know if you hear anything.'

'Don't worry, I will,' said Ruby.

Once he was gone, she turned round and came over to Crystal.

'Hi, Crystal, sorry I'm a bit late. He likes a long session.' Ruby laughed. 'Maybe it's because he's usually the one doling out the punishment so he likes to have a change.'

'How d'you mean?' asked Crystal.

Ruby seemed to hesitate before answering her. 'He's a DI,' she whispered. 'On the drugs squad. But keep it to yourself. I only found out because another client recognised him and told me who he was.'

Crystal nodded. 'Blimey, you've known me long enough, Ruby, to know that I won't go blabbing off to anyone. What was he on about anyway?'

Ruby whispered again, 'Tell you when we get outside. But only if you promise not to blab. Don't forget, it wasn't so long ago you were ready to confess about Gilly's death.'

'Yeah, but that was when I was on the drugs. It's different now, Ruby. You know that.'

Ruby smiled and they both said their goodbyes to Tiffany before heading out of the door.

'Well?' asked Crystal.

'Bloody hell!' said Ruby, laughing. 'You're not gonna let this go are you, girl?' She breathed in sharply before continuing. 'I help him out from time to time, with information.'

'What do you mean?'

'Well, if I spot anything dodgy or if he's looking for someone who might be a client?'

'What? You mean you're a grass?'

'Not really. I prefer to think of it as damage limitation. We get some bad sorts in the club sometimes and it helps to have the police onside. If there's someone knocking about who could harm my girls or the business then I prefer to know about it. You could say it's a mutual arrangement. But keep it to yourself.'

'Yeah sure,' said Crystal before focusing on what she had come here for. 'Where do you want to go for a drink?'

'Rose and Crown?'

'Yeah, why not.'

It didn't take Crystal and Ruby long to walk the few streets to the Rose and Crown and as they made their way they made small talk, with Ruby complimenting Crystal on her appearance and how well she was doing. They were soon amongst the pub's clientele. As they walked inside, they spotted three of the working girls – Amber, Sapphire and Angie – seated around a table and they went over to join them.

'Bugger! We're just going,' said Angie. 'No offence, girls, but we were just finishing our drinks when you walked through the door.' She stood up and drained the last of her glass.

'Sure we can't tempt you to have another?' Crystal asked.

'No, sorry. We've got to go. We won't make much money sat around here doing nothing, will we?'

'No worries, maybe another time,' said Crystal.

'Come on, let's get a drink,' said Ruby. 'See you again, girls.'

By the time Ruby and Crystal returned from the bar the others had gone. 'Actually,' said Crystal, 'I'm glad in a way that it's just the two of us because I've got something to tell you.'

'Sounds interesting,' said Ruby.

'Erm, it is.' Crystal looked around to make sure no one was listening then leaned in closer to Ruby. 'I've come off the game,' she said.

'Really? How come?'

'Well, I've thought of another way to earn money and if I play my cards right I'll probably earn even more than I would on the game.'

Crystal paused a moment, enjoying the look of intrigue that passed across Ruby's face before she continued. 'This is strictly between me and you, Ruby, so please don't tell anyone else.'

'As if I would. You know me, girl.'

'OK, well, for the last few weeks I've been collecting stuff from clients.'

'What kind of stuff?'

'Credit cards, debit cards, business cards; that sort of stuff.'

'What the fuck are you doing that for?' asked Ruby.

'Because I want to have as much information on them as possible.'

Ruby sat up in her seat and pulled her shoulders back, her expression one of amazement and curiosity.

'Not all of them,' continued Crystal. 'Just the bad ones or the sick bastards. I'm gonna fuckin' target them, Ruby.'

'Jesus Christ! What the fuck's brought this on?'

'I've had enough – standing about in all weathers freezing

my tits off, being treated like shit, not to mention the abuse. I'm not fuckin' having it anymore and it's about time some of those bastards paid for what they've done to me.'

'Wow! This doesn't sound like you, Crystal.'

'I've just reached my limit and, besides, I don't want Candice to grow up feeling ashamed of who I am. I want to make her proud. If I make enough money I could provide a nice future for her.'

Crystal could feel her eyes welling up as she said the last few words but she fought the tears back. She'd had enough of tears. From now on she was going to be strong.

'Fuckin' hell, I'm gobsmacked,' said Ruby. 'But in a way I can understand it. Some of the bastards deserve all they get. How will you do it anyway?'

'Well, there must be a lot of ways of getting money out of someone with a dirty little secret, mustn't there? Especially if you know how to get in touch with their wives or bosses.'

'Jesus! Have you got enough on them for that?'

'Well, I've got enough to start with but I'm hoping to find out even more.'

'Fuckin hell, Crystal! You're serious about this, aren't you?'

'Deadly! And some of them are gonna pay in more ways than one too. Especially the bad bastards. I'm gonna make them sorry for what they've done to me.'

Then Ruby became grave, placing a hand on Crystal's as she said, 'I don't blame you one bit for what you're doing, but have you thought it through?'

'What do you mean?'

'Well, there are some nasty people out there and you

don't want any of it coming back on you. I think it would be better to leave it alone.'

'Don't worry, I'll be careful,' said Crystal.

' Well, if you're dead set on this then you make sure you do and let me know how you get on.'

Crystal then switched the conversation, asking Ruby, 'Do you know anyone called Spud? I've heard of him but I can't place him.'

'Yeah, course I have. He's over there,' said Ruby, pointing to one of the pub's regulars, a youth aged around twenty wearing a pair of skinny jeans and a smart fitted shirt with a designer logo.'

'Aah, so he's Spud. I didn't realise that was the name he went by. Do you know what his real name is?'

'Yeah, Tommy,' said Ruby. 'What do you want him for anyway?'

As soon as Ruby had told her that his real name was Tommy, she knew she had the right man and she was eager to approach him and find out more. She grinned as she said to Ruby, 'Well, let's just say he's the first step in tracing one of my targets. Are you OK here for a bit while I go over for a chat?'

'Sure,' said Ruby, 'But, like I said, Crystal. Be careful.'

and VISTA volunteers. For specific information on Older American Volunteer programs, such as Foster Grandparents, Senior Companions, and Retired Senior Volunteer programs, call 1 (800) 424-8867; Washington, DC: (202)634-9355.)

Volunteers of America
340 West 85th Street
New York, NY 10024
(212) 873-2600

American Association of
   Retired Persons (AARP)
1909 K Street NW
Washington, DC 20049
(202) 434-2277 (202) 872-4700
(Publications, informative
   brochures about health,
   travel, social security,

Medicare, and more. Lobbies for age-related issues.)

Health
American Association of Homes
   for the Aging (AAHA) and
   Continuing Care
   Accreditation Commission
   (CCAC)
1129 20th Street NW, Suite 400
Washington, DC 20036
(202) 296-5960

Council of State
   Housing Agencies
400 North Capital Street NW,
   Suite 291
Washington, DC 20001

National Association of Housing
   and Redevelopment Officials
2600 Virginia Avenue NW
Washington, DC 20037

Index

Vision problems, driving and, 176

Walking devices, 119, 120

Weight loss, causes of, 71–72
Wheelchairs, 122–123
Will, Living, 200–202
Wills, 209–210

Crystal approached the table at which Spud was seated with two friends. Although she hadn't connected the name Spud to him, she already knew that he was a small-time dealer who regularly peddled his drugs amongst the clientele of the Rose and Crown as well as other city-centre pubs. The three lads were noisy, laughing loudly and talking incessantly over each other.

'Hi. Spud, isn't it?' asked Crystal.

'Yeah. You alright?' he asked, recognising Crystal by sight.

'Yeah, good thanks. I wondered if I could have a word.'

'Sure,' said Spud, getting up from his seat then looking around the pub, his limbs constantly moving. 'I'll grab us another seat.'

Crystal looked at his two friends before turning her attention back to him. 'No, it's OK. I'd prefer us to talk in private if you don't mind sitting somewhere else.'

Spud grinned and flashed her a knowing look. 'Yeah, course. There's a table free over there.'

He headed towards the vacant table and Crystal followed behind. Once there he plonked himself down in a seat. Then his foot shot out and he wrapped it around the leg of a stool, pulling it out from under the table with a fast jerking movement.

'Thanks,' said Crystal, sitting down next to him.

'Before we start,' he said. 'Any business has to be done outside the pub. I can't fuckin' risk being spotted by the landlord. And no giving the game away. You never know who's gonna dob you in.'

As he spoke Crystal noticed how twitchy he was and how dilated his pupils were. She guessed he had recently had a cocaine fix and the small dab of white powder just inside his right nostril confirmed it.

'No, it's not that I'm after,' she said.

'What you after then?' he asked, his head jerking backwards and forwards as he spoke rapidly.

'Information.'

'Aah, right. OK. But it'll cost you.'

'Are you joking? Come on. It's not as if I'm a copper or summat. I just want to know if you've heard of a guy.'

'It'll still cost. Knowledge is power, and all that.'

As he waited for Crystal's response he sniffed repeatedly and tapped his fingers on the table.

'Alright,' said Crystal, becoming mildly irritated by his fidgeting. 'I'll give you twenty but that's it. I only want to know if you've heard of someone.'

Spud sniffed again. 'I'll take the twenty but if you wanna know anything about them it'll cost you more.'

'OK,' said Crystal, pulling a twenty-pound note out of her purse and passing it to him. 'His name's Justin Foster. Do you know him?'

She saw Spud blanch and his movements became even more rapid as he quickly said. 'No. Never heard of him.'

'You sure?'

'Course I'm sure. I wouldn't fuckin' lie, would I?' Crystal looked suspiciously at him as he stood up. 'Look, I'm sorry you've wasted your money,' he continued. 'But, like I said, I've never fuckin' heard of him. I'm going back to my mates. We were having a good laugh till you came over.'

'Wait,' said Crystal, placing a hand on his arm.

He glared at her. 'What?' he demanded.

'Sit down a minute unless you want your mates to hear what I have to say.'

She could tell the name Justin Foster had made him uneasy and guessed correctly that he wouldn't want her to make his involvement with him become public knowledge. He kicked his stool moodily before he sat back down on it then Crystal carried on speaking, deliberately keeping her voice calm but firm.

'You might not know him but he definitely knows you.'

'Nah, doubt it.'

'Really? Well, why would your name be on a list that he carries around with him?'

Spud's expression changed to one of alarm as his jaw dropped open slightly and his eyelids flickered.

'Shush!' he ordered. 'Now you listen to me. Yes, I do know him. Alright. But I wish I'd never fuckin' set eyes on him. And if you've got any sense you'll keep the fuck away from him too. You don't wanna go getting involved with someone like Justin Foster.' He stood up again.

'Why?' asked Crystal even though she thought she already knew the answer.

Spud leant down towards her and whispered, 'Because he's a bad bastard. But you never heard that from me, right?

Like I say: stay the fuck away if you know what's good for you.'

Then he left her sitting there while he dashed from the pub.

'You alright?' asked Ruby when Crystal joined her again.

'Yeah.'

'Well it doesn't fuckin' look like it.'

Crystal shook her head before responding. 'Oh, it's nothing,' she said. 'It's just that he knows my first target but he's warned me to stay the fuck away.'

'Oh. Did he say why?'

'Yeah, he reckons he's a bad bastard.'

'And d'you think he's right?' asked Ruby.

'Oh yeah, definitely. I know he's right.'

Ruby grabbed hold of Crystal's hand. 'What did he do to you?' she asked, with the perception of someone who knew how things worked on the streets.

'It was bad, Ruby,' said Crystal, her voice quivering as she relived the ordeal while describing it to her friend.

'Shit!' said Ruby. 'It sounds like you're playing with fire, Crystal. I think Spud's right. You might want your revenge but it's best to leave it the fuck alone and try to put it behind you. You don't wanna make matters even worse for yourself, do you?'

Crystal shrugged. 'I suppose so,' she said but she had already decided that, although she'd leave Justin Foster alone for now, she would move on to her next target. With a bit of luck he'd be easier to deal with.

She'd been planning this for weeks and there was no way she was going to abandon her scheme, not when her future plans depended on it.

Target 2

<u>Name</u>: Wayne Winters

<u>Profession</u>: Kids' TV Presenter

<u>Description</u>: Aged early thirties, average height (about 5 foot 9), black hair cut in a trendy style, wears trendy clothes

<u>Address</u>: Unknown

<u>Personality</u>: Vain. He loves himself and thinks he's the bee's knees. Obsessed with a well-known female presenter

<u>Phone number</u>: Unknown

<u>Bank details</u>: Yes – has a credit card

<u>Information/Items</u>: Credit card, mobile phone, photograph and name of well-known female TV presenter – Naomh Tranter

<u>Aim</u>: Extortion/blackmail

Crystal could still clearly remember the first time she dealt with Wayne Winters a couple of years back. He had pulled up in his car on Aytoun Street and invited her back to his hotel room. At that point she didn't know who he was but the picture on the bedside cabinet gave her a clue that he might be connected with the television industry. It was of Naomh Tranter, the well-known and popular TV presenter.

'Is she your partner?' Crystal asked, glancing admiringly at the attractive photograph.

She was expecting a rebuff. Crystal didn't often ask clients questions. Knowing that most of them preferred to keep their private lives under wraps, she allowed them to do the talking and responded accordingly. But Wayne seemed happy to answer her.

'I wish,' he said, in answer to her question. 'Gorgeous, isn't she?'

'Yes, she is.'

'I know her, of course,' Wayne continued. 'I've just done a TV show and she was working at the same studios so we had a bit of a chat. She's with someone at the moment though. But I'm just biding my time till the day she's mine. And it'll happen; I'm sure of it.'

Crystal just nodded, feeling uneasy that he should keep a photo of someone he had designs on. It was immediately apparent from his manner that he thought a lot of himself. Otherwise, why be so sure that Naomh Tranter would be his eventually?

Wayne carried on prattling. 'You get to meet a lot of big names in my job. But I suppose it's a novelty for someone like you to meet a TV star.'

Crystal didn't say anything but she picked up on his patronising manner. He also spoke with a Liverpool accent but he was doing his best to tone it down.

This guy was a pretty boy too who had obviously spent a lot of time on his appearance; his hair cut just right in a trendy style and his clothes designer casuals that fit perfectly.

'So, you're in TV as well?' she asked, curious about this new client.

'Yeah, I'm Wayne Winters. I'm surprised you didn't recognise me. I present *Twinkle*, the kids' TV show.'

'I remember that one,' said Crystal. 'My daughter used to watch it when she was little. I don't remember you presenting it though. It was an older man and a woman.'

'Oh, that must have been a while back,' said Wayne. 'I've been on the show for the last two and a half years.'

'Aah, right.'

'We've made some changes since then too, all for the better, obviously.'

Crystal smiled, thinking about how willing he had been to reveal his identity so easily considering he was a well-known TV presenter. But then, she supposed that if she had recognised him from the TV, she'd have known who he was anyway.

Wayne crossed the room and grabbed a backpack from inside the wardrobe then unzipped it. 'Put these on,' he said.

It was a demand rather than a request but Crystal was used to that from clients. She walked over and picked up the items he was handing her: a bandage dress, size 10, and a blonde wig. She could tell the dress had been worn as it smelled of expensive perfume and she guessed straightaway that it belonged to Naomh Tranter, especially as the wig was in a similar hairstyle to that of the famous TV presenter.

Wayne must have picked up on the expression of doubt that flashed across Crystal's face as he quickly said, 'I've borrowed it. I'm sure she won't mind.'

Crystal recognised that it was just the sort of thing Naomh Tranter would wear. She felt a bit uneasy about the scenario at first; she'd never been asked to dress as the object of someone's desire before. But in this industry she was used to dealing with strange tastes and being asked to dress up wasn't that unusual in itself, so she decided to go along with it.

The dress was fitted and, although Crystal was a bit slimmer than Naomh, her breasts were huge following a boob job and the outfit clung to them.

'Nice,' said Wayne. 'You've got curves, just like Naomh. Now,' he added, walking around her and gazing lustfully at her body. 'I want you to peel the dress off slowly, just like Naomh would do, and then do the same with your underwear.'

'OK,' said Crystal, stifling the urge to giggle.

She complied with his wishes, noticing how excited he was becoming, pulling his own clothes off frantically then flinging himself on the bed, his hand clutching his genitals.

'Get here, for fuck's sake!' he ordered. 'I'm ready.'

He got straight down to business and it wasn't long before he climaxed. She could tell when he was about to do so as he insisted on letting her know.

'I'm gonna come, I'm gonna come!' he yelled. 'Aaah, Naomh. You were fuckin' brilliant.'

Then he rolled over and lay on his back, spread-eagled across the bed and leaving no room for her to lie alongside him. But Crystal was done anyway. She stood up and began putting her own clothes back on. Once Wayne became aware that she was getting ready to go, he sat up.

'Well, how does it feel?' he asked.

Crystal looked at him nonplussed. 'What do you mean?'

'To have bedded one of the hottest celebs on TV.' When

Crystal didn't respond, apart from casting a curious glance his way, he said, 'Oh, I know you probably don't think I'm a big shot now but, believe me, this guy is going places.'

His tone demanded a response so Crystal obliged, knowing it was important to keep the customer happy. 'Good for you, I hope you do.'

'No doubt about it. Producers are dying to employ me but I can't oblige them at the moment. I'm too busy fulfilling my contract. But, once I'm through with it, just you watch. They'll be lining up.'

'Couldn't you take on other work on top of *Twinkle*?' she asked.

'Not much, I'm too busy. It takes longer than you think, y'know, to produce a decent kids' show. I mean, I could probably do it in less time but I like to do things properly and offer my own input.'

'Do you not get much time off then?'

'Well, yeah. Some. But, all work and no play and all that...'

As he spoke he got up from the bed and put his clothes back on then walked over to the full-length mirror, smoothing down his hair then puffing his chest out as he checked his physique. He made her wait till he'd finished admiring himself before he passed her the money.

After that first session Wayne phoned her regularly and it was always the same scenario. He brought the same outfit with him each time and asked Crystal to dress up as Naomh Tranter. Something she noticed was that he used a different phone number each time he got in touch. So, although he was happy to reveal his identity, perhaps he had at least taken some steps to protect himself.

Aside from Wayne's obsession with Naomh Tranter, Crystal found him unlikeable and pretentious. He also badmouthed anyone who was having more success than him on TV. In his fantasy world he and Naomh were the two best presenters on television and they deserved to be together.

Crystal had chosen him as a target because of his fake personality and his weird and scary obsession with Naomh Tranter. The man was detestable! And the other reason she had chosen Wayne Winters was because she knew non-exposure would be really important to him. If his obsession with Naomh Tranter and his nefarious activities ever came out in the media, it would ruin his TV career. She was therefore confident that she would have no problems in blackmailing him.

Crystal was in her bedroom going through the items she had collected and she placed all those collected from Wayne Winters on the bed in front of her. She had a credit card but knew it was a waste of time attempting to use it; she'd already tried and failed. It seemed that in the time between her taking the card and trying to use it the next day, Wayne had already placed a stop on it. Nevertheless, the name on the card confirmed that he was probably the person he claimed to be.

She also had a photograph of Naomh Tranter. It wasn't the one he kept in a frame and placed on the bedside table of whichever hotel he was staying at. It was another smaller one, which had been autographed. Crystal had another photograph too; one that she'd taken on her phone, and she knew it would come in very useful.

Crystal had taken a phone from him as well but it was a cheap one, which fitted in with the fact that he used a different number whenever he rang her. Maybe he had purchased several of them.

Fortunately she'd been able to charge the phone up as she'd bought a collection of different chargers especially so that she could carry out her plans. She switched the phone on but there was very little information on it. The only contact was her; maybe she was the only prostitute he used or maybe he used a different phone for each.

Crystal went into the list of calls but, again, she was the only person he'd rung and there was no record of any incoming calls. Likewise, there were no texts whatsoever. That was about the extent of the phone's features; no stored photographs, notes or anything else that might give her something to go on. She decided to try using the phone but it was dead and she surmised that it must have been a pay as you go phone, which hadn't been topped up.

She didn't have any other phone number for him because his number changed all the time. So, although blackmailing him shouldn't be too much of a problem, the main challenge lay in how she was going to make contact with him.

Crystal pulled her laptop out of the wardrobe and switched it on. She keyed Wayne Winters' name into an Internet search engine and his Wikipedia profile appeared at the top of the screen. She clicked on it and scanned through the details. It was mainly a record of his TV career to date; his role on *Twinkle* and a few one-off appearances on kids' TV shows.

The only personal details were his date of birth, where he was born and where he went to school. She took a note of them anyway in case they might prove useful. As he was born in Liverpool there was a good chance he might still live there. But Liverpool was a big place so it would be difficult to find him unless she could pinpoint a precise area.

Next she looked at any other information that appeared on the Internet. There were a few news items that didn't reveal too much, and he had a couple of social media accounts. She took note of the latter and brought them up on the screen.

Crystal decided not to follow him on social media, preferring to exercise caution. But that meant she couldn't send him a private message. He also had privacy settings on some of his social media accounts, which meant she couldn't see a lot of his posts. She'd hoped that he might reveal where he was filming on any particular day but, from the details she could access, he was always vague about his whereabouts and didn't give much away.

But she still hadn't looked at any information relating to the TV programme, *Twinkle*. A quick search of Wikipedia revealed the name of the broadcasting company that aired it and the particular studios where it was filmed, in London. Crystal sighed. London was a long way to go and there was no guarantee she would find him when she got there. The TV studios were probably huge and security was unlikely to let her get through the doors. Apart from all that, she didn't know when exactly the show was filmed and she guessed that it was probably filmed well in advance of the dates when it appeared on TV.

She shut down her laptop. It was getting late and she was tired. She'd had enough for tonight and wondered if her plan was going to prove more challenging than she had anticipated. She'd already hit a brick wall with her first target and now she was having trouble getting hold of the second. She'd sleep on it then decide in the morning whether it was worth making the trip to London.

It was the following morning when she woke up that it came to her. The last time she had seen him he had been bragging about his big chance coming up next month. Apparently it was an opportunity to do something other than kids' TV and it was bound to catapult him to super stardom.

He was going to present a well-known reality TV show called *Song Stars*. He'd explained that it was just for two episodes starting from mid-month while the usual presenter was unavailable. But he'd told her they were bound to ask him to do more on the strength of it. She remembered thinking at the time that the way he'd gushed about it made her feel as though he was trying to convince Naomh Tranter herself of his merits.

Crystal quickly grabbed her laptop and, once she had started it up, she entered the name of the TV show into the Internet. It didn't take her long to find out what dates filming would take place and she was thrilled to find that there were two audition dates next month. And, even better, they were both taking place at Media City, in Salford Quays, Manchester.

The only trouble was, that was three weeks away and she didn't want to wait that long. But the answer to that was easy; in the meantime she would start work on one of her other targets.

13

Target 3
Name: Nigel Swithen
Profession: Restaurateur
Description: Aged around fifty, very overweight and unattractive
Address: Unknown home address but restaurants at Deansgate and Alderley Edge, both called Swithen's
Personality: Egotistical, bragger, hypochondriac, woman hater and bullshitter. Likes prostitutes, overeating and drinking to excess. Repulsive to look at and irritating to listen to. Very unlikeable.
Phone number: Yes
Bank details: No
Information/Items: Restaurant leaflet and cash
Aim: Blackmail/extortion and revenge

Nigel Swithen had been visiting Crystal for a number of years as well as many other prostitutes. On this particular occasion he had rented a hotel room, a preference of his since it meant he didn't have to rush as much because when Nigel Swithen was talking about himself he never rushed.

'So, I said to him,' he drawled, in between quaffing on the hotel's best champagne without offering her any. 'I said if that's the way you want to behave then you'd best start looking for alternative employment. Honestly, the youth of today; there's no work in them. He should have thought himself lucky to be working for an upmarket international restaurant chain, but no...

'And talking of the restaurant chain, I'm so glad that bitch of an ex-wife of mine can't get her hands on it. Thank God I set up the restaurants after the divorce. She leeched off me enough as it was. I tell you what, you won't find me remarrying. Oh no! Women are only good for one thing if you ask me...'

Crystal felt as though she had ceased to exist as a human being; she seemed to have become nothing more than a sounding board for all his gripes. Had he overlooked the fact that she was a woman too and therefore one of the people he was denigrating?

She was tempted to put him straight but she bit back the sharp retort that was ready to spill from her mouth. Nigel Swithen annoyed her so much that she could spend hours arguing with him but that wasn't what she was here for. So, instead, she said, 'OK, do you want to start undressing?' aware of the fact that the hour he had paid for was ticking away.

'In a moment,' he said with a dismissive wave of his hand. 'I haven't finished telling you about my diabetes problems yet. My readings have been right of the scale this week, y'know. The doctor's told me to cut down on the food and drink but what does he know?'

'Alright,' said Crystal. 'I just wondered if you were aware

of the time. Would you like me to book you in for another hour?'

'Oh good God, no! It's costing me enough as it is.'

'Right, well we'd best get started then.'

Crystal's reference to the time seemed to do the trick and he quickly shed his clothes.

'I'm afraid you'll have to get on top again,' he said with a chuckle. 'My gout's playing me up something shocking. You wouldn't believe the pain I suffer.'

Well ditch the fuckin' booze and go on a diet, you fat bastard, thought Crystal but instead she said, 'No problem.'

She looked across at him: Nigel Swithen, the upmarket restaurateur. *Well, he certainly has the girth to show for all that food he eats,* she thought as she looked at his surprisingly small appendage almost swallowed whole by the wide expanse of fat that surrounded it.

Not for the first time she was thankful that at least he didn't have any particular proclivities apart from the fact that he liked to lie back and let her do all the work. She was convinced that the main reason he hired call girls was because they provided him with a chance to belittle women as well as a captive audience while he droned on endlessly about himself.

Crystal shut down the irritating memories of Nigel Swithen and focused instead on the task in hand. She turned to the items relating to him, which she had laid out on the bed.

There was quite a bit to go on really including a leaflet with the names of his restaurants. He hadn't had any cards on him last time she'd seen him but she did have his phone number. Although she hadn't found out his home address, she knew it would be easy to find his restaurants as he'd egotistically named them Swithen's, Deansgate, and Swithen's, Alderley Edge. The restaurant leaflet didn't give the exact addresses but it would take no more than an Internet search to find them.

Crystal started up her laptop and it wasn't long before she had the restaurant website on screen. She noticed the restaurants were described as 'haute cuisine'. It brought a smile to her lips as she recalled him bragging about how it gave him a good excuse to serve minuscule portions at high prices and therefore maximise his profits.

She checked to make sure there were no more than the two restaurants she was aware of but, just as she had suspected, there were only the Deansgate and Alderley Edge branches, which had now been operating for eleven and nine years respectively. That would have given him ample time to expand, she thought ironically, if he hadn't been so busy squandering his profits on prostitutes, booze and 'fine food' as he described it.

The worst thing about her plan to blackmail him was the chance that she might actually have to speak to him again; the man was a tiresome bore. But Crystal was confident that it wouldn't come to that. After all, unlike Wayne Winters, she had a regular phone number for Nigel Swithen. Surely, therefore, it was just a matter of sending a text or making a call and arranging for him to deliver the cash. Deciding there was no point in delaying matters, Crystal fired a text off to him:

> How would you like your friends and family to find out what you get up to in your spare time? I've got plenty of tales to tell. But if you want me to keep silent then you'll have to pay. £5000 should cover it.

A text arrived back within the space of five minutes.

> Who is this?

To which Crystal replied:

> You know me as Crystal.

His next reply came back just as quickly.

> Do you really think a cheap little slut like you can upset me? For your information, it wouldn't bother me in the slightest if you blabbed. I don't have a wife or partner and it's highly unlikely that customers will stop coming to my restaurants just because of what I do in my spare time. Now I suggest you go away before I contact the police.

Crystal wasn't going to be put off so easily. He might not have a wife or partner but it was obvious, from the way he'd bragged in the past, that he cared what his customers thought. They might not bother about his personal reputation but they'd definitely be concerned about the reputations of his restaurants. Dealing with the man brought back to her the repulsion she had felt every time she'd met him but at least she didn't have to have sex with him anymore. Things were different now and Crystal knew she had the upper hand so she pushed those feelings aside.

The next step was straightforward. She set up several email addresses under false names then posted a negative online review for his Manchester restaurant from each of the fake emails. Altogether there were six reviews, each showing a different name. Once she had done that, Crystal sent him another text.

Have you checked your online reviews lately?

She didn't tell him which online sites she'd posted the reviews to. It amused her to think of him frantically clicking away at his keyboard trying to find them. This time she waited a little longer for his response but when it came back it said:

How many reviews do you think you will need to post before you bring my review average down substantially? And, more importantly, how long do you think it will take the police to work out that these spurious reviews have all been sent from the same IP address? Now, I suggest you remove them before I report the matter.

Shit! thought Crystal. She hadn't looked that far into it. She might have to get a bit more creative with this target; perhaps he would be harder to crack than she thought. But she wasn't giving up yet.

*

It was Saturday night and just a few days after Crystal had made her initial approach to Nigel Swithen. Currently he was waiting in a hotel bar to meet another prostitute before going up to the room he had booked. As he waited he thought about what had happened a few days earlier. Cheeky little slut! Did she really think she could get one over on him? Not a chance. Crystal's actions had rattled him but there was no way he was going to let them affect the way he lived his life.

He was pleased when the girl arrived and took a seat next to him. She was prettier than most and was wearing a black figure-hugging dress. Rather tantalising he thought. She had an air of expectation but he crushed any thoughts she might have of getting a free drink straightaway. He was paying enough for tonight as it was!

'I think we might as well go straight up to the room,' he said. 'No point in delaying things.'

Then he downed the rest of his own drink while the girl waited patiently. Once he had finished the last dregs, he stood up. 'Come on, follow me,' he said, and he headed for the lift with the girl trailing behind.

When they reached the room the girl stripped off straightaway and was soon ready to get down to business. Nigel couldn't help an amused smile as he looked at her. These little bitches were all the same: just tits and arse. They were interchangeable at the end of the day and only fit for one thing. But all of them were willing to do whatever it took to get their grubby little hands on his money.

That thought brought Crystal to mind again. He didn't think it was the end of things with her and had a feeling he'd be hearing from her again. But he wasn't fazed by the prospect. Just the opposite, in fact. He was determined to put up a fight and teach her that she wasn't going to get the better of Nigel Swithen!

14

Crystal had had a couple more ideas for how to deal with Nigel Swithen. She knew that he was going on holiday soon because he had talked about nothing else during the last few weeks that she had dealt with him. She also knew that he never took phone calls while he was away. The man was so full of his own self-importance that he'd often bragged about how he had the best staff including a brilliant manager at his Manchester restaurant who was more than capable of taking care of things in his absence.

Whenever he stressed the importance of not being disturbed while he was away he had leered in that sickening way of his. Just the thought of it made Crystal want to retch as she thought about their last conversation, or rather, his monologue about his holidays.

'Thailand's the place to go now, y'know. Those Thai birds are gagging for it and they could certainly teach you British tar... erm prostitutes a thing or two. I was telling a mate of mine, "These British prostitutes need to up their game." You've got competition now, y'know, from this influx of Eastern Europeans. They're well up for it; anything you want, anything at all, and a damn sight cheaper too. They haven't had such an easy life as you lot over here. I'm only telling you for your own good; it pays to keep ahead of things.'

The mere recollection made her seethe but she tried to quash her anger while she focused on her latest plan for revenge. Nigel's absence would give Crystal the opportunity to take advantage, and the fact that he couldn't be contacted would work even more in her favour. A smile played on her lips as she thought about her cunning idea while she made her way to Alderley Edge in a hire car. She wasn't going to wait until he was away; she had another trick in store first.

It didn't take Crystal long to find Nigel Swithen's Alderley Edge restaurant; she'd already been previously to check it out. She couldn't avoid being impressed the first time she had spotted it. The restaurant had screamed Alderley Edge to her with its affluence and upmarket vibe, just like the other venues in the town.

Located in a prime position on the high street it occupied a beautiful old red-brick building, which had been well maintained. It looked spectacular lit up at night and there was a buzz around the place from the diners who occupied the few outside tables, all smart well-dressed people who she could tell had money to burn.

Swithen had kitted it out well too. Expensive-looking wooden planters – well stocked with evergreens – lined the front of the restaurant, forming a casual barrier between the diners and any passers-by. At each side of the entrance stood two decorative large stone pillars, and a neat canopy ran across the whole of the restaurant's frontage. It was in a muted shade of grey with the words 'Swithen's, Alderley Edge' printed across the centre in a classic font.

Crystal hadn't actually been inside the restaurant but she surmised that the interior would be just as impressive as the outside.

She passed the front of Swithen's and made her way to the rear where there was an entrance for customer vehicles to access the car park as well as for deliveries. Having checked out the restaurant over several days and asked around, Crystal knew the exact days that deliveries were made and she'd deliberately chosen a time when the restaurant was due to receive a big delivery. It wasn't the busiest time in terms of custom, but it was a time when she was likely to cause the most disruption.

She had also chosen the biggest car available from the hire company. Cost was no object as she'd given the company a false name and address and used a stolen credit card.

Once she had reached the back of the restaurant, Crystal parked the car across the entranceway leaving no room for any cars or vans to pass through. She switched off the engine, locked the car and turned to walk away. Crystal caught the eye of a motorist who was waiting to drive into the restaurant's car park and saw the look of incredulity on his face.

He wound down the window, shouting at her as she walked briskly away. 'What the hell do you think you're doing?'

But Crystal kept walking, knowing that by the time the man had decided whether to pursue her and, if so, what to do with his car, she would be well away. She made her way to the train station, thankful that it was out of view of Swithen's restaurant, and waited for a train in to Manchester. She had intended to wait until she reached home before she sent Nigel Swithen a text but one arrived from him before the train had even pulled in to Manchester:

I suppose this is your idea of a joke?

Crystal fired a text back straightaway:

No, I'm deadly serious. Are you ready to reconsider yet?

Not at all. In fact, I've already called the police. They've just arrived and are arranging for your car to be towed away. In the meantime I can see one of the officers on his radio, probably checking for the vehicle owner's address so it shouldn't be long now till they catch up with you.

She smiled as she typed her reply.

Good luck with that. It isn't my car.

By the time the train arrived in Manchester, Crystal had received no further texts. She slipped the car keys into an envelope she had already prepared together with a note detailing where she had left the car, and she posted them off to the hire company. Then she boarded a bus to her home in Longsight.

There were still no further texts when she arrived home so she removed the SIM card from the phone and disposed of it. She had already bought a replacement, anticipating that he would get the police involved at some point. Crystal wasn't too worried about Nigel's lack of response; she had already planned her next move.

It wasn't long before Candice was home from school and she burst into the house full of exuberance, and handed Crystal a letter. 'It's about the school disco. Can I go, Mum, please?'

Crystal had a quick look at the letter, checking they were free on that date before replying. 'Course you can, love.'

'Aw, brilliant!' said Candice, bending over to where Crystal was sitting on the armchair and giving her an affectionate hug. 'I love you, Mum.'

'I wondered when I was going to get my hug,' said Crystal, smiling back at her daughter.

She loved it when Candice was like this, all happy and excited. But then, as Candice drew away, her mood seemed to change and she had a look of worry on her face.

'What's the matter?' asked Crystal.

'Well, all my friends will be wearing new clothes for the disco and I don't really want them to see me in what I wore last time.'

'It's no problem, love. Don't worry, I'll get you something nice. We can go at weekend if you like.'

'Aw, can we? Brilliant!' Candice gushed.

Crystal couldn't help but think back to how things had been before, especially when she had been with Gilly. What little money he had left her with was taken up by drugs and struggling to pay the bills. At one time she would have had to say no to Candice's new outfit and then watched the disappointment on her face. She was such a good kid that she would pretend it didn't matter when Crystal knew that really it did.

It was so gratifying now to be able to give Candice the

things she wanted. Why should she have any less than her friends had? Candice deserved it; she was a little angel, and it gave Crystal immense pleasure to be able to treat her. She felt a warm glow inside knowing that once her plans were complete Candice would want for nothing in the future.

15

Three weeks after she had drawn up plans for targeting Wayne Winters, Crystal turned up for filming. Although she'd arrived early there was a large queue outside the TV studios. She clutched the ticket she'd managed to acquire at short notice through a contact at the Rose and Crown, and waited for the doors to open.

She cursed her choice of footwear; the high heels made her feet throb as she stood in the queue. The incessant chatter from people around her was also making her a bit irritable. Their enthusiasm for the forthcoming show was lost on Crystal whose reason for being there was something entirely different.

It soon became apparent to Crystal that most of these people were real aficionados who followed the show around the country so she decided to use that to her advantage. Knowing her aim would be more successful if she blended in with the crowd, she struck up a conversation with a group of teenage girls who were in front of her in the queue.

'Do you know who's presenting the show this week?' asked Crystal once she had gained their interest.

'Same as every week,' said a tall girl with a nose ring. 'Naomh Tranter.'

'Ah, right. Is Wayne Winters not presenting it?' asked Crystal.

'No,' said the girl. 'Why? Do you like him?' Her friends giggled at her boldness.

'Not exactly,' said Crystal. 'But I've come across him in the past and I just want to be in the audience to support him.'

'What, you mean you know him?' asked the girls, excitedly. 'How come he didn't get you in for free?'

'It's a surprise,' Crystal added. She was beginning to regret telling them so much.

'He might be on the after show,' said the girl's friend. 'The usual presenter isn't gonna be on it for two weeks because he's filming another big show. Maybe he's the stand-in for him.'

Crystal nodded knowingly. It sounded like Wayne's style, leading her to believe he was presenting the main show when he was on the after show. She looked at her ticket, her expression one of concern.

'Oh, it's OK,' said the girl. 'That ticket will get you in both but the after show is filmed a bit later and it's in a studio further down the corridor from where the main show's filmed. Just follow the signs.'

Crystal smiled. 'Thanks.'

The queue started moving and Crystal was soon inside the building. She followed the signs as the young girls had instructed and grabbed herself a seat well back from the front. She didn't want Wayne to see her yet; she needed to take him by surprise once she could get him on his own.

*

At the end of the show Crystal followed a group of dedicated fans who were trying to make it backstage. She was disconcerted to discover that the security staff were holding them back. Crystal edged her way to the front of the group hoping to convince the two burly men on the door to let her through.

'Hi, I'm a friend of Wayne's,' she said. 'Mind if I go through to see him?'

'You got a backstage pass?'

'Not exactly, no. But I know he'll want to see me.'

'What's your name?' growled the doorman.

'Erm, it's Laura,' said Crystal, opting to use her real name rather than the street name Gilly had given her during her days on the game. She knew that if she used the name Wayne knew her by, it would alert him.

'Laura what?'

'He, he doesn't know my surname but, trust me, I know him. And I prefer it if you don't give him my name. I want to surprise him.'

'Nah, you're not coming in,' he said.

While Crystal remonstrated with the burly man, a young woman standing next to her was trying to persuade the other doorman to let *her* through. From what Crystal could hear she wasn't having any success either. After pleading with the doorman she turned to Crystal.

'We're wasting our time here. We might as well call it a day. I'm gutted. I love Wayne Winters and I was really looking forward to meeting him.'

Crystal tried not to display her repulsion as she went along with the young woman. 'Me too.'

A young woman behind them spoke up. 'Well, I don't

know about you two but I'm going to Studio. Loads of the stars hang out there. He might go there after the show.'

Crystal turned round and looked at her, confused. 'It's a bar,' said the woman.

'Where is it?'

'Only about two doors down. Come on, let's go.'

Crystal followed the handful of people who made their way to Studio but then she hung back, pretending she had to make a phone call. She didn't want to be in the company of others when she confronted Wayne. What she had to say to him had to be done surreptitiously.

After waiting a couple of minutes, Crystal walked into the bar. She noticed the group of people who had come from the TV studios and deliberately plonked herself on a bar stool well away from them then ordered herself a brandy and soda. Although Crystal still enjoyed a drink, she had cut down drastically. Now, instead of drinking to excess she found she was able to enjoy a couple of drinks socially. Thank God her drinking hadn't got to the stage where she daren't touch another drop! It was different where drugs were concerned; she knew she couldn't risk ever taking drugs again otherwise she would end up back in that dark place she had escaped from.

She scanned the room on the way in, noting where the group of fans from the TV studios were sitting and also noticing that Wayne Winters didn't seem to be in the bar yet. Crystal had her back to the fans, hoping they wouldn't notice her. But she was also near enough to pick up on their excited chatter once Wayne Winters entered the bar. And she knew it would happen if he was to enter; these women were fanatical, although God alone knew why. She felt sure that if they learnt what Wayne was really like, they'd soon change their opinions of him.

She had already reached the bottom of her glass when she heard an enthusiastic cheer amongst the crowd of women. She glanced over her shoulder to see Wayne Winters break away from a group of people and saunter up to the bar with a smug grin on his face. As he reached the bar she jumped down from her stool and walked over to him.

'Hi, Wayne, fancy buying me a drink?' she asked, holding out her empty glass.

Wayne's expression was one of shock and for a moment he stared at her with his mouth and eyes wide open before he spoke. 'What the fuck do *you* want?'

'Buy me a drink and I'll tell you,' said Crystal, provocatively, noticing with satisfaction how he quickly turned his head to see if any of his colleagues were watching. He seemed to weigh up his options before he sighed and asked again, 'What do you want?'

'Ooh, let me see. About two grand for my silence.'

He glared at her. 'You must be fuckin' joking!'

'Not at all. Oh, and I'll have a double brandy and soda too seeing as how you're buying.'

Wayne ordered the drinks then slammed his money on the bar. After the barman had finished serving, Wayne turned to Crystal. 'Right, you've got your drink so now you can fuck off! There's no way I'm letting you blackmail me. Nobody would fuckin' believe you anyway.'

'Believe what, Wayne? That you've been visiting a prostitute or that you've got a weird obsession with Naomh Tranter?'

She watched him visibly cringe. 'None of it. They won't believe fuck all coming from a cheap tart like you.'

'Oh, won't they?' asked Crystal, pulling out her phone then bringing a photograph up on the screen.

She smirked as she spotted his reaction. The look of sheer terror on his face told her she had him. 'Recognise this?' she asked, showing him a picture she had taken in the bathroom of one of the hotels they'd visited. It showed her from the shoulders down wearing Naomh Tranter's dress. 'Yes, I'm sure Naomh Tranter would too, and how do you think she'd react if she was to discover what happened to the dress that went missing from her dressing room?'

Wayne glared at her. 'I can't fuckin' afford that much! *Twinkle* doesn't pay that well, y'know. Anyway, how would she know it was hers? There could be loads of people with the same dress.'

'I doubt it. There's not many people can afford a dress like that. It's not exactly high street, is it?' Then she showed him another photograph of the designer label attached to the dress, and added, 'So, two grand is what I'm after, and you'll be getting off lightly.'

'And how do I know you won't fuckin' come back for more once I've given you that?' His voice had now changed. Instead of sounding angry it had a panicked edge to it.

'Because you have my word for it, Wayne. Besides, I've got much bigger fish to fry than you.'

Just that moment they heard one of Wayne's friends shouting, 'Where's those drinks, Wayne? We're dehydrating here.'

Wayne turned around. 'Won't be a minute,' he said.

Crystal knew she had to act quickly before his friend came over so she pulled a handwritten note from her handbag and slipped it into Wayne's hand. 'There's the details of where and when to make the payment.' Wayne nodded then stuffed it in his pocket and picked up the round of drinks from the bar. 'Don't let me down, Wayne,' she said as he walked away, 'Otherwise I might have to tell the world about your dirty little secret.'

He snarled at her as he went to join his friends but Crystal wasn't bothered. She knew he'd pay up and she smiled to herself as she downed her drink then left the bar.

16

It was just over a week later when Crystal began to execute the next stage of her plan relating to Nigel Swithen, having waited until he was on holiday.

'Oh hello,' said Crystal into her phone. 'My name is Melanie O'Brien from Swithen's restaurant in Manchester.'

'Oh hi, Melanie. It's Robyn. How are you?' said the person on the other end of the line.

Crystal could feel the flutter of nerves. Robyn clearly knew Melanie O'Brien. 'Hi, Robyn. I'm good, thank you,' she replied. 'I hope you are too.'

'Yes, thanks. You don't sound so good if you don't mind me saying.'

'No, I'm full of a cold,' said Crystal, relieved that she had used a voice changer to imitate someone with a cold. Hopefully that would disguise her voice enough so that Robyn wouldn't know the difference between her and Melanie.

'And how's that little rascal of yours?' asked Robyn.

Shit! thought Crystal. *What's she referring to: a child, a dog, a cat?*

She was quick to deflect. 'Not too bad, thanks. Listen, Robyn, it's a bit mad here today so I hope you don't mind if I get straight to the point.'

'Sure, no probs.'

'OK. I need to change our order.'

'Right, I'll just grab a pen. What would you like?'

'I want to double up on the steaks, please, for the next three weeks at least.'

'Wow! OK.'

'Yeah, we've suddenly got really busy following an online ad and we keep running out. We have to keep offering the customers an alternative, which means we're running short of a lot of the other meat too.'

'Right. Would you like to increase the amount of anything else?'

'Yes, the chicken and the lamb.'

'How many?' asked Robyn.

Crystal had no idea how much meat Swithen's restaurants went through. 'Well, I wouldn't say double exactly. Maybe just increase everything by a third.'

'OK, so what are we talking about in terms of numbers exactly?'

'Oh, I'm sorry, Robyn. I haven't had chance to work it out. Like I say, we're mad busy here and having this stinking head cold doesn't help. I can't think straight, my head's aching so much.'

'Aw, poor you,' said Robyn. 'I tell you what, leave it with me. I'll work it out and get them off to you.'

'Thanks, Robyn. That would be brilliant. And I'll come back to you in a couple of weeks to let you know if we want to carry on with the increase in supplies.'

'Sure, thanks for your custom. I'll let you get back to it.'

Crystal put the phone down and grinned to herself. She'd done it and she couldn't help but feel a sense of smug satisfaction. It was strange to feel like this. For so much of her life she'd put up with bad treatment from people without hitting back. She had never thought herself capable of such deceit, let alone such vindictiveness, but now she found she was quite enjoying it. After all, she'd specifically chosen each of her targets and they all deserved everything that was coming to them.

It wasn't until almost two weeks later that Crystal witnessed the results of her call to the wholesalers. She waited until Nigel Swithen was due back from his fortnight away then texted him.

Hi, it's Crystal. I thought you might want to know my new number.

He had presumably returned from his holidays to find chaos in his Manchester restaurant, and he had guessed straightaway that she was responsible for the increased meat order and the resultant waste of money. As soon as Crystal received his first text she could tell he was starting to crack, and she was quick to respond.

Just what the hell do you think you're playing at? Your stupid pranks are costing me a bloody fortune!

I'm not playing at all. I've told you before, I'm deadly serious. And if you don't pay the £5000 I've asked you for then things are going to get a whole lot worse.

That's what you think! I've already got the police involved and it's only a matter of time before they catch up with you. And when they do, I personally will look forward to seeing you locked up behind bars where you belong.

Good luck with that.

Crystal disposed of the phone yet again when he didn't make any further comeback to her last text.

Once she had finished with the phone, she spent a few minutes deep in thought. As she had already surmised, Nigel Swithen was proving to be a much bigger challenge than she had at first predicted. And, if she was honest with herself, she was running out of ideas.

But she still wasn't ready to give up on him. Nigel Swithen was a weak man and there was no way she was going to be beaten by someone like him, especially after she had invested so much time already. And she knew she was near to breaking him; it was obvious from the tone of his texts that he wasn't taking things coolly anymore.

Crystal thought about the steps she'd already taken. She'd threatened to expose him, posted online negative reviews, blocked the entrance to one of his restaurants and cost him a small fortune by ordering excess meat supplies. And yet he still hadn't given in to her demands! But he would, soon, she was sure of it. She just had to come up with something that would really make him crack.

17

A week later Crystal still hadn't thought of a way to make Nigel Swithen respond to her threats and she was becoming frustrated. She had therefore decided to push it to one side for now and give herself a well-deserved night out. She headed for the Rose and Crown where she knew many of the regulars, and was pleased to see a group of friends there. Three of the street girls – Amber, Sapphire and Angie – were all seated round a table having a chat and they looked up as she approached them.

'Oh, hello. We weren't expecting to see you here tonight,' said Amber.

'Well, I just fancied a night out.'

'Aw, that's a shame because we'll be off to work in a bit.'

'Shit, never mind,' Crystal said, looking around the pub to see if there was anybody else around who she knew.

Then Sapphire chipped in. 'Actually, I'm not going straightaway. I fancy having a couple more drinks before I go off to work.'

Crystal smiled. 'Great. We can have a few drinks together and a catch-up.'

It wasn't long before Amber and Angie went off to work,

hugging Crystal as they left and asking her to pop in again soon. Once they were gone, Sapphire turned to Crystal.

'Actually, I'm glad you've come in,' she said. 'I was going to ring you to cancel our get-together next week.'

'Why? What's wrong?' asked Crystal, who had been looking forward to a get-together at Sapphire's place. She was good fun to be around, and they generally stayed up till the early hours having a gossip and a laugh.

'The bloody flat's overrun with cockroaches. I'm sick of it. The little bastards are everywhere.'

'Haven't you been on to the council about it?'

'Yeah, loads of times. But, as per usual, they're dragging their bloody feet. Anyway, they've finally arranged to come round in a couple of weeks to fumigate. Hopefully that'll get rid of the little buggers but it just means I'll have to put off our get-together till after the council have been round.'

'Why?'

''Cos of the cockroaches, you daft cow.'

'Don't be stupid. As if that would bother me. Sod the cockroaches. I've had a lot worse than that to deal with in my fuckin' life. A few bloody cockroaches aren't gonna bother me.'

'Aw, so you'll still be coming round then?'

'Course I will.'

The following Saturday Sapphire was having a night off work and was sitting inside her flat with Crystal necking wine while they played music and had a chat. Sapphire was currently telling Crystal about a recent client who had asked her to dress up as a young child.

'So, what did you do then?' asked Crystal.

'Well, what could I do? I put the fuckin' dress on, tied my hair up in pigtails, stuck the dummy in my gob and got on with it. He was offering me a lot of money when all said and done so I thought, what's the harm?'

'Didn't it feel a bit weird though, dressed like that?' asked Crystal.

'Course it did, especially when he asked me to wear a pair of bloody ankle socks and call him Daddy.'

'You're joking!' said Crystal. Then a mental image of Sapphire dressed as a young child flashed through her mind and she burst into laughter.

Sapphire couldn't help but join in with the laughter. They'd both had a fair bit to drink and were feeling merry. But after they'd calmed down, Crystal was gripped by an attack of conscience.

'Thinking about it though, Sapphire, we shouldn't really be laughing. I mean, the guy's probably a fuckin' paedophile, and if he's asking you to dress up as a young kid then God knows what he'd do if he could get his hands on a child. In fact, he might have even done it already.'

'Fuck! I didn't think of it like that,' said Sapphire. 'But now you've pointed it out I'll piss him off next time he asks to see me and I'll put the word out to the other girls.'

'Good for you. We don't need perverts like him in the world.' Then Crystal reached over to the coffee table and grabbed the wine bottle, which was empty. Alongside it was another bottle she'd brought, but that was also empty. 'Shit, it looks like we're out of booze.'

Sapphire stood up and grinned. 'Don't worry. There's plenty more where that came from.'

She walked to the back of the living room, opened a cupboard door then reached inside it. 'Shit!' she yelled. Crystal turned round to see Sapphire jumping back from the cupboard in panic and disgust, shouting, 'It's full of the little bastards!'

Crystal rushed to Sapphire's side where she could see hordes of cockroaches crawling all over the booze Sapphire had stored in the cupboards and scurrying across the floor. The sight of them with their hairy legs and wriggling antennae made her itch, and the stench coming from them made her gag. She instinctively jumped back as well, then danced around on her tiptoes as she tried to avoid them.

'Fuck! Haven't you got anything to kill them with?' she asked Sapphire.

'Yes, I'll get some spray,' said Sapphire, dashing through to the kitchen.

Crystal realised that this was the chance she had been waiting for. While Sapphire was gone, she dashed back to the coffee table, grabbed her bag and rooted inside it for the large matchbox she had brought with her. Then she rushed back to the cupboard and, fighting back her gagging reflex, she scooped as many cockroaches as she could fit into the box and shut it. She could hear Sapphire in the kitchen and the sound of tin cans jangling as though she was searching through a cupboard for the spray.

Then the jangling sound stopped and Crystal could hear Sapphire's footsteps as she made her way back to the living room. She shoved the matchbox inside a polythene bag and pushed it back inside her handbag. Crystal was just putting her bag back on the floor when Sapphire walked into the room.

'Aw, I'm sorry, Crystal,' she said. 'They've not got inside your bag, have they?'

'No, it's OK. I've just checked it and it's alright,' said Crystal. 'Don't worry; I'll give it a good shake before I go home.'

'Make sure you do,' Sapphire replied. 'The last thing you want is to take them home with you. I can't tell you how bad it feels having those little bastards running about all over the place.'

18

Crystal was enjoying her time at Swithen's, Manchester. It was rare for her to eat in such a high-class restaurant and she would have liked to have taken her time but it was so expensive that she'd decided to have only a main course. The food was delicious, better than anything she had ever tasted, but the portions were minute and it didn't take her long to finish it. She was tempted to order a sweet but decided that, at these prices, she would be better off filling her stomach with some toast and biscuits when she got home.

As she waited for the bill, she contemplated doing a runner but that would only draw attention to herself and she wanted to avoid that if possible. So she paid the waitress then gathered her things together. Crystal could feel her heart racing in anticipation of what she was about to do. But she knew she had to act quickly because the restaurant staff would want her out of the place now she had settled her bill.

Picking up her bag, Crystal grabbed the matchbox that was tucked inside, and placed it on the table. Then she took out her phone and brought up the camera function. It was a tricky manoeuvre, opening the box and getting the picture in focus at just about the right time. But she did it, releasing the cockroaches and managing to keep the matchbox out of the shot while capturing the repulsive creatures as they scuttled about on the table top.

She heard a screech from the next table. A customer had spotted the cockroaches. Without waiting for a reaction, Crystal slipped her phone back inside her handbag and dashed from the restaurant. She could hear a commotion in the background but she didn't turn round. Her aim was just to get away as quickly as possible.

Crystal waited till she was home before she checked out the photo on her phone. It was perfect; she had most of the table top in the shot, including the decorative brass number plate, and the distinctive plush seating could be seen in the background. They were both so individual that they would easily verify that the restaurant was Swithen's.

Using a false name, it was easy to post the picture on social media sites. She also added suitable comments from her as an outraged customer. After she had done that, Crystal posted some more negative reviews about Swithen's being overrun with cockroaches. Then, all that was left to do was to wait for the reaction.

The next day, when she checked the various websites, Crystal was amazed to find that she wasn't the only one who had spotted the cockroaches. Two other customers had posted equally outraged comments on one of her social media posts about seeing cockroaches inside Swithen's restaurant and one had even added her own photograph of a cockroach running across the restaurant floor. In addition to that, there were several negative reviews from customers who had spotted the cockroaches and other outraged responses from people who hadn't even visited the restaurant.

Swithen's management had been quick to respond, claiming that it was a prank by a mischievous customer who was seen running out of the restaurant, but it was obvious from the angry backlash that the public weren't convinced.

Crystal was shocked to realise just what a stir she had created. She couldn't believe how easy it was to bring a well-respected restaurant into disrepute and, although she had achieved her objective, she couldn't help but feel a pang of guilt. She was also nervous; if she was found out she'd probably end up in serious trouble.

But she wouldn't be found out because she had told no one. Even if someone from the restaurant could describe her to the police, she was confident they wouldn't be able to trace her because she had covered her tracks. Once again she had used a false name when she had made the booking and she'd paid in cash.

Thinking of how well she'd pulled it off, Crystal began to relax. Although she was still feeling a little nervous she also felt a tremendous buzz. Nigel Swithen was an arrogant, pompous bore who used women like her to satiate his own needs and expected them to pander to his every whim despite their revulsion towards him. Well now he was getting his comeuppance. It was her turn to make him suffer and she surprised herself by just how much she was enjoying it.

'Ah, here you are,' said Melanie O'Brien, manager of Swithen's, Manchester. It was the morning after the fiasco with the cockroaches, and she was still engaged in a damage-limitation exercise. They'd decided to close the restaurant to the public until the problem with the cockroaches was dealt with, and Melanie had been waiting to speak to Nigel about further action.

Nigel didn't like her tone, and immediately became defensive. 'I already told you on the phone, I was busy on business last night.' Melanie gave him a knowing look, which made him more irate. 'This isn't the only restaurant I own, you know,' he snapped.

'No, Nigel, but it is the only one that's become overrun with cockroaches.'

'Overrun? Don't be ridiculous! I thought you said she'd brought them in a matchbox. How many of the damn things could she fit inside a matchbox, for heaven's sake?'

'It was one of the large matchboxes, and she released enough of them to cause a great deal of disruption. We had to shut the restaurant because customers were leaving in their droves and queuing up for refunds.'

'Right, well, you'd best tell me what action you've taken about the matter up to now.'

Melanie sighed before detailing how they'd dealt with the customers, trying their best to reassure them it was a one-off, how they'd called the police as soon as possible to report the incident and how, once everything else was dealt with, she had sat up till the early hours trying to counter negative reviews and comments on social media.

Nigel listened to what she had to say but he wasn't really focused on her words; he was too het up at the thought that he had been maliciously targeted once again. He was livid and he needed someone to blame. Melanie just happened to be there.

'And have you called in a pest control company?' he demanded.

Melanie sighed, 'Not yet, no.'

'Well I suggest you do so, and ask them to come as soon as possible. The entire bloody place wants fumigating. Oh, and shop around. I want the best price; we've lost enough damn money as it is. Let me know when they're coming and, as soon as they've taken care of matters, we can reopen.'

'It isn't as straightforward as that,' said Melanie, with attitude. 'We need to think about what to do with the food. Obviously there's a chance that the cockroaches might have worked their way into some of the perishables. Tinned food should be OK but, even then, we will need to store it away from any poisons used by the pest control company otherwise we risk the food becoming contaminated once the tins are opened.'

'Oh, for heaven's sake, Melanie! Stop making a mountain out of a molehill. We're only talking about a few tiny bloody insects when all's said and done. Just get on the phone to the pest controllers. They should advise you what to do about the food.'

He turned to walk away before giving Melanie chance to respond, letting out a loud belch as he did so. He'd heard enough and didn't think he could take any more. The stress was playing havoc with his digestive system as it was. But Melanie's next words made him turn back.

'I thought you might like to know,' she shouted. 'Health and safety have already been on the phone. They want to come and inspect the place.'

'Jesus! When?' Nigel couldn't believe that health and safety were onto them so soon. He'd hoped to get the matter cleared up and avoid them even finding out but they must have been alerted either by a disgruntled customer or because of the online reviews and comments.

'I don't know. They haven't set a time yet. I thought perhaps you might like to talk to them.' She passed him a slip of paper. 'Here's the number. They're waiting for you to ring back and arrange a visit.'

Nigel made to grab the piece of paper but, as he did so, he spotted something moving on the ground near his feet. He let out a loud screech and tried to dodge it but the little bugger crawled onto his shoes. Its speed was frightening and before he knew it the damn thing had latched onto his trousers and was making its way upwards.

'Aah!' he yelled. 'Get the bloody thing off.'

But Melanie walked away. 'I'll leave you to deal with it,' she shouted over her shoulder. 'After all, it's only a tiny bloody insect when all's said and done.'

Nigel grabbed a place mat and swatted the cockroach till it dropped off his trousers and sped along the ground away from him. The sight of the thing had given him the creeps. Thank God the place mat had been handy otherwise he'd have had to touch the damn thing. The thought of it made him shudder but at least it would have been preferable to letting it make its evil little way up his body.

He went over to the bar area and grabbed himself a drink, despite the fact that it was still only eleven in the morning. His nerves were shattered with these latest events. The episode with the meat had been bad enough. How on earth could the wholesale company have mistaken some tart's voice for that of Melanie? Nigel cursed their foolishness. Was he completely surrounded by incompetents? Still, at least the wholesalers had eventually capitulated and refunded him some of the money but only after he'd kicked up a fuss and threatened to take them to court. Damn imbeciles!

Of course, he knew who was really responsible for everything that was going wrong. That hard-faced little tart! He only wished he could have got his hands on her. And what exactly were the police doing to track her down? The fools! He made a mental note to contact them and apply a bit more pressure. Surely, it was only a matter of time before they caught up with her. Otherwise, God alone knew what she was about to do next.

Nigel tried to put his trust in the police, hoping they would eventually put a stop to all this. He had to believe in them because there was no way he was going to be beaten by some tacky, malicious street girl. But what if they didn't manage to trace her? What if things got even worse?

19

Ironically, the same day that Crystal read in the news about Nigel Swithen's Manchester restaurant being shut down by the health and safety inspector, she also received a text. Having heard nothing from him since she'd released the cockroaches, Crystal had texted him the previous day using another throwaway phone.

Are you ready for the next stage?

she had asked but Nigel hadn't responded.

She had almost given up on him, deciding that it would be better to find an easier target and focus on them instead. But then her phone pinged. Crystal knew it was a text from him. She hadn't given this number to anyone else.

Right, you win! I want an end to all this nonsense. But I can't afford £5000, not with the money I'm losing at the moment, thanks to you. It'll have to be £3000. Let me know where you want the money delivering.

Crystal smiled as she read the text. She knew she had him and there was no way she was going to settle for three thousand pounds, not with the amount of time and effort she had already spent on him.

'What are you smiling at, Mum?' asked Candice, looking across from where she was sitting on the sofa. 'Can I have a look?'

'No, it's nothing. It's not for your eyes, love. It's a grown-up joke.'

Crystal smiled again on hearing Candice reply, 'Whatever.' It always amused her to hear her daughter coming out with the latest expressions as they sounded so out of place from Candice. To someone else the term might sound dismissive but Crystal knew her daughter; she was just imitating her peers but not meaning any offence.

Once she was satisfied that Candice's eyes were fixed once again on the TV screen Crystal fired a text back.

It's £5000, non-negotiable, or we go to the next stage. And I want you to promise you won't turn up with the police when we arrange the drop-off point. I've already left instructions with a friend to take it to the next stage if I get arrested. And there's no way you'll be able to find her.

While she texted, Crystal kept looking over at her daughter, worried in case she had an inkling of what she was up to. She'd be mortified if Candice found out she was a blackmailer as well as a former prostitute but she was doing it for the right reasons. Anyway, it wouldn't be forever and they'd both gain from it in the end.

The next text took a while to come back and she could picture Nigel cursing and stomping around as he deliberated over what to do. Eventually she heard the phone ping again.

Right, I'll agree to £5000 but I want you to promise that you'll put a complete stop to all this.

Crystal smiled as she typed her response.

You have my word.

OK, where and when do you want me to deliver the money?

Crystal sent him the details then smiled smugly. She'd done it! She'd broken that pompous prat Nigel Swithen. And now she was five thousand pounds richer. Crystal was surprised by the tremendous buzz that she felt at her triumph. It was addictive and she couldn't wait to start on her next target.

When Justin Foster answered his phone he could hear Phil Thomas on the other end of the line.

'Hi, boss,' he said. 'I've got a bit more info for you about that tart.'

'Yeah, go on.'

'She's called Crystal.'

'For fuck's sake! We already know that. I was the one who gave you her fuckin' name.'

'Yeah, but there's more. Apparently she doesn't have red hair anymore so it's no wonder I couldn't find her. They reckon' she's not on the game anymore either and looks completely different. Anyway, I've found out where she hangs out. It's a pub called the Rose and Crown but from what I've been told she doesn't go in there as much as she used to. The guy I spoke to said Crystal was the name she used for business when she was on the game.'

'So, what's her real name then?'

'Laura apparently.'

'Laura? OK. Laura what?'

'Sorry, boss, the guy didn't know that.'

'For fuck's sake! Haven't you got any more than that?'

'Not yet, no. But at least we know where she hangs out now.'

'OK, here's what you're gonna do. I want you in that fuckin' pub day and night. You need to find out more. I want you to find the bitch and where she lives, and when you do, I want you to let me know so I can decide how to deal with her.'

'Sure,' Phil Thomas began, but Justin had already cut the call.

20

Target 4

<u>Name</u>: Joseph Abrahams

<u>Profession</u>: Doctor

<u>Description</u>: Aged mid to late fifties, around five foot six, slight, grey hair, unattractive

<u>Address</u>: Unknown

<u>Personality</u>: Really weird

<u>Phone number</u>: Yes

<u>Bank details</u>: Yes

<u>Information/Items</u>: Debit card, cash and mobile phone

<u>Aim</u>: Revenge and safeguarding the public

Crystal still found it difficult to think about this next client without shuddering, despite the fact that he had only visited her once a few weeks ago. Unlike Wayne Winters and Nigel Swithen, this guy wasn't just unlikeable, he was creepy and he took repulsion to a whole new level.

Like many of her other clients, he had taken her to a hotel room. A lot of clients preferred the privacy that it afforded them but it soon became apparent why privacy was so important to this particular man. He wasn't scary in the physical sense, being only slight and not particularly tall. But there was definitely something weird about him. That wasn't too worrying in itself; a lot of her clients were a bit odd. But, the longer she spent with him, the more she realised just how peculiar he was.

'Before you undress, I would like you to remove your makeup; it's all wrong, I'm afraid,' he said. 'Instead, I'd like you to wear some that I've brought.'

'OK,' said Crystal, holding her hand out so he could pass over the plastic bag he was carrying.

'Actually, I'd prefer to put it on you myself, if that's alright. I find that a lot of girls tend to overdo it.'

'Fine,' said Crystal, thinking that he clearly thought she wore too much makeup, and trying not to be offended.

'If you would like to lie down, it'll be easier for me to apply the makeup. But I'd like you to undress first. It'll stop your clothes from becoming covered in it.'

Crystal did as he asked then watched as he leant beside her on the bed and took some face powder out of a bag. She noticed how pale it was and thought that it wouldn't really suit her skin tone. But she wasn't overly concerned; she'd just clean it off in the bathroom when they had finished.

Once he had covered her face with the powder he said, 'Right, I need your eyes closed for the next stage.' When Crystal drew her head back, he seemed to sense her alarm as he added, 'It's alright, no need to worry. It's just so that the powder doesn't go into your eyes.'

'Let me see what else is in that bag!' demanded Crystal, worried in case he might try to tie her up.

He opened the bag and she peered inside, satisfied that it

held nothing other than makeup. But, just to make sure, she said, 'I want to know what's inside your pockets too.'

The man sighed and turned out the outer pockets of his jacket, which were empty. Then he took a handful of items from his inside pocket: a mobile phone, wallet and pen, and placed them on top of the dressing table. Once he'd removed the items, he turned out that pocket too to let her know there was nothing else inside.

'Fair enough,' she said, shutting her eyes.

Crystal was still a bit ill at ease but decided to go along with it. When she felt the soft makeup applicator gliding under her eyes, she relaxed a little. It seemed he was keeping to his word after all. She thought he was perhaps using highlighter or concealer but then he seemed to use the same applicator to also add some makeup to the crease above her eyes although he left the rest of her eyelids alone.

'Right, you can open your eyes now,' he said, 'But I want you to stay very still while I apply some eyeliner.'

She didn't notice the colour as he quickly took an eyeliner pencil and ran it underneath her eyes, seemingly satisfied with the results. Crystal felt her eyes water and she blinked a few times.

'Don't worry, the next stage is far more comfortable,' he said. 'We're just going to do a bit of contouring.'

With the exception of her watering eyes, there was something strangely relaxing about having her makeup applied by someone else and Crystal began to unwind and enjoy the attention. She could feel him running a makeup sponge over the outside of her face and down the sides of her nose.

'Just the lips to do!' he then said. He had now become quite animated – his voice full of enthusiasm – and it was evident to Crystal that he was getting some sort of kick from applying her makeup for her.

Ah well, whatever turns you on, she thought.

'Can you pucker your lips for me please?' he asked. Crystal instantly stretched her lips wide, thinking he'd probably been mistaken, but he soon put her right. 'No, I said pucker.'

She opened her eyes, and stared at him. 'But, it won't go on properly.'

'Trust me; I know what I'm doing. I've done this a few times before,' he said. So Crystal obliged.

When he had finished, she was curious to see the result of her makeover and she started to get up from the bed so she could check herself in the mirror.

'No!' he said, a bit too quickly to Crystal's mind. 'Leave it, you can check out your makeup later. At the moment I just want you to lie still.'

She did as he instructed and he watched her for several seconds, his eyes roaming over her face and then down to her body, before he removed his own clothing. Then he said, 'You're nice and pale. I like that.' His hands began to stroke her body, and he added, 'You're warm though. I want you cold. You should be cold.'

He got up off the bed and crossed the room then opened the window before returning to the bed and stroking her body again. Although it was summer, there was a slight chill in the night air. She felt herself shiver and couldn't resist saying something.

'I'm cold. Can't you shut that window?'

'Shush,' he said. 'Keep still. I don't want you to speak, just keep still.'

'But I'm bloody cold.'

'Quiet, please. You should be cold. It's important for you to be cold. Now keep still. It'll all be over soon.' Then he continued speaking as he stroked her body once more. 'That's better. You're nice and cold now. And still. I want you to stay still. Don't be tempted to move or speak again. I don't want you to spoil it.'

Crystal stared at him with a puzzled expression on her face. This man was strange! But he wasn't hurting her in any way so she complied with his wishes, resisting the urge to speak and staying quiet while he carried on commenting.

'You're soft at the moment. But that will change. Your body will become hard and stiff. But then you'll go soft again.'

Crystal thought he was talking about orgasm and when he prised her legs apart it confirmed her supposition because it wasn't long before he was inside her. But what he did next made her realise that it hadn't been about that. As he drew nearer to his own orgasm his speech became fast and disjointed.

'I love your lips. Cracked and dry. Your eyes, I love your eyes! Still. Nice and still.' Then he yelled, 'Stiff, stiff, stiff! The perfect corpse,' just as he climaxed.

'Shit!' shouted Crystal. 'What the fuck?'

In her alarm she forgot about lying still and she shot up out of the bed, pushing him aside in her haste to get away.

'You fuckin' weirdo!' she yelled, grasping at her clothes ready to put them back on.

The man lay cowed on the bed, as though he was embarrassed now the spectacle was over.

'Just what the fuck is wrong with you?' she yelled.

But instead of replying the man got up, grabbed his wallet from the dressing table and slung some money at her. Then he sat back down with his back turned to her, his legs hanging over the other side of the bed and his head bowed low in shame. Against a barrage of verbal abuse from Crystal he muttered, 'Just go, will you?'

Crystal continued her verbal assault. 'Don't worry; I'm out of here as soon as I'm dressed. I'm not hanging around a fuckin' weirdo like you!'

She quickly got her clothes on and as she did so she noticed something. In his haste to extricate himself from the embarrassing situation, he had slung his wallet back on the dressing table and left his phone there too. Crystal grabbed them while he still had his back to her then fled through the door. By the time he realised the items were gone, and got himself dressed, she would be long gone. And after what he'd just put her through she deserved every penny.

Crystal was so shaken by the experience that it wasn't until she was well away from the hotel that she thought to check her makeup. She walked into a bar and went straight to the ladies, noticing the curious looks from people she passed. As soon as she was in front of a mirror she realised why. Jesus! She was shocked. No wonder he'd used such a pale colour of face powder. She hadn't noticed the other colours he'd applied but now it was all apparent.

As well as a deathly pallor she had bluey-grey colouring under her eyes and in the creases above, emphasising the sockets so that her eyes appeared deep-set. They were also red-rimmed from the eyeliner he'd used. The contouring was reddish black, making her cheeks appear sunken and, as she stared at her lips, she realised why he had wanted her to pucker them. The pale colour had missed the creases in her lips, which emphasised them and made her lips look dry and cracked. The perfect corpse!

As she stared in shock at her mirror image, she felt an odd sensation in the pit of her stomach. She heard a giggle, which made her jump, and she looked across at a girl who had stepped in front of the sink next to her.

'You going to a fancy dress?' she asked.

But Crystal ignored her. Feeling an urge to vomit she switched on the cold tap and ran it over her face, experiencing some relief as the morbid colours drained away and ran into the sink.

'Has someone played a trick on you?' asked the girl, realising something was amiss, but Crystal was too stunned to reply. The girl reached into her handbag. 'Here, have a wipe,' she said. 'It'll bring it off better.'

Crystal muttered her thanks and grabbed the wipe then scrubbed vigorously at the makeup until every bit was gone. She was relieved when the girl seemed to grow tired of being ignored and went away.

Afterwards, it took Crystal a while to calm down. Although she'd heard of necrophilia before, it still horrified her to think that she had just had sex with someone who had such perversions. But, from that day, there was something else about the experience that troubled her. If he was the sort of man who got his rocks off by pretending to have sex with a dead person then who knew what lengths he would go to in the future? And the fact that he was a doctor made it all the more worrying.

*

Crystal stared at the debit card she was holding in her hand: Dr Joseph Abrahams, the pervert who had made her up as a corpse and really freaked her out. By the time she had stolen his card, she had already begun her mission to get revenge on the worst of her ex-clients. But with Joseph Abrahams she knew it was about more than just revenge; she knew she had to safeguard the public against his depraved and perverted behaviour before he went too far.

21

Crystal was spending some time with her friends – Amber, Sapphire and Angie – inside the Rose and Crown.

'Well, we're off to work,' said Amber. 'But I can stay with you while you finish your drink if you like.'

'No, it's fine,' said Crystal. 'There's somebody I want a word with anyway.'

'Ooh, sounds interesting.'

'Not really,' said Crystal, but she didn't elucidate.

Holly, a ravaged drug addict and prostitute who Crystal spoke to from time to time, was sitting a few tables away. She was on her own, as she often was, unless she was so high that she became indifferent to people's repugnance towards her and insisted on joining them. As soon as Crystal's friends left the pub, she went over to her.

'Hi, Holly. Mind if I join you?' she asked.

Holly looked up and smiled, displaying her discoloured and decaying teeth and the gap in the front two, her greasy hair hanging like rats' tails around her shoulders. Crystal smiled back, trying to ignore the unwashed stench of body odour that emanated from Holly. It always struck her as sad that such an attractive girl should come to this and, since she'd been off drugs herself, she was becoming increasingly aware of the abject misery and desperation of people like Holly.

'What d'you want?' asked Holly, knowing that people generally avoided her except for the most depraved of clients who would overlook Holly's flaws if the price was right.

'I'm after a favour,' said Crystal.

'What sort of favour?'

'Well, do you remember the other week when I was telling you and the girls about that client who freaked me out? The one whose name you recognised when I mentioned it?'

'Oh, yeah,' Holly drawled. 'The necrophiliac you mean?' A faint smile of amusement fleetingly lit up her features, giving a hint of the girl she once was.

'Yes, that's the one. You said he was a doctor at the surgery you go to.'

'Yeah, that's right. I knew as soon as you said the name. Always thought he was a bit weird but you could have fuckin' knocked me over when you told me what he's into. I was telling my mate about him and...'

Crystal quickly cut in to stop her rambling. 'I've got a job for you but I want it to stay between you and me. Oh, and one other person, if she agrees to help too.'

'That depends if you make it worth my while,' said Holly.

'Oh, I'll definitely make it worth your while, and your friend's too,' said Crystal.

Crystal knew Holly would do almost anything for money, and she hoped her friend was like-minded. But, as she looked at the withered features of the young girl, Crystal felt a twinge of conscience, knowing that by paying her she would be helping to feed her many habits. But she reasoned that Holly was a lost cause anyway. And, after all, it was for the greater good.

It was late when Phil Thomas arrived in the Rose and Crown. If he was honest with himself, he was getting a bit sick of hanging out in that dive doing Justin Foster's dirty work for him so he'd met up with some mates beforehand and had a few pints and a game of pool. It wouldn't matter anyway because Justin would never know how often he'd visited the Rose and Crown.

He walked up to the bar and caught the eye of the barmaid. He'd seen her a few times before, a woman in her sixties wearing a short skirt, a revealing top and too much makeup, a fold of fat hanging over the waistband of her skirt and visible through the tight-fitting top she wore; the epitome of mutton dressed as lamb.

'A pint of lager is it?' she asked, leaning over and giving him a glimpse of her cleavage.

'Yeah, that's right,' replied Phil.

He might not have been in there day and night as Justin would have wanted, but he was obviously going in enough to be recognised by the barmaid. He decided to take his chances with her when she returned with his pint and handed him his change.

'Has Crystal been in tonight?' he asked.

He could tell she was immediately suspicious, her eyes narrowing as she asked, 'Why, is she a friend of yours?'

Phil knew Crystal's former profession so he decided to play it cagey. 'Let's just say we've had some dealings together.'

The barmaid nodded in recognition. 'She was in earlier but if you're thinking of any future dealings I think you might be disappointed. She isn't in that game anymore.'

'Oh, she'd want to see me,' said Phil.

The barmaid smiled flirtatiously, despite her advancing years. 'Why's that?' she asked and Phil tried to hide his repulsion as he played along with it.

'Let's just say we had a special arrangement,' he said, enigmatically.

'Really? Handsome lad like you, I wouldn't have thought you'd have had to pay for it. I bet you could have your pick.'

He laughed. 'Who mentioned paying? I told you, we had a special arrangement.' Before she could chip in with any more of her flirtatious banter, he quickly asked, 'When did she leave? Do you know?'

'About ten minutes ago.'

'Did she say where she was going?'

The barmaid's eyes narrowed again, all thoughts of flirtation temporarily put aside. 'Why don't you ring her and find out? Presumably you've got her number, haven't you, what with you two having a special arrangement?'

She emphasised the last two words and then walked away before he could quiz her anymore. The barmaid obviously wasn't fooled; he guessed that in a place like this she'd probably heard it all before.

He looked about him. This place really was a dive and he didn't want to spend any longer here than necessary. If Crystal had already been and gone then there wasn't any point hanging around. He decided to drink his pint then leave and try his luck again the next day. He'd just taken a swig when he felt someone join him at the bar, and he could feel their eyes on him.

Phil swallowed the mouthful of beer then put his pint down on the bar and turned to the side almost gagging on his drink when he caught a malodorous whiff of body odour. He flashed a look of contempt when he saw the person standing there. It was a girl, scruffy, with rotten teeth and a face full of sores, and he knew straightaway that she was a junkie; he could spot them a mile off.

'You lookin' for Crystal?' she asked.

'Yeah, what's it to you?'

'She's a mate of mine, that's what.'

'Yeah sure,' he said, dismissively before turning his back to her.

'Moira!' the girl shouted to the barmaid. 'Isn't Crystal a mate of mine?'

'I suppose so,' said Moira.

Phil turned back round and gazed at the girl. *Jesus!* he thought. *This Crystal must have been a piece of work if this was what she called a friend.* Before he could say anything, she asked. 'What do you want to know about her?'

He realised it would pay him to be nice to her now. 'Let's sit down,' he said, nodding towards the nearest available table. 'I'll get you a drink. What do you want?'

Once he'd bought the drink and joined Holly at the table, she said, 'It'll cost you more than a drink if you wanna find out about Crystal.'

'I thought as much. Name your price and tell me what you know.'

'Twenty quid.'

He was relieved – small price to pay really, even if

she didn't know much. But Holly wasn't as stupid as he thought. She'd obviously spotted his look of relief as she quickly added, 'And that's just for starters.'

'OK. What do you know?'

'I know her real name.'

'OK, what else? Phone number? Address?'

'Nah.'

'Well, it's not much to go on, is it? And as I already know her real name there's not much point in continuing this conversation.'

He could see a look of disappointment on the girl's face till she seemed to think of something and her expression changed.

'I don't know where she lives but she's got a daughter living with her called Candice. She's always going on about her.'

'Really? How old?'

'Only young. Eleven I think Crystal said.'

'Interesting,' said Phil. 'What else do you know?'

'Er, well, she's got me doing a job for her,' Holly replied.

'What kind of job?'

'Give me the twenty quid and I'll tell you.'

Phil sighed then pulled a note from his pocket and handed it to her. She examined it before putting it away. 'OK, she's called Laura.'

'Yes, I already told you, I know that. Laura what?'

'I don't know her second name, only that she's called Laura.'

Phil raised his eyes in consternation. 'OK, what about this job she's got for you?'

'She wants me to stitch a doctor up,' she said without hesitation.

'Why?'

''Cos he's a fuckin' weirdo that likes tarts to play dead.'

'OK, so how does this help me?'

'She's going to pay me once the job's been done.'

'Ah, so you do have her phone number?'

'No, she wouldn't let me have it. Crystal's careful about who she gives her number to these days, ever since she came off the game... But she's meeting me in here in a fortnight to pay me for the job.'

'OK, what day?'

'Give me another twenty and I'll tell you.'

Phil tutted but handed over another twenty pounds, knowing this was the information he had been looking for. She gave him the date and he asked, 'What time?'

'Dunno, she just said early doors.'

'OK, put my number in your phone, and I'll take yours,' he said, pulling his mobile out of his pocket. 'And as soon as she steps inside this pub I want to fuckin' know about it. There'll be another twenty in it for you if she's still in the pub when I get here.'

22

Crystal was enjoying being the owner of a laptop. It had opened up a whole new world to her and, because she had always been adept with computers, it hadn't taken her long to find out how to set up her own blog. It was called, 'A Street Girl's Life' and, in the few weeks since she'd set it up, it was already attracting a lot of traffic.

Through her blog posts, Crystal had told of some of the dire experiences she'd had as a prostitute. It would serve as a reminder to her of what she'd been through and, should she ever risk going back to that life, it would dissuade her. Hopefully it would also act as a warning to other women who were being lured into the industry.

But running her blog wasn't just about that. She knew she could also use it to deliver important messages to the general public and, at the moment, her message concerned Dr Joseph Abrahams. She looked at the words in front of her and read it back to make sure she was happy with it:

One of the scariest experiences I had in my time as a street girl was with a client who didn't actually do me any physical harm, believe it or not. At the time I didn't realise what his perversions were. It freaks me out when I remember what he shouted just as he climaxed because his words told me that he was imagining having sex with a dead person.

I feel so foolish now because at first I hadn't realised why he had opened the window so I'd be cold and why he wanted me to keep still while he had sex with me. It was only what he later said that gave him away. He called me 'the perfect corpse'.

Not only that, but he'd made me up to look like a dead person. I didn't realise at the time what the makeup looked like, as he wouldn't let me check it out until afterwards. I know I probably sound like a complete idiot but as a prostitute you have to deal with all kinds. Sometimes it's just a relief to have someone who doesn't want to beat the crap out of you so you just get on with it.

Later, the more I thought about this client, the more it freaked me out. If he wanted me to play dead then he must have been into necrophilia and, even though he might not have killed anyone yet, who's to say what might happen in the future?

And that's why this client needs to be named because the public should be protected from people like him. So I'm naming and shaming him. He's Dr Joseph Abrahams. He works at Torbrook Medical Centre in Harpurhey and, from what I can make out, it isn't the first time he's acted like this with a woman.

Crystal read through the post once again, nervous about taking that final step and publishing it. Then her hand hovered over the publish button, her heart beating rapidly as she thought about the consequences once it went live. But she'd covered herself, making sure everything was anonymous and she had used a false name for the blog.

She knew the police would be able to trace her through the laptop's IP address but that didn't really concern her because it wasn't a false accusation. The main concern was that the mad doctor didn't find out her identity because there was no way she wanted a man like him coming after her. But she knew he had to be stopped before he went any further so she took a deep breath and clicked 'publish'.

Two weeks after his first meeting with Holly, Phil Thomas received a text from her. True to her word she was letting him know that Crystal had turned up in the Rose and Crown. He was already in a nearby Manchester pub, since it was the day when Crystal was due to meet Holly, so it didn't take him long to walk the short distance to the Rose and Crown.

By the time he arrived Crystal had got a round in and was putting the drinks down on the table in front of Holly. He stood at the bar drinking his pint and watching the two women through the mirror on the back wall. It wasn't long before Crystal passed some money to Holly. *Good,* he thought. *That would mean she was almost ready to go.*

But she didn't seem to be in a rush. He watched as she stood up, said something else to Holly then went to join some women at another table. Unfortunately that meant he could no longer see her through the mirror and he had to keep turning his head to the side to check she was still there.

For over an hour Phil continued watching as the women gossiped and shared jokes. Crystal stayed for another two drinks, and he grew irritable each time one of the women left the table to buy another round. He had swapped his beer for water by this stage; he needed to stay sharp for what he was about to do.

Phil became conscious of the barmaid surveying him each time he glanced sideways and he wished Crystal would just hurry up and leave the pub. He couldn't afford to hang on much longer in case the barmaid started asking him awkward questions.

Then he noticed Crystal exchange phone numbers with one of her friends before the women left the pub. Crystal was now alone but she still had a drink in front of her, and it was almost full. When she got up from her chair, picked up her drink and started walking towards the bar, he quickly looked away. Phil felt uneasy as she slid into the space by his side. But she didn't say anything to him. Instead she laughed and joked with the customers standing to the other side of her.

'What brings you here after all this time?' asked one of them.

'I fancied slumming it,' she replied, laughing.

He continued watching through the mirror as she turned, face forward, and called to the barmaid. 'You alright, Moira?'

He held his breath, willing Moira not to tell her about him asking questions, and ready to deny everything. But, for whatever reason, she kept schtum about their previous meeting. Maybe she'd forgotten. After all, the old bird was getting on a bit.

When the guys next to Crystal resumed their conversation about football, Crystal started downing her drink more quickly. *This is it,* he thought. *Maybe she's ready to go at last.* She finished the last dregs, then said goodbye to Moira and the other customers, promising them she'd be back to see them soon. And then she went.

Phil quickly finished the last of his drink, not wanting to look too suspicious by leaving mid-pint. Then he stopped off at Holly's table and, checking no one was looking, he slipped a twenty-pound note into her hand. Without saying anything to her he carried on out of the Rose and Crown, eager to catch up with Crystal.

The barmaid, Moira, had seen Crystal walk into the pub; it was the first time she had seen her for a couple of weeks. She watched as Crystal went to join Holly then, after chatting for a few minutes, she handed over some money to her. The landlord served Crystal so Moira didn't get chance to chat but she decided that when Crystal came to the bar again she would tell her about the strange man who had been asking about her, and about his conversation with Holly. Crystal wasn't a bad kid and she didn't like the thought of her running into problems.

But then Moira also saw the man arrive. She served him and watched as he stared into the mirror at the back of the bar, taking in everything that was going on between Crystal and Holly. She also thought she saw a look of acknowledgement pass between him and Holly but she couldn't be sure; she was too busy serving other customers by then.

Moira knew it would be difficult to tell Crystal about him now because he would overhear her, and she didn't want any comeback. There was obviously something dodgy going on and, at her age, she didn't want the hassle of getting involved.

She'd been working in the Rose and Crown for a while now. It wasn't the first pub she'd have chosen but there weren't many others willing to employ an ageing ex-prostitute who was no longer nimble on her feet. Moira had become wise to the goings-on in the Rose and Crown, and she had always found it best to keep her own counsel in a pub like this.

She was still deliberating over whether to tell Crystal about him, and how she would go about it, when Crystal left. She went to serve another customer and, by the time she had finished, she noticed the man had left too. Moira had a feeling of dread. What if he was following Crystal?

She was tempted to call the police. But what would she tell them? She didn't actually know anything; it was just a suspicion. So she carried on with her work hoping to God that Crystal would be alright.

23

Once he was out of view of the barmaid Phil sped through the pub doors and looked left and right to see if there was any sign of Crystal. She wasn't to his left and he couldn't see anything to his right but the view was blocked by a group of youngsters walking towards him. He changed position until he had a good view of the road. There was nothing on his side but a lorry was blocking his view of the opposite pavement. He waited a few seconds for it to pass then checked the view on that side. Nothing.

Phil dashed round the corner and looked down the side street, and there in the distance he just about spotted her. He was tempted to turn back for his car, which he'd left parked close to the Rose and Crown but he didn't want to risk losing sight of her. Crystal's head was bobbing up and down as she weaved in and out of the throngs of people who were now starting to crowd the Manchester streets as day turned into night. Thank God for that; he was beginning to think he'd lost her.

He took to his heels, determined to catch up with Crystal. For a moment she went out of view and he tried to increase his speed till he reached the point where she had disappeared. It was at the junction with another street so he was fairly confident that she had headed that way. But he still couldn't see her. He raced down the connecting street till he came to the next junction and peered in the direction she had been walking. And there she was, still weaving her way through the evening crowds.

Phil was relieved that, not only had he spotted her but he'd also shortened the gap between them. But she was still some distance away. Feeling out of breath by now, he stopped running but instead walked at a brisk pace, hoping to close the gap even further.

Then she stopped at another junction and looked about her before crossing the road. As she turned her head, Phil could almost feel her eyes on him and he quickly ducked into a shop doorway so that she didn't spot him. Once she was across the road he set off after her again but this time he maintained a steady pace. He couldn't afford to get any nearer in case she saw him and recognised him from the pub.

The problem was, because of the crowds, she kept slipping out of view. He kept a keen eye out for her, letting out a breath of relief each time he saw her again. Then he lost sight of her once more but this time it was a while and she still hadn't come back into view. He sped up, but not too much, telling himself he'd spot her again as soon as she passed a large crowd that had been walking near to her. But he didn't.

Phil began running. He couldn't afford to lose her, even if she saw him. He'd just have to take his chances. But when he reached the point where she'd disappeared, he still couldn't see her. He stopped and searched frantically around but he couldn't see any sign of her on the pavement.

His eyes drifted towards the road in case she'd crossed over again. There was a red Golf parked up on the other side with a pink panel on the driver's door as though the driver had had a bump and tried to patch it up on the cheap. And then he saw Crystal. She was getting into the passenger side of the red Golf. Shit! How was he going to catch her now? He'd left his car near the Rose and Crown and there was no time to go back for it.

He watched with dismay as the car sped off down the road then he looked about him for some way of following the car. A taxi. He needed a taxi. He spotted one parked only a few metres up the road and raced towards it. Someone had beaten him. But not quite.

He continued running towards the taxi and pulled the door open wide just as it was about to set off.

'What the bloody hell's going on?' shouted the taxi driver.

'Urgent business!' said Phil, taking a twenty-pound note out of his wallet and throwing it at the woman sitting on the back seat.

'This one's mine, love. You'll have to get another,' he said, taking her arm and pulling her from the seat.

He didn't know whether it was the money or his sense of urgency but the woman got up from her seat and stepped outside the taxi.

'Where you off?' demanded the taxi driver.

'I'll tell you as I go along,' said Phil, refusing to give too much away. 'But don't worry; I'll give you a good tip.'

'Suit yourself,' said the driver, sniffing and then setting off.

Phil could tell the driver was already mellowing towards him. It was amazing what the promise of a few quid could do. 'Drive to the end of the road and turn left,' he said, following the direction the red Golf had taken.

They were soon round the corner. 'Where to now?' asked the driver.

'Keep going, straight ahead,' said Phil as he scanned the vehicles in front, searching for the red Golf.

The driver carried on, taking the left lane. Then Phil spotted it, on a road off to the right.

'Turn right, quick!' he shouted.

The driver tutted and pulled out, just missing an oncoming car. 'For fuck's sake!' he cursed. 'Make your mind up, mate.'

'Sorry. Just keep going for now,' said Phil, keeping his eye on the Golf, which was about five cars ahead.

When the Golf switched lanes, he instructed the driver to do the same, making sure they were ready to follow the car as soon as it took another right turn. But they'd lost some ground as the taxi driver tried to find a gap in the traffic. The Golf was now about seven cars in front and kept dipping out of view. It wasn't long before the car turned again; its driver seemed to be taking a short cut through the maze of narrow Manchester backstreets.

Phil managed to just about keep tabs on it till they reached the junction to Oxford Road. He wasn't even sure which way the driver had turned but he'd last spotted the car in the left lane so he ordered the driver to turn left. He couldn't see anything at first until, eventually, as they left the city centre and the traffic became less dense, he spotted the Golf in the distance.

'Can you go a bit faster please?' he asked.

'I'll do what I can, mate, but I'm already pushing the speed limit as it is.'

Despite his complaints the driver sped up and Phil was relieved when he overtook several vehicles until the Golf wasn't far ahead of them. They kept pace with it until they got to Fallowfield and it stopped outside a terraced house. Two people emerged but neither of them was Crystal. Perhaps she was still inside the car.

Phil got the taxi driver to pull over a short distance ahead then he paid him and got out of the cab. It sped off as soon as he stepped outside. The two people he had seen were entering the terraced house and he knew they'd be indoors by the time he reached the Golf. Good. That would be the best time to get hold of Crystal – when no one else was looking.

He hurried, concerned in case the car set off again with Crystal inside. He surveyed it from the other side of the street but he couldn't spot Crystal. Surely that couldn't be right! He ignored his caution of earlier and crossed the road, continuing to walk until he was by the side of the Golf. But as soon as he reached it he found that it was empty!

Refusing to acknowledge what he was seeing, Phil walked around the car and peered in through all the windows in case Crystal was hiding in the foot well. But there was nobody inside. By this time he was standing on the driver's side of the Golf. Then he noticed something. The pink patch was missing. Damn! He'd somehow managed to follow the wrong car.

24

'Are you OK, Crystal?' asked Amber when Crystal answered her phone, two nights after her visit to the Rose and Crown.

'Yeah, why wouldn't I be?'

'Well, me and Sapphire have just been talking to Moira and she reckons a man followed you out of the pub last time you were in there.'

'Really? I didn't see anyone. I was with Sapphire anyway for most of the journey home. She stopped her car when I was on the way to Piccadilly and gave me a lift.'

'Yeah, she told me.'

'Well she should know if I'm alright then.'

'I know, but we were worried he might have caught up with you after Sapphire dropped you off.'

'Nah, I'm fine. What did he look like anyway?'

'In his twenties, tall and good-looking with dark hair according to Moira.'

'I think I'd have remembered him,' said Crystal, giggling, but when Amber didn't return her laughter, she asked, 'Did Sapphire see anyone that looked like that when she gave me a lift?'

'Nah. She said she saw nothing iffy.'

'Well then. Are you sure Moira's not imagining things? I mean, she is getting on a bit, isn't she?'

'She seemed really worried though, Crystal. According to her it isn't the first time he's been in the pub either, and he's already been asking about you.'

'Asking what?'

'Whether you'd been in the pub and where you were going after the pub, that sort of thing.'

'Really?' asked Crystal, feeling a cold prickle of fear.

'Yeah. And there's something else… She reckons this man has been cosying up with Holly and doing some sort of a deal with her. Moira saw him give her money.'

'You sure?' asked Crystal, deliberately not mentioning her own deal with Holly. 'But why would he do that? Maybe he's a client.'

'No, not according to Moira. She said he didn't look rough enough to be one of Holly's clients. But I don't know why he'd be giving her money; maybe you'd better ask Holly. Don't you have her number?'

'No, and I haven't given her mine either.'

'How come?' asked Amber. 'I thought you and her were mates.'

'Because I don't bloody trust her, that's why. I mean, she seems OK but you know what these smack heads are like. They'll do anything for their next fix.'

Crystal realised the irony of her words as soon as she said them considering that she also used to have a bad drugs habit.

'What you gonna do then?' asked Amber.

'I dunno. But thanks for warning me anyway.'

'No problems, see you soon. Bye.'

'Bye, Amber.'

When Crystal finished the call she sat looking at her mobile for a while, deep in thought. She had played down her own concern but, in view of her latest escapades, she was worried that maybe there was some comeback from one of the clients she had been targeting.

She felt a rush of terror at the thought that one of her targets had perhaps traced her to the Rose and Crown and, even now, might be thinking about ways in which he could get back at her. For a few moments she let her thoughts run away with her, imagining all the ways in which he could exact his revenge. Then she stopped herself. There was no point letting her imagination run riot. This man might have been totally unconnected to her targets.

But she couldn't think of any other reason why someone would be searching for her in the Rose and Crown, and striking up some sort of a deal with Holly. So, just as a precaution, she decided to avoid the pub for a while. It wouldn't stop her targeting other ex-clients, though, because even if the man was connected to one of her previous targets, the damage had already been done.

She wished she knew what Holly was up to but how could she ask her when she daren't risk going in the Rose and Crown? She only wished now that she had taken Holly's phone number. Perhaps she could get Amber or Sapphire to ask Holly what was going on. But she doubted whether Holly would tell them, especially if it was something dodgy involving her. And, for the same reason, she doubted whether Holly would give her phone number to Amber or Holly so that Crystal could ring her.

*

A few days later Crystal stared with satisfaction at the computer screen in front of her. She had been checking the news reports daily since her first meeting with Holly and now, here it was:

Doctor Accused of Indecent Assault

A doctor accused of indecent assault by two patients is due to face a medical tribunal. Doctor Joseph Abrahams of Torbrook Medical Centre in Harpurhey, Manchester, is under investigation by the General Medical Council following claims from two patients that he indecently assaulted them at his surgery in Harpurhey.

There are also concerns relating to his private life amid reports to the GMC about irregular sexual practices. Dr Abrahams will be expected to respond to the two indecent assault allegations as well as allegations relating to his private life. If found guilty of misconduct, Dr Abrahams could be struck off the medical register.

Pending the investigation by the General Medical Council, Dr Abrahams has been suspended from his duties at the Torbrook Medical Centre. The police have also been called in to investigate the two allegations of indecent assault.

A spokesman for the Torbrook Medical Centre said, 'We are concerned about matters that have been raised in relation to Dr Abrahams' conduct. However, as an investigation is currently underway, we are not at liberty to discuss details relating to the case.'

Dr Abrahams was unavailable for comment.

She was relieved that it was finally out there and that Holly hadn't let her down. Knowing of Holly's reputation, Crystal had been worried that she might just squander the money on drugs without having done the job she was supposed to do. But no, it had been done.

Crystal had paid Holly for her and a friend to each report Dr Abrahams to Torbrook Medical Centre for indecent assault. As well as concerns that Holly might not have done as she asked, Crystal had also been worried that the medical centre might not take sufficient action against the doctor so she had contacted the General Medical Council direct.

In an anonymous call Crystal had informed them of Dr Abrahams' perverse sexual practices during his time as one of her former clients. That way, the General Medical Council would probably speak to the medical centre. Hopefully that would force the centre to take Holly and her friend's claims more seriously as well as prompting them to raise their own concerns with the General Medical Council.

Using a photograph from the medical centre's website, Crystal had then circulated Dr Abrahams' details to all the street girls she knew, warning them not to deal with him, and asking them to spread the word.

She was satisfied that, short of reporting him to the police herself, she had done everything else in her power to put a stop to Doctor Abrahams. Crystal hadn't really had sufficient evidence to contact the police directly and, apart from that, she didn't want them raking up her past or looking too closely at her personal affairs. But she was satisfied that she'd created enough of a stir to open up an investigation regarding Dr Abrahams.

She hadn't earnt much money from him other than the

bit of cash that had been in his wallet, as he'd put a stop on the debit card before she got chance to use it. But financial reward had never been her aim with this client. Ever since the incident in that hotel room, she had felt that she had a duty to protect the public from Dr Abrahams.

Hopefully, now that the police were involved, they would be keeping a close eye on him in the future. She realised that his future would be destroyed but she felt no guilt at all. Her sympathies lay with possible future victims who she hoped would now be protected from him.

As she thought about the perverted doctor, she reflected on how well things had been going up to now. It was good to know that some of her worst clients were finally getting what they deserved. She'd spent enough years putting up with abuse. With her new-found confidence also came the realisation that Gilly had been a large part of that abuse. She'd been so high on drugs half the time as well as being so wrapped up in him that she had refused to acknowledge his faults.

Although she hadn't earnt much from this client, she'd got plenty from the others who she'd managed to blackmail. But it was still nowhere near the amount she would need to start a new life. She still had two more clients listed, though, and there were countless others she could target once she had finished with these two.

Crystal took out her list of targets and her eyes ran down to the next name on the list, Gerry Patterson. What a nasty piece of work he was! She felt a rush of excitement as she thought about gaining the upper hand with him and her mind explored the possibilities for revenge. Yes, she'd definitely enjoy toying with this one, and he would deserve everything that was coming to him.

25

Target 5

<u>Name</u>: Gerry Patterson

<u>Profession</u>: Policeman

<u>Description</u>: Aged in mid-forties, tall and confident with an air of authority. Light brown hair, which is greying, a big nose and ruddy complexion

<u>Address</u>: Unknown

<u>Personality</u>: Arrogant and condescending, talks to women like they're a piece of dirt, is rough during sex

<u>Phone number</u>: Yes

<u>Bank details</u>: No

<u>Information/Items</u>: A photo of him with a woman (presumably his wife), mobile phone

<u>Aim</u>: Blackmail/extortion and revenge

Crystal knew Gerry Patterson was a policeman because one of the other street girls had told her after her first meeting with him. As soon as Crystal had drawn up her list of targets, she'd known he would be on it. It wasn't just because he was a copper and therefore one of the very people who regularly arrested her and her friends or moved them on. It was also because he was arrogant, aggressive and condescending.

The bile rose in her throat as she thought about her meetings with him. Unlike all the other clients on her list up to now, this target had preferred sex in the back of a car to the luxury of a hotel room. He was careful though and used a different car each time. A lot of them were beaten-up old wrecks although he'd once used a BMW and a smart Audi another time. She guessed that these vehicles probably didn't belong to him and had wondered once or twice how he managed to acquire them.

She didn't notice anything amiss on her first meeting with him, but it was the second meeting that stuck in her mind. She had been chatting to another of the girls on Aytoun Street when the car pulled up and the driver wound down his window.

'Oy, you!' he shouted.

Crystal's friend stepped forward.

'No, not you. Her!' he said, nodding in Crystal's direction.

Crystal's friend stepped back and flashed Crystal a look of concern as she walked towards the car.

'It's OK,' whispered Crystal. 'I've had this one before.'

She got inside the car and he slammed the door shut then looked across at her with an expression of distaste on his face.

'Was she fuckin' serious?' he said. 'I'd be mad to go with that. She looks diseased. And we all have our limits.'

As he said the last words, he continued looking her up and down, the expression of distaste still on his face, as though conveying the idea that he'd reached his limit with her.

It wasn't long until they'd reached a patch of waste ground behind some old factories. Crystal was familiar with this particular location; it wasn't the most scenic but was popular with street girls and their clients because it was out of view. He stopped the car and started to get out. Crystal remained in her seat, baffled.

'Well, come on!' he demanded. 'I haven't got all night.'

'What?' she asked, returning his aggressive tone.

'What d'you fuckin' think? Get out!'

She did as he asked and by the time she had emerged from the car, he had run round to the passenger side and grabbed hold of her arm.

'In the back,' he said. 'There's not enough room in the front of this car, is there?'

'Oh, right,' she said, eying a dog faeces on the ground and trying to step round it. 'Hang on!' she shouted as he dragged her by the arm, trying to rush her into the car. 'I don't want fuckin' dog shit all over my shoes, do I?'

'Hurry up before some bastard sees you,' he ordered, letting go of her arm while he opened the rear door but then pushing her inside. 'Slide over there,' he said and when Crystal did as he said, he slipped into the seat beside her.

'Same as last time?' she asked.

'No. I want you to go down.'

'OK,' said Crystal, pulling a condom from inside her jacket, and tearing the wrapper open.

'What the fuck's that for?'

'Protection.'

'It's alright. I can see you've got nowt on your lips, not like that other tart we've just left.'

Crystal tutted. 'It's to protect us as well as the clients.'

'Are you fuckin' joking?' he asked, affronted.

She realised she might have offended him and tried to backtrack. 'It's best to be on the safe side and you'll find that most of the girls won't do it without.'

He grunted. 'Go on then,' and continued complaining as she slid the condom over his erect penis.

Crystal wasn't happy with the client's attitude but reasoned to herself that she was here now so she might as well just get it over and done with as soon as possible. But as soon as she started work on him, he got hold of the top of her head and pushed her down so hard that she thought she might choke. Gasping for air, she struggled to pull her head back but he wasn't having any of it. Just as she'd reached the point where she was starting to panic, he grabbed hold of her hair and yanked her head back while letting out a loud groan of satisfaction.

'You nearly fuckin' suffocated me!' she complained.

'Oh, don't be such a fuckin' drama queen!' he yelled. 'You're OK, aren't you? Anyway, I thought you would be used to it in your line of work.'

Crystal ignored him and made to open the rear door.

'Hang on,' he said, grabbing her arm again. 'You need to get rid of this first.'

He nodded towards his now flaccid penis, a contemptuous smirk on his face, and Crystal realised he was enjoying belittling her. She pulled off the condom, opened the car door and slung it outside then got out so she could get back into the front seat.

They didn't speak a word as they made their way back to Aytoun Street. Crystal knew it would do her no good to complain; he hadn't paid her yet. When they reached her usual spot his car screeched to a halt and he slung the money at her. One of the notes floated into the foot well so she had to bend to retrieve it.

'Hurry up. I haven't got all fuckin' day!' he complained.

As soon as Crystal had retrieved the money, she got out of the car and slammed the door shut, fully intending never to bother with him again. But then, the next time, he'd been different.

He pulled up in her usual spot and wound his window down then shouted, 'Crystal!'

She wondered momentarily where he had got her name from since he'd not bothered asking the previous times. Then she'd turned away and tried to ignore him. But he was persistent.

'Come on, Crystal. What's the matter?'

'No chance!' she shouted back. 'Not after last time.'

'Well at least come here and talk to me so I don't have to shout.'

She stepped tentatively towards the car, taking care not to get too close.

'What's wrong?' he asked, surprising her by the note of concern in his voice.

'You nearly bloody choked me, that's what's wrong.'

'Sorry, didn't mean to. I suppose I must have got a bit carried away, that's all. We don't have to do that this time if you don't want. How much for straight sex?'

His change in attitude, plus the fact that business had been a bit slow that night, was beginning to win Crystal round and she named her price.

'Tell you what, jump in and I'll bung you an extra tenner.'

The lure of the money was too much and Crystal got

inside. She was relieved that he kept to his word and even more relieved that it was over quickly. He wasn't exactly mindful of her comfort let alone her pleasure but that was no worse than many other clients who were only there for their own enjoyment.

After that third time it became a pattern. He'd overstep the mark, his treatment of her rough and condescending, but he'd be careful not to inflict any real damage. Then, once he'd appeared conciliatory and considerate, she'd go off with him again.

Crystal realised now how crafty he'd been, stopping just short of actual violence and then persuading her to go with him again. It took a few times before she came to her senses and refused to have any more dealings with him. Looking back, she realised how foolish and desperate she must have been to put up with that sort of behaviour. But that's what drugs did to you.

As she replayed her experience of him over in her mind she could feel herself tensing. Crystal had no qualms about choosing him as a revenge target. She would make sure she got plenty of money out of him and see to it that he was punished too. He was going to pay dearly for his mistreatment of her and all other women. And now, she just had to work out how she was going to go about it.

26

Crystal took another look at the photo she had taken from Gerry Patterson's pocket. Looking back, it had amused her to think how she'd got away with lifting both the photo and his phone. But, after a few dealings with her, he'd carelessly slung his jacket on the back seat one night. Once he'd finished with her and got out of the car to get back into the front, she'd quickly slipped her hand into the inside pocket of his jacket and taken what she could. Then, once she was outside the car, she'd pretended to be adjusting her clothing while she slipped the items inside her underwear, out of view.

She knew by now that he usually kept his wallet in his trouser pocket. That meant he probably wouldn't discover his loss of the other items until much later. By that time he could have lost them anywhere and she hoped he'd never guess that it was her who had taken them. But, just as a precaution, she made sure she never went off with him again after that night. She only saw him once more and she took care to keep hidden in a shop doorway until he had picked up another girl and driven away.

The photograph was of him and a very attractive woman, presumably his wife, at some sort of event – he in a smart dinner jacket and she in an evening gown. Her dress looked expensive, as did the gold that dripped from her, and Crystal figured that it must have been a special event for them to go to so much trouble. Not only that, but he must have held a senior position with the police to be able to afford such lavish jewellery and be invited to such a special occasion.

The photo was a revelation in another way too: the way he held the woman so tenderly, a proud smile painted on his face as he stared into the camera, showing off his stunning wife. It was ironic, thought Crystal, when she considered how badly he had treated her, and she wondered whether his wife was aware of that other side to him.

It was obvious, looking at the picture, that the best way to get at Gerry Patterson would be through his wife. Crystal was pleased that she had also taken his phone and felt confident that this one shouldn't be too much of a problem.

She looked at the phone next. Unsurprisingly, it needed charging up but Crystal was already prepared for that. She connected it to one of the chargers she'd bought and plugged it in. Then she busied herself with other things until the phone had charged up.

After waiting a while she took the phone from the charger and switched it on. Damn! As she looked at the screen she recalled something she'd noticed when she'd first taken the phone. It was locked and she needed a pass code to access the contents. But she wasn't going to lose heart yet, knowing it was possible to find a pass code. It was just going to take a little longer.

Crystal needed a four-digit code to access the phone so she started with the most obvious ones: 999 plus an extra nine. But that didn't work. Unsurprisingly, he wasn't going to make it that easy for anybody to access his phone. Being a policeman, and a senior one if her suspicions were correct, he would probably take a bit more care than that. But she continued trying it anyway, using a combination of the three nines plus another digit, then another digit followed by the three nines until she had exhausted all the single digits.

Next she did the same thing for the US emergency services number but had no luck. Then she tried the Spanish one, recalling how he'd once mentioned in passing that he wouldn't be around for a while as he was going to Spain. But she had no luck with that one either so she gave up on that idea and decided to focus on dates of birth instead.

She figured that he would either use the date and month or the month and year. Therefore, starting with 01 for January she tried 31 combinations for each of the days in that month e.g. 0101, 0201 and so on. For February she entered 02 preceded by the 29 days in that month. She carried on in this way until she had tried all twelve months but she still didn't have any luck.

Crystal tried not to get too disheartened; after all, she still had the years to try. She estimated his age to be around mid-forties so she therefore started on the basis of him being forty and used the birth year of 1972, using only the last two digits. *At least there are only twelve combinations for each year,* she thought as she started at January and keyed 0172 into the phone.

By the time she got to the year 1974, Crystal had had enough so she packed it in for the day. She was becoming frustrated and beginning to think she would never break the code. As she sat drinking tea and flicking through the television channels, Crystal wondered about the wealth of information that would be contained on that mobile should she be lucky enough to access it. She felt a hint of excitement at the prospect of what might lie ahead if only she could hack into the phone. But this was countered by her lack of enthusiasm when she thought about pointlessly spending hours going through all the different combinations.

She didn't try the phone again for several days but, in the end, her curiosity got the better of her and she decided to have another go. It was when she reached 1966 that she finally cracked it. July 1966, in fact, that's assuming that the code of 0766 related to his date of birth. It made sense as that would mean he was forty-six this year (2012), round about the age that she had estimated.

As soon as the screen blanked then reappeared showing several icons, Crystal felt exhilarated. She'd done it; she'd gained access to Gerry Patterson's phone! And now she was eager to check it out and see what information she could use to her own advantage.

But there wasn't much to go on. There were no emails and no social media accounts. All she really had were a few contacts and some text messages. She looked at his contacts first but they weren't really giving anything away. There were no full names, just single names, presumably of friends or relatives. But the names that she guessed were the important ones were coded as Op1, Op2 and so on. Sometimes he had added a letter, such as Op4F, presumably to remind himself who was who.

Next she looked at his text messages. She went straight to those listed under the coded names but none of them meant anything to her. It was all acronyms and talk of jobs, operations and meetings. But he never revealed the destinations of the meetings or the names of the people who would be there. A quick glance at some of the proper names told her they were probably friends or relatives, just as she had assumed.

But then she noticed that he had exchanged flirty messages with a couple of the females. Then she skipped to one called Lyndsey. Here the messages took on a different tone; occasionally flirty but more complimentary and loving, and there was also reference to their children. She guessed straightaway that this must be his wife, the attractive woman in the photograph.

It occurred to Crystal that Gerry Patterson must have been using more than one phone for whatever reason. Was it because he was cheating on his wife? But that wouldn't have made any sense seeing as how her details were stored on this phone alongside the women he had been trading flirty messages with. Maybe it was because he kept a separate phone for work. But then, why would he have the coded names on his personal phone?

Crystal couldn't think of any answers but she tried not to ponder too much. At least she had his wife's phone number and that was a good place to start. She couldn't send him a message as she had his phone and, even if he had another phone, she didn't know the number. So she fired off a message to his wife:

Ask your husband if the name Crystal means anything to him.

Then she put the phone down and got on with other things while she waited for the fallout.

27

Crystal had noticed that her number wasn't among those stored on the phone she had taken. She remembered giving him the number she was using at the time when he had asked for it but he had never rung her, which was strange considering that he'd picked her up a few times after that. Maybe the thought of cruising the red-light district was more appealing than ringing her. But the fact that she wasn't in the contacts confirmed her suspicions that he probably had more than one phone.

None of that mattered now, though, because she had his wife's number and she felt sure that, once his wife received her text, it wouldn't be long before he got in touch. But it was his wife who made contact first.

Who on earth is this?

read the message.
Crystal sent a message straight back:

Ask your husband.

Then she didn't hear anything more for a while but,

when she did eventually hear from him, his message was a let-down.

When Gerry Patterson returned home that evening he got a very hostile reception from his wife. He walked into the kitchen where she was cooking their evening meal, one of her tantalising stir-fries.

'Ooh, that's looks delicious,' he said, peering into the pan.

She lightly smacked the back of his hand. 'Keep off! You're lucky to be getting anything at all after the message I received today.'

'What do you mean?' he asked.

Lyndsey walked over to the worktop where she had left her phone and brought the text message up on the screen. Then she crossed the room again and held it up for him to see.

'So, tell me, who is this Crystal?'

Gerry's mouth dropped wide open and for a few moments all he could do was stare at the phone's screen.

'Well, come on. I'm waiting.'

Gerry quickly recovered, and adopted an annoyed tone. 'Sorry, love. I was just so shocked. How on earth did she get your number?'

'Quiet!' she hissed, flicking her head upwards. 'I don't want the kids to hear you.'

'Where are they?'

'In their rooms. And don't change the subject. I want to know what exactly has bloody well been going on.'

'Sorry, love,' he said. 'It was a stupid prank on a night out with the lads. But it wasn't my fault. This stupid little slapper was hanging around us and the lads thought it would be a good laugh to give her my number.'

'A likely story. And how the bloody hell did she manage to get *my* number then?'

'I've no idea, honestly. Unless…' He seemed pensive for a moment before adding, 'Unless they decided it would be an even bigger laugh to give her your number.'

'And who exactly was it that played such a nasty little prank?'

'One of the lads at work.'

'Who? I want to know.'

'I need to get to the bottom of it first and find out which one of them gave her your number. Don't worry, Lyndsey. They won't bloody get away with it. I'll have it out with them. They're lucky I'm not reporting them to personnel. But don't you worry,' he repeated, 'by the time I've finished with them they'll think twice before pulling a stunt like that again.'

He looked at his wife and he could see that his act of outrage was having an effect. She was beginning to mellow, her beautiful eyes no longer narrowed and the harsh lines around her lips beginning to soften again. He decided to play on that.

'I'm so sorry about this, Lyndsey. I can see it's upset you and it should never have happened.'

She shrugged. 'Just sort it. I never want to see another message like that again.'

'Don't worry, love. I'll see to it that you won't have to. Oh, and let me take a note of the number she used. I want to give *her* a piece of my mind too.' His wife showed him Crystal's new number on her phone and he took a note of it.

Then, after a pause, he added, 'I'll go and tell the kids their tea's nearly ready, shall I? Oh, and keep mine in the wok for a bit, I need to use the bathroom.'

He fled up the stairs, glad to get away from his wife's accusations. Gerry was relieved that he had managed to convince her of his innocence. But he was also furious. How dare that little tart send messages to his wife? Lyndsey was worth a million of her and he was livid that some little slapper had managed to invade his private world and upset his wife.

Once he had greeted his kids and sent them down for their dinner, he went into the bathroom and locked the door. He put the seat down on the loo and plonked himself on it. Then he took out his other phone where he had just entered Crystal's latest number, and he called her details up on screen. The cheeky bitch wasn't going to get away with this!

28

Crystal heard her phone ping and she rushed to look at the text. It was obvious straightaway who it was from.

How dare you message my wife! You cheeky little slapper,

the message read.

She smiled as she read it, amused by his reaction. The insults didn't bother her; it was no more than she'd expected and she'd put up with a lot worse in her time as a street girl. At least she had his other phone number now, which would make things easier.

She fired a text back to him.

If you want the messages to stop then you'll have to pay for my silence.

The reply came almost straightaway and Crystal was happy to continue the chat.

Not a fuckin' chance! Do you really think I'm daft enough to fall for that?

We'll see how you feel once your wife's had a few more messages.

It won't make any fuckin' difference. She thinks my mates gave some little slapper her number for a laugh. So there's no way she'll believe a thing you say. Now, I suggest you do one.

Or else?

Or else I'll get someone at the station to trace your address from the phone company records. And when I find out where you live, you'll be in big trouble!

Good luck with that. It's a throwaway phone.

Then the texts stopped and Crystal looked at her phone, disheartened. She could have carried on texting his wife but something told her she was probably wasting her time. This guy was obviously good at manipulating people and he had his wife convinced of his cover story.

Crystal was in two minds about taking things further. He was a nasty piece of stuff and there was something about him that made her nervous. But she didn't like to think he'd beaten her.

She thought about the men she'd targeted up to now. Yes, she'd had some success with Wayne Winters, Nigel Swithen and Joseph Abrahams but this was the second client who looked like getting away scot-free. It seemed to be the aggressive ones that she couldn't pin down, and it didn't sit easy with her. There must be a way to fix Gerry

Patterson and that other nasty piece of stuff, Justin Foster. But how?

After puzzling over things for a while she took to her laptop and entered Gerry Patterson's name in the search engine. But nothing of any significance came up. Then she entered Justin Foster's name, even though she had done so before but, again, nothing of any relevance came up in the search.

While her mind was on Justin Foster she recalled the list of names that she had taken from him. Surely that list must have some significance. She remembered searching for some of the names on the Internet but she had stopped when she had recognised the name Spud. Then, when he had warned her off, she hadn't taken things further. She wondered now if perhaps it would be worthwhile to look up some of the other names.

She pulled the list out from her hiding place and read it once again. *Dennis Atkinson, Phil Thomas, Roger Purvis*, it began. She remembered doing a search on Dennis Atkinson and Phil Thomas, which had been fruitless but she hadn't got as far as Roger Purvis. She quickly typed the name into the Internet and there, at the top of the search results was an article entitled, *Chief Inspector Receives Award for His Part in Drugs Bust*.

Crystal clicked on the heading and quickly scanned the article, but it wasn't the words that caught her attention; it was the accompanying photograph. It was a picture of Detective Chief Inspector Roger Purvis receiving his award. She recognised him straightaway but did a double take just to make sure. Yes, there was no doubt about it; the police officer in the picture was Gerry Patterson. He had given her a false name.

Once she had recovered from the shock of her discovery she read the article in detail. It related how DCI Roger Purvis had led a covert operation to bust a major drugs ring. They had arrested several men including Dan Matthews, the main player on the UK side of things. He later received a hefty sentence for his part in the importation of class-A drugs. However, it was suspected that some of the people taking part might have fled abroad to evade capture. Nevertheless, the authorities saw the arrest and imprisonment of Dan Matthews as a success story.

Roger Purvis commented in the article that they were regarding it as a triumph to have captured the man in charge of the UK side of things. Although it was suspected that some criminals may have evaded capture, they were likely to have fled back to their country of origin, making it difficult for the police to pursue them.

Crystal was amazed to find that the man who had treated her so contemptuously was being hailed a hero. With her curiosity raised she continued to search through the Internet, trying to find out as much as she could about Roger Purvis. It seemed he wasn't shy of the limelight and was often quoted in news articles appealing for information from witnesses or commenting on particular cases.

Then another photo caught her eye. It was at a charity event attended by prominent businessmen and other pillars of the community and the photograph was one of many recording the prestigious event. Roger Purvis was pictured with his wife and another couple. The body language told her that they were all good friends, probably used to socialising together.

Roger and his wife were wearing the same clothes as

they were in the picture Crystal had stolen from his jacket and she guessed that it must have been taken at the same event. But in this picture they weren't alone and Crystal's eyes were drawn, not to them, but to the other couple in the photograph. It was the man in particular that had caught her interest because she realised with startling clarity that she also recognised him. It was none other than Justin Foster.

Crystal recalled how Justin had told her a friend had recommended him. She wondered whether Roger Purvis could have been that friend, seeing as how they had both been clients of hers. It was ironic how both of them were derogatory towards women too. Did Roger Purvis perhaps know what Justin was into and had he earmarked her as being submissive enough to put up with it?

A shiver of fear ran down her spine at the realisation that two of the nastiest clients she had ever dealt with were in some way connected, and she thought about the implications. Why had she been followed home from the pub? Did that have something to do with Justin Foster? He seemed the most likely of her targets to have been involved in something like that, especially when she thought about the way Spud had warned her off. And, if Justin Foster was behind her being followed, was Roger Purvis somehow involved too?

She thought about Roger Purvis threatening to find out her address from mobile phone records. Thank God she had used a throwaway phone! But what if there was another way of finding out where she lived? As a senior police officer he must have access to all sorts of records. Crystal knew she'd definitely be on the database because of her convictions for soliciting but, fortunately, Roger Purvis only knew her as Crystal.

Nevertheless, it was a frightening thought that these two men were involved with each other. And by the looks of things, they were participating in some sort of criminal activity. Otherwise, why would Justin Foster be carrying a list of names, which included Roger Purvis and Spud, a known drug addict?

Crystal stared at the computer screen for a few moments and, as the shock of this discovery hit home, an ominous feeling came over her, settling like a lead weight in the pit of her stomach. She realised that what had started out as a revenge mission had now taken a very sinister turn.

29

Phil Thomas pulled the phone sharply away, his ears still ringing from the sound of Justin's yelling and cursing.

'What do you mean she hasn't been in the fuckin' pub for weeks?' he raged. 'I thought it was her local! You should have nabbed her when you had the fuckin' chance. Fancy following the wrong car, you useless bastard.' His anger had left him panting and he paused to regain his breath before he resumed. 'Eh, I hope that fuckin' junkie you paid hasn't warned her off.'

'No, I don't think so,' said Phil, trying to placate him.

'How d'you know she can be trusted?'

'Well, I did let her know what would happen to her if she grassed.'

'I don't care. I'm taking no fuckin' chances! I want her out of the picture. She's too much of a fuckin' liability.'

'OK, what do you want me to do?'

Justin was quiet for a moment and Phil guessed he must have been thinking of something.

'You said the junkie goes in the pub nearly all the time, didn't you?'

'Yeah, seems to hang out there a lot, boss.'

'Right, well I want you in there tomorrow night. As soon as she leaves the pub you ring me straightaway, right?'

'OK. And what do you want me to do after that?'

'Fuck all, seeing as I can't trust you to get anything right.'

Phil felt a tremor of nerves. It didn't pay to get on the wrong side of Justin Foster so it was important to keep being useful to him.

'No, I mean, what's the next job?' he asked tentatively.

'Never mind that, I've got other things to concentrate on at the moment. Just be there tomorrow night, and don't fuckin' let me down, then I'll think about what to do with you after that. But there's no way I want you in that Rose and Crown once we've dealt with the fuckin' junkie. Too many people know your face. Anyway, I've got someone else working inside the pub.'

'Who?'

'You ask too many fuckin' questions! It's nobody you know, just a guy who's worked for me before. And, if I'd have known that that pub was his local, I would have put him onto it in the first place. I might have had a fuckin' result by now!'

Phil felt put out at the implication that this other employee was more efficient at his job than him but before he could say anything in his defence, he noticed that the line had gone quiet; Justin Foster had cut the call.

Phil Thomas had an uneasy feeling when he stepped inside the Rose and Crown the following night. If he was honest with himself, he didn't really want to do this, but he knew that with Justin Foster you had no choice. If he said he wanted a job done then you did it or otherwise you faced the consequences.

'A pint of the usual, is it?' asked the ageing barmaid when he walked up to the bar.

He nodded and, when she put the pint down on the bar, he passed her the money and told her to keep the change. She muttered her thanks but didn't stay to make conversation as she used to do when he first started going into the pub. In fact, ever since he had been asking questions about Crystal, and been seen talking to Holly, she had been curt with him.

He knew he'd come under suspicion if anything happened to Holly but it was a chance he'd have to take. Once he'd done what Justin had asked he'd stop going in the Rose and Crown so hopefully nobody could catch up with him.

Phil glanced in the mirror at the back of the bar and saw that Holly was sitting at a table on her own. She'd tried to catch his eye as he walked in but he'd blanked her. The last thing he needed tonight was to be seen in conversation with Holly. So, when she went to join some women at another table, he was relieved.

Holly was now sitting nearer to him and he could hear some of what was being said. From what he could make out she was either stoned or pissed or both and was making a bit of a nuisance of herself with the other women.

'Shouldn't you be going soon?' asked one of the women.

'Where the fuck would I be going?' Holly drawled.

'To earn some money off a few clients.'

'Nah, not tonight. I'm in no mood for the fuckers. I'm here to enjoy myself.'

Then she was up out of her seat and dancing alone to Lady Gaga's 'Edge of Glory' despite the fact that the pub didn't have a dance floor. Phil dreaded her coming over and asking him to dance; that would really have drawn attention to him. But she seemed oblivious to his presence by now as she carried out her own alternative moves while singing along tunelessly and bumping into surrounding tables, a vacant expression on her face. Phil willed this night to come to an end so that it would all be over and done with.

Once the song had finished, one of the other women stood up and took hold of Holly's arm. 'Come on, Holly, sit down. You're in everybody's way here.'

'Fuck 'em!' said Holly, glaring about her at the other customers, her glazed eyes fortunately missing him.

A row broke out between Holly and the woman till another of the women started trying to persuade Holly to sit down. Between them the two women grabbed hold of Holly and forced her into a seat at the table. But Holly was having none of it. She was soon back up out of the chair and yanking her arms away from them so viciously that she lost her balance and keeled over, bumping into the neighbouring table and knocking the drinks over.

'Right, that's it!' shouted the landlord, dashing over to Holly who was still on the floor.

The two women pulled her up between them and Holly stood swaying, her eyes now trying to focus on the landlord who was speaking to her.

'Let's have you out, Holly,' he said, grabbing her arm and tugging her towards the door. Holly complained but nevertheless allowed him to lead her away. 'You can come back another night when you've sobered up,' he said.

As the landlord led her away, Phil headed in the other direction towards the gents. He was relieved that there was nobody inside as he pulled out his phone and quickly rang Justin Foster.

'She's just left,' he said.

'OK, thanks,' said Justin before he cut the call.

Phil went back into the bar intending to stay for at least another hour. That should ensure that he wouldn't be connected to whatever was going to take place tonight. But the hour dragged and despite downing another two pints Phil couldn't shake the anxious feeling that had dogged him all night.

Holly stumbled out of the Rose and Crown and turned down the narrow road that ran alongside the pub. She was so drunk that she barely registered the dark saloon with tinted windows as she staggered in the direction of Piccadilly. She had almost passed the car when she felt somebody grab her from behind. But she had consumed so much alcohol and drugs that they had bundled her in the back of the car before she realised what was happening.

She crashed down hard onto the back seat where there was a man sitting at the far side. He was leaning over and dragging her towards him while the man who had bundled her into the car slammed the door shut and plonked himself down on the other side of her. In front of her were two other men: one driving and the other in the passenger seat.

Holly immediately sensed danger knowing that four strange men hadn't dragged her into the car for nothing. Her first thought was that they were going to gang rape her and she began screaming and shouting for help.

'Shut the fuck up!' yelled the man to her left who was

bulky and menacing. Holly glanced at his fierce expression but she was too drunk to exercise caution.

'No! Let me out, you bastards,' she shouted.

'You heard what he said!' shouted the man on the other side of her. Unlike the man who had thrown her into the car, he wasn't so bulky but the scowl on his face made him just as intimidating. His tense muscles and taut facial expression spoke of a barely contained anger but Holly refused to cower.

She looked across at him then spat in his face. 'Fuck you! Now let me go or I'm calling the police.'

But Holly didn't even have chance to pull her phone out of her pocket before the nasty-looking man struck her with a savage backhand.

'Do as you're fuckin' told!' he yelled before shouting at the gorilla sitting to Holly's left. 'Fuckin' sort her out, will yer?'

His mate responded by clamping his hand round Holly's mouth and trying to pin her down with his other hand. Holly continued to struggle, pushing against him and wriggling her arms and legs frantically. But then she felt the chilling sensation of solid gunmetal against her throat and she tensed, her body now pressed up against the back seat and her breath coming in short gasps.

'Right, now are you gonna shut the fuck up and keep still?' demanded the man while his friend let go of her, knowing that Holly had given up the struggle.

'W-w-what do you want?' she asked. She suddenly felt sober and her voice was now a mere whisper. 'What are you gonna do to me?'

She could feel her voice cracking as fear consumed her

but she tried not to cry. She wouldn't give these bastards the pleasure of seeing her fall apart.

'What I want is for you to keep fuckin' quiet. In a minute I'm gonna take the gun away from your throat and when I do I want you to keep still because, if you don't, I'm gonna have to use it.'

The way he spoke was so emotionally detached that it made Holly even more terrified. She had no doubt that he would waste no time in doing exactly what he threatened. She could feel her stomach growl and she had a sudden urge to empty her bladder but she tried to keep control.

'Yeah, OK,' she said, trying to minimise her movements as best she could for fear of the gun slipping. 'But what do you want with me?'

'You don't need to fuckin' know that,' said the man. 'But you'll find out soon enough, don't worry. Now, are you gonna do as I ask?'

'Yes,' said Holly, relieved when he took the gun away and desperately hoping that this wasn't going to be as bad as she anticipated.

30

Crystal had kept away from the Rose and Crown for weeks ever since Amber had told her about the man who had followed her out of the pub. Her discovery about the connection between Justin Foster and Roger Purvis had given her even more reason to be cautious.

The more she thought about things, the more she was convinced that there was something very sinister going on. Otherwise, why would Roger Purvis be on the list of names that Justin Foster was carrying around? And why would Justin Foster be carrying such a large amount of cash around with him? She had also discovered that Dan Matthews, the man who had been arrested in the drugs bust led by Roger Purvis, was on Justin Foster's list of names.

Whatever was going on, it was something she didn't want to be a part of as it sounded too dangerous so she decided to forget about those two targets for now. But she still intended to pursue other targets and she was just putting together a profile for the sixth man on her list when her phone rang. She sighed and looked at the screen. When she saw it was Amber she quickly answered the call.

'Hi, Amber. You OK?' she asked.

But Amber sounded agitated. 'No, I'm fuckin' not. Have you heard about Holly?'

'No. Why, what's happened?'

Amber sobbed into the phone, 'She's fuckin' dead, Crystal!'

'No!' said Crystal. 'How? What's happened?'

'I don't fuckin' know. They think someone's done her in. She was found on some waste ground yesterday with a bullet in her head.'

'No!' Crystal was screaming now. 'Why? Why the fuck would someone do that to Holly?'

'I don't fuckin' know,' said Amber before she broke down sobbing.

'I can't fuckin' believe it,' Crystal kept repeating. 'I can't understand why someone would do that to her.'

Amber seemed to recover her composure a little as she then said, 'They're all talking about it in the pub. A lot of people are saying it's probably to do with drugs but Moira reckons it might have something to do with that guy that used to come in the pub.'

'What guy?'

'The one that fuckin' followed you that night.' Crystal felt a cold chill on hearing Amber's words. 'He was in the last time Holly was in the pub too and nobody's seen fuck all of him since.'

'Jesus! That's terrible but thanks for letting me know anyway.'

'No worries, but you take care, Crystal. I don't mean to scare you but whoever's done Holly in might be after you too.'

'OK, thanks,' said Crystal, before cutting the call, but she didn't really feel thankful.

Crystal noticed as she put her phone down that her hands were trembling and her throat had gone dry. Apart from leaving her shaken the call had also roused her curiosity again. Just what the hell was going on? Why had Holly been killed? And why had this man been following her? Were Justin Foster and Roger Purvis somehow involved? If so, she needed to know why. It was important to make sure she could protect herself.

Crystal took to her laptop, banging down hard on the keys in a frenzied attempt to find answers. She still couldn't trace anything on Justin Foster; whatever he was involved in, he had covered his back well. Then she keyed Roger Purvis's name into the Internet search engine again. She scrolled through the search results but it was all items she'd already seen so she clicked onto the second page looking for anything else that might shed any light. And then a heading caught her eye.

She clicked on it and read through the report. It didn't surprise her to learn that Roger Purvis had previously been suspected of involvement in a police corruption cover-up. In the article the reporter had interviewed a man arrested for possession of cocaine several years previously. The man claimed that the drugs had, in fact, been planted on him by one of Roger Purvis's officers. When questioned the officer denied the claims and Roger Purvis backed up the officer's denial.

Crystal continued scrolling through the headings but when nothing else came up in the search results for Roger Purvis she decided to try another name: Dan Matthews. As his was one of the names on Justin Foster's list, and he was also the man who Roger Purvis had arrested for playing a key role in a major drugs operation, Crystal was keen to find out more.

There wasn't anything about him in the national press other than the drugs bust of which she was already aware. But there were a few articles about him in the local press and they were all related to petty crime. One of them was drugs-related on a small scale but there was nothing in any of the articles to suggest that he was a major player in any drugs operation.

As far as Crystal was concerned, that could mean one of two things: either Dan Matthews was a career criminal who had progressed from minor crimes to something much bigger or he had been used as the fall guy. From what she had read and learnt so far, Crystal suspected that it was the latter. In fact, the more she read, the more suspicious she became of Roger Purvis and Justin Foster.

Crystal switched off the laptop and sat deep in thought for some time. She was troubled. There was no doubt in her mind that something underhand was going on but she wasn't sure what. She was also puzzled and very worried that either Justin Foster or Roger Purvis had sent the man to the Rose and Crown to find her. But why? The only explanation she could think of at first was that they had discussed what she had done to them and were therefore both out to get her. But how did the list of names fit in with all of this?

Thinking about the names took her mind back to Spud who was also on the list. Last time she'd approached him, he'd warned her off getting involved with Justin Foster so she'd left well alone. But that had been before Holly had died. Surely, if she explained about the man who had hung about the pub and then been seen chatting to Holly, he might relent and give her some clue as to what was going on.

Crystal deliberated at first over whether to delve into things further. It was risky in view of Spud's connections to Justin but she couldn't think of a better alternative. Besides, she'd already spoken to him once so if he was going to tip Justin off about her asking questions surely he'd have done it by now.

She could have just reported matters to the police but she didn't really have anything concrete to go on apart from her own suspicions. And what if they asked her to explain where she had got the list from? No, it was best leaving them out of it; she didn't want the whole thing to backfire on her.

In the end she decided that she'd have to take some sort of action. For starters, she needed to know what she was dealing with. And then there was Holly; she owed it to her to try to find out more about the circumstances surrounding her death. So, she'd go to the Rose and Crown and see if she could have another word with Spud; maybe that would shed some light on matters.

She felt a flutter of nerves as she reflected on her decision. But then she reassured herself that at least the man who had followed her no longer went into the Rose and Crown. So surely it had to be worth taking a chance if she was going to get to the bottom of things.

31

'Hiya, Crystal,' greeted Moira when she walked up to the bar of the Rose and Crown. 'How are you? OK?'

'Not bad,' said Crystal, forcing a weak smile.

Moira served her a drink then, while she was passing Crystal her change, she closed in and spoke softly. 'Shocking news about Holly, isn't it?'

'Yes, terrible,' said Crystal.

Then Moira seemed to lower her voice even more. 'I suppose Amber told you about that guy that followed you, didn't she?'

'Yes,' said Crystal, feeling a shudder of fear but trying to disguise it as she didn't want anyone from the Rose and Crown to find out what she was involved in. 'We don't really know that he followed me though, do we? Only that he left the pub just after I did.'

Moira was quick to elaborate. 'Aye, but he'd been asking a lot of questions about you beforehand.'

'Yeah, Amber said.'

'And him and Holly were as thick as thieves a few weeks before she disappeared.'

Crystal was just about to respond when Moira continued, 'He was in here that night, y'know.'

'What night?'

'The last night anybody saw Holly.'

Crystal shrugged. 'Could be a coincidence.'

'Maybe. Anyway, I've told the police what I know but it doesn't seem like they've come up with anything up to now. There was something not right about that fella though, you mark my words. He was definitely up to no good... Poor Holly being found like that, on a pile of bloody rubbish from what it said in the news. What a way to die; even she didn't deserve that! And those poor children that found her, I feel dead sorry for them. They'll probably never get over the shock...'

Then Crystal suddenly thought of something and she interrupted Moira's rambling. 'What was this guy's name anyway?'

'What? Oh, Phil something or other,' said Moira before another customer grabbed her attention and she went to serve him.

The name hit Crystal like a gale-force wind, almost knocking her off her feet. Phil! There was definitely a Phil on Justin Foster's list. She remembered searching the name on the Internet but she had come up with nothing. Jesus! What if it was the same man? Then that would mean he was definitely connected to Justin Foster and Roger Purvis. This realisation made her even more determined to find out more.

Crystal turned away from the bar to see Spud sitting across from her. She nodded in acknowledgement and when he nodded back she made her way over to join him.

★

Spud saw Crystal when she walked into the pub and his eyes followed her as she approached the bar and chatted for a few minutes with Moira. He had been sitting with a group of friends on another table but he extricated himself from their company after Crystal arrived so that he could watch her, uninterrupted.

He was perturbed to see her coming to join him and grew agitated as she drew nearer.

'Hi, Spud,' she said when she reached the table where he was sitting. 'Mind if I join you?'

He presumed it was more of a statement than a question as she pulled out a chair straightaway and sat opposite him. It didn't take her long to come to the point and he could feel his anxiety levels spiralling as soon as she spoke.

'Last time I spoke to you, I asked you about someone and you told me to keep away.'

'Yeah, that's right,' he said, the reference to Justin Foster making his usual twitchiness even more pronounced.

'Well, I know this might be going against what you advised, but I need to find out what he's up to. You see...'

'No, I don't see,' said Spud, deciding to put an end to this conversation before she said anything more. He grabbed hold of the back of her wrist, desperate to impart his words of warning. 'You should have fuckin' listened to me last time. Get the fuck out of here if you know what's good for you!'

'What? You mean out of the pub? Now?'

Spud could see the look of alarm on her face and he felt bad even though he was trying to do her a favour. 'Yes. Honest, you don't know what you're dealing with. You need to leave the fuck alone! I'm telling you for your own good.'

He was becoming really jittery now but he stopped himself before he gave away too much. He was desperate to warn her but, at the same time, he was terrified of doing so.

'I only want to ask…' she began again but Spud shut her down straightaway.

'No! Shut it,' he snapped, pulling his hand away then pulling back his stool as though ready to leave.

'No, it's OK. You stay where you are. I'll go,' said Crystal. He could see by the expression on her face that she had resigned herself to the fact that she wouldn't get anything more out of him and he watched as she sloped off out of the pub, dejected.

He could feel himself becoming even more worked up and, after a few minutes had passed, and he was still feeling jittery, he took himself off to the gents for a fix. Spud had just entered a cubicle when his phone rang, making him jump. He looked at the screen and noticed the name Justin. Shit! It was as though the guy had now become psychic as well as psycho, he thought, sardonically.

Spud pressed the call-receive button and came out of the cubicle so he could check there was no one around.

'Can you talk?' Justin barked into the phone.

'Yeah, it's OK at the moment,' said Spud.

'Right, well what's happening? Have you seen the bitch yet?'

'No,' said Spud, praying Justin wouldn't find out that he had been talking to Crystal tonight.

'Well you need to fuckin' step things up then.'

'What can I do? It's not my fault she hasn't been in!' said Spud, trying to sound affronted but coming over as insolent, his anxiety levels affecting his restraint.

'Use your fuckin' brains, that's if you've got any! Ask around. You're supposed to know everyone in that dive. And she must have mates if she's a regular. One of them must know summat about her – where she hangs out or where she lives. For fuck's sake!'

'OK, OK, I'll do it.'

'You better fuckin' do it! I was relying on you to get results but it seems you're as fuckin' useless as the last idiot I had looking for her. And you know what happened to him. Do you wanna go the same way as him and Holly?'

'No, no, I'll do it. I promise. Look, I've got to go now, someone's here.'

Spud was shaking by the time he'd got Justin off the phone. He stared at the sombre walls of the Rose and Crown men's toilets as he tried to steady his breathing. There was nobody else there; he'd told Justin that to get him off the phone. He needed a fix and Justin's threats had done nothing to lessen that need.

Spud went back into the cubicle and locked the door, feeling some relief once he felt the coke entering his blood stream. Jesus! Now he was calmer he could think about the situation he had found himself in. He was an idiot! He should have taken Crystal to Justin when he had the chance. But now she had left and he didn't know when he'd get another opportunity.

Spud knew why he'd let her go. Because he was soft. Crystal was a nice girl and he didn't want her to be on the receiving end of whatever Justin had lined up for her. But then he thought about what would happen to him if he didn't take her to Justin or at least lead Justin to her. As Justin had said, he'd go the same way as Phil and Holly.

Nobody in the Rose and Crown knew about what had happened to Phil. As far as they were concerned he'd just stopped coming into the pub. But Spud knew and the thought of it terrified him. Like Holly, Phil had been shot in the head and dumped. But his body would take a while to find. At Justin's insistence, the man who had shot him had then buried him under a mound of rubbish on a council tip.

Justin had told his men that Phil had become another liability. The police were bound to link him to Holly's disappearance and Justin reasoned that he couldn't take that chance. But Spud also knew that Justin had ordered such a callous and demeaning end to Phil's life to set an example to anybody else working for him. If you let him down, you paid the price.

As Spud imagined his own brutal death he felt a tremor of fear so intense that tears of desperation filled his eyes. He sank to the cold, hard floor of the cubicle and sobbed in torment. It took him a while to pull himself together but when he did he reached a decision.

Spud wished he'd never have agreed to it in the first place. But he'd needed the money, and Justin was paying him handsomely. Aside from that, Justin had insisted that Crystal had done something very bad to deserve punishment. And he could be very persuasive when he wanted to be.

But Spud knew he couldn't take Crystal to Justin, he just couldn't do it. He'd have to give him something though. So, he'd lead Justin to her instead as soon as he found out where she lived. He still wasn't happy with his decision but at least that way was less direct and with Justin on his case he didn't feel he had a choice.

32

It was late when Crystal arrived home; still disturbed by the way Spud had reacted when she'd tried to speak to him about Justin. He'd come over very aggressive but she could tell that his anger was trying to mask the fear that she had recognised straightaway. It was in his body language, his rapid speech, the startled look in his eyes and the clenched muscles despite his twitchiness, which was even more pronounced than usual.

She poured herself a drink and for a while she sat going over everything that had happened. The whole situation troubled her: the connection between Justin Foster and Roger Purvis, the death of Holly and her connection with this guy called Phil, the apparent stitch-up of Dan Matthews (if her suspicions were correct) and, worst of all, Spud's abject terror at the mention of Justin Foster. It took a while for her to calm her racing mind but eventually the brandy flooded her bloodstream making her feel more relaxed.

The following day Crystal decided to do more research. It was the only way she would get to the bottom of things and, at the same time, hopefully find a way to protect herself from whatever Justin Foster had planned.

Crystal opened up her laptop, recalling that Justin had

mentioned he was in the fast food industry when she had seen him. She had heard somewhere that you could find out a lot about a company from the Internet. Perhaps it was something Ruby had mentioned when she had been doing some admin work for her. At the time she hadn't taken much notice but now she decided it might come in handy.

She typed 'find company information' in the Internet search engine. It led to a link for Companies House, which she followed. Next she followed the 'find company information' link and clicked on the start button. Crystal then carried out a search. Assuming 'officer name' referred to a company director, she entered Justin's name on the off chance that something might come up.

There were a few Justin Fosters listed and she scrolled down the list, looking for any involved in the fast food industry. She was relieved to find there was only one situated in Manchester. The business was called *Fries and Pies* and the correspondence address was given as Levenshulme.

Crystal couldn't believe how near it was to her own home and she wondered whether Justin Foster lived there or whether it was the address of one of his shops. She could feel her heart thudding in her chest, partly from excitement at the prospect of tracking him down but partly through fear that she was getting so close to a potentially dangerous man.

She was tempted to go along to the shop and see what she could find out but the thought of it terrified her. Crystal was unsure just what she was dealing with but, from what she had discovered, she knew it wasn't good. In the end she decided to leave it for now, sleep on it tonight, and then see what she thought the following day.

★

'So, what was so secretive that you couldn't even tell me in front of Tiffany?' asked Ruby, stepping inside Crystal's lounge and plonking herself down on the sofa.

Crystal was fiddling with the cushion at the side of her, dreading how her friend would react when she told her what she'd been up to. 'Well, do you remember weeks ago when I told you I was going to target some clients?' she began.

'Yeah,' said Ruby. 'And I told you to leave the fuck alone, didn't I?'

'Yeah. Well… I didn't,' said Crystal.

'Hmmm, I guessed you were gonna say that,' said Ruby, with a hint of mild reproach.

'Well,' said Crystal again. 'A lot of the damage had already been done by then.' Ruby sat up straight in her chair, her full attention on Crystal, but she allowed Crystal to finish what she was saying. 'It's that first client I told you about: Justin Foster.'

'That bad bastard who did that to you in the hotel room, you mean?'

'Yeah, that's the one,' said Crystal, feeling a tug of repulsion as her mind shot back to her ordeal. 'Well… it turns out him and another guy, Roger Purvis, are connected. This Roger Purvis is a nasty bastard too and he's a copper. He was on a list of names that I took off Justin Foster when I stole his money. I thought he was called Gerry Patterson but he'd given me a false name. The thing is…'

'Hang on, hang on!' said Ruby. 'What's this list of names and why would you steal it?'

'I didn't mean to. It was in Justin's pocket with his money and I just rushed to grab what I could before he woke up. I've got it here,' she said, taking the list out of her purse and handing it to Ruby. 'Have a look.'

Ruby scanned the list of names before she spotted one that was familiar. 'Spud?' she asked. 'Is that why you wanted a word with him?'

'Yeah, that's right. Anyway, this copper, Roger Purvis, is a bit dodgy.'

'How do you mean?'

'He's been suspected of corruption in the past but it looks as though it was all covered up. And, after that, a guy called Dan Matthews was sent down after Roger Purvis made a big drugs bust. They had this Dan pegged as the main man but I think he was just the fall guy.'

Ruby interrupted her again. 'Hang on a minute, Crystal. Aren't you getting a bit carried away? How do you know all this?'

'No, there's more, Ruby, a lot more. Let me finish. Right, so this Dan Matthews had only ever been done for petty offences before the drugs bust so he doesn't look like a big drug baron to me.'

'OK, but he could have worked his way up to it.'

Crystal shrugged. 'Yeah, but it's not just that. A while back Amber told me about this guy, Phil, who Moira reckoned followed me out of the Rose and Crown. I spoke to Moira about it after that and she reckons he'd asked about me a few times. Then she saw him and Holly as thick as thieves. The next thing you know, Holly's been fuckin' killed and nobody's seen hide nor hair of this Phil bloke ever since. There's a Phil on that list of names as well so it might be the same guy.'

'Phil Thomas?' asked Ruby, reading the name from the list. 'Can't say I've heard of him.'

'No, you won't have done. He hadn't been going in the pub all that long when Holly disappeared, which sounds suspicious if you ask me.'

'You're right, that does sound suspicious.'

'It's not just bloody suspicious, Ruby. It's shitting me up. What if one of these two dodgy ex-clients is after me?'

'Steady, Crystal. You don't know that they're connected with this Phil. It might be a completely different Phil who was asking about you, for all you know.'

'I can't think of any reason anyone else would follow me though, can you? And I don't know anyone else called Phil. And, besides, these two are bad bastards. And when I tried to blackmail Roger Purvis, he threatened to find out my address so he could get back at me.'

She could feel a hint of hysteria in her voice as she confided in her friend. Somehow, voicing it out loud made it all the more frightening.

'For fuck's sake, Crystal! Why haven't you told me all this before?' Then Ruby's tone softened as she said, 'Jesus, girl, you don't believe in having an easy life, do you? Why does trouble always seem to follow you round?'

Crystal could feel her lip tremble but she held herself together while she spoke. 'I couldn't tell you, not after you'd told me to stay the fuck out of it. Turns out you were right, doesn't it?' Her voice was also breaking now, but she carried on speaking, determined to tell Ruby everything that had been happening. 'This Justin told me he's a businessman so I did a bit of research. He runs a chain of fast food shops, and I think he might be using them as a front for drug dealing.'

'You don't know that though,' said Ruby, handing the list back to Crystal.

'Yeah, but, don't forget, Spud is on that list of names too. And he's a known junkie and a dealer. Apart from that, he's shit-scared of Justin Foster. I've tried to get some information out of him twice but he's frightened to death of telling me anything about Justin in case it gets back to him, and he's warned me off.'

Ruby didn't speak for a while. She just stared at Crystal as though she was trying to take it all in. It was Crystal who broke the silence.

'I'm fuckin' petrified, Ruby. But I don't want to go to the police. I'll only be even more in the shit if they find out what I'd been up to. And that Roger Purvis might put a spanner in the works anyway. Can't you get your copper friend to look into things, and keep my name out of it?'

Ruby looked puzzled. 'Who?'

'That client of yours. You said he was a DI on the drugs squad.'

Ruby's manner switched rapidly from recognition to refusal. 'Ray? No! No he'd never do it. He'd be risking his career if people found out how he spent his spare time. Think about it, Crystal. I'm a fuckin' dominatrix who runs a brothel. Do you really think he'd want to be linked to me in the press? Anyway, I always promise my clients confidentiality so he wouldn't exactly be thrilled if he knew I'd told you what he gets up to either.'

'Well what else can I do, Ruby?'

'Why don't you just walk away and leave it?'

'Because it's already gone too far. They're after me for some reason, otherwise why would they have this Phil following me out of the pub? It might be because I've got the list of names that connects them all. And I need to make sure I do them before they do me.'

'Why not get in touch with this Justin and offer to give him his list back then?'

'I wish it was that easy. I've already seen it, haven't I? So, if they're doing what I think they're doing then the list could be... what d'you call it?' Crystal racked her brains for a few seconds trying to come up with the correct term.

'Incriminating evidence, do you mean?'

'Yeah, that's it. Incriminating evidence. He'll know I've seen it so he won't just be after the list, he'll be after me too.'

Ruby blew out a puff of air. 'You've got yourself in one hell of a fuckin' fix, girl.'

Crystal looked at her, beseechingly, willing her to come up with some way of helping her. Ruby didn't let her down.

'I tell you what we'll do. If you believe this Justin is involved in drugs with the copper, and he's using his legitimate businesses as a front, we'll go and visit one of these fast food shops to see what we can suss out. Then we'll decide what to do about it. But we've got to be careful. If these men are as fuckin' dangerous as you say they are, then I ain't taking no chances, girl.'

Crystal forced a smile despite her trepidation, knowing she had wanted to go to one of the shops herself but had been far too frightened to do it alone. Thank God she had a friend like Ruby. She might not have found an end to her problems yet but at least it was a start.

33

Roger Purvis stared impatiently at his phone waiting for Justin to pick up the call. After several rings he heard his voice on the other end of the line.

'Thank Christ I've got you!' said Roger. 'I've been trying to get hold of you for days. What's happening?'

'Relax,' said Justin. 'The job's not for a few weeks yet.'

'OK, fair enough. But I'll still need to know what's going down and who's involved.'

'Yeah, I think we've hit a bit of a snag there, mate.'

'What do you mean?'

'Well, remember that time when I was due to meet you and had to cancel?' Without listening for Roger's response, Justin carried on. 'I had a list of names all written out ready. It was a list of everyone involved in the job as well as some contacts who often come in useful and people I've dealt with in the past. I thought it would be handy for you to know who they all are. I put you down on it too 'cos I took a photocopy for myself.'

'OK, well can't you send it to me?'

'Ooh, no. I'd never fuckin' send anything like that, Rog. That's why I had it all written out by hand ready to give to you.'

Roger sensed a but… 'Go on, what's happened?'

'I think it's been nicked.'

'Nicked? Who the hell would want to nick a list of names?'

'I don't think it was the list of names she was after. She was just looking for anything of value and in the rush to get her mitts on my fuckin' cash she took the list as well.'

'She? Who? Who the fuck are we talking about?' demanded Roger. He didn't like the sound of this one bit.

'That little tart you recommended to me. Crystal, wasn't it?'

'Eh? What the hell? That was ages ago? Why wasn't I told about this? If that list gets into the wrong hands it could fuckin' destroy me. Can't you get it back?'

'I'm working on it, mate. And I didn't tell you because I didn't want to fuckin' worry you. But it's OK, I've got it covered. I've found out where her local is and I've got someone in there looking for the bitch.'

'Jesus! I can't believe this. She must be one hard-faced little bitch 'cos, as well as robbing you, she's been trying to blackmail me!'

'Are you fuckin' serious?'

'Straight up. The little tart even contacted Lyndsey and told her I'd been messing about.'

'Shit! She maxed out one of my credit cards too, would you believe? And she took all the cash I had on me. Over seven hundred fuckin' quid! The bitch. Thank Christ she didn't get her fuckin' hands on my wife's phone number! I bet it left you in the shit with Lyndsey, though, didn't it?'

'I just told her some little tart had latched onto us on a night out and the lads thought it would be a laugh to give her my number. She seemed to buy it.'

'Fuck! That was a close shave.'

'Yeah, it was.' Roger was worried. 'Eh, you don't think she's twigged the connection between us, do you?'

'Nah, come on! You're Gerry to her anyway, aren't you? And she's a fuckin' street girl, for Christ's sake. What would she know? It's probably just a coincidence that she's targeted both of us. She'll have just decided to go round robbing clients for whatever reason.'

'But still, I'm not happy about her having the list. If it gets out that I've been involved in your... affairs, then I'm well in the shit!'

'We'll all be in the shit if she susses out what we're up to, Roger. But don't worry, she's just an opportunist. She might have even binned the fuckin' list by now, for all I know.'

'But we can't afford to take that chance, Justin.'

'I know. That's why I've got someone looking for her.'

'Well, if there's any way I can help, just let me know. I would have had her traced from mobile phone records but it seems the crafty little bitch has been using throwaway phones.'

'OK, well for a start you can let me have the number of whatever phone she's using at the moment; it might come in handy. Don't worry, it's only a matter of time before I catch up with her and when I do she'll wish she'd never crossed me.'

Roger could sense where this conversation was going and he didn't want to hear any more. He knew Justin used violence; it was part of the reason he'd become such a powerful man. But he'd rather not know the details. In fact, the less he knew about that side of things, the better; he was up to his neck in it as it was. So, Roger quickly rounded up the call and hoped to God Justin could retrieve the list before it was too late.

Two days after Crystal's panicked conversation with Ruby they were sitting in Ruby's car over the road from one of Justin Foster's fast food shops. They had parked a short distance away so they would be able to watch the comings and goings at the shop without being spotted. Crystal was really nervous in case Justin might put in an appearance but, as Ruby had pointed out, that wasn't really likely as he had a chain of shops and, besides, he'd probably be at home with his wife and kids at this time of night.

After half an hour they hadn't spotted anything untoward. The customers that entered the shop seemed typical fast food customers: families out for a treat or singles who couldn't be bothered to cook, all emerging with their bag of goodies and a look of eager anticipation on their faces. Nevertheless, Crystal was becoming increasingly uneasy.

'Come on, Ruby. We might as well pack it in, I don't think we're going to see anything that might tell us what Justin's up to.'

'Are you joking?' asked Ruby. 'Look, you've not dragged me all this way for nothing. If there's nowt going on at this shop then we might as well try one of the others.'

'But I don't even know where the others are.'

'Right, well it's time to find out then, isn't it?'

Ruby pulled the keys out of the ignition and made to open the car door.

'What are you doing?' asked Crystal.

'I'm going round the back to root through the bins, that's

what.' Crystal didn't like the sound of that and she pulled a face till Ruby spoke again. 'Come on, you can find out some useful stuff from what people throw away, y'know.'

Then she was out of the car and Crystal followed suit, partly because she felt she had no choice but also because, despite her trepidation, she needed to get to the bottom of things.

There was only one bin but it was one of the large industrial types and the prospect of rummaging through it appealed to Crystal even less than earlier. But it was her mess and Ruby had taken the trouble to drive her here so she could hardly expect her to rummage through the bin for her.

'Come on, let's get it done with,' said Ruby, nodding at Crystal and waiting for her to make the first move.

As soon as Crystal opened the bin lid, the smell hit them: a mix of rotten food and greasy chips. Crystal tried to hold her breath as they sifted through the waste. It was mostly discarded food items – crusty, rotten pies and oily battered fish – amongst the broken polystyrene cartons. But then she felt some paper underneath the smelly, congealed mass.

She grabbed hold of a bundle and pulled it to the top of the bin so she could examine it. There was a stack of discarded leaflets, which she presumed were out of date. She threw the greasy stained ones on the top to one side and pulled out one from the middle of the stack. A quick scan of it told her that this shop was one of six that were dotted around Manchester. She passed it to Ruby and continued digging, convinced that she had felt something else underneath the leaflets.

Crystal soon discovered that it was a letter. It had been

handwritten by someone from *Fries and Pies* but they'd stopped after only a few words then screwed it up. She couldn't understand why anyone would be sending a letter in this day and age when they could email but she saw that it was on letter-headed paper so maybe that was why they'd opted for snail mail.

The handwritten words didn't tell her much, '*Dear Sir/Madam, After careful consideration we have decided to withdraw…*' And that was it. Crystal kept it anyway thinking that it might come in handy at some point.

They carried on searching the bin for a bit longer but when they didn't find anything else of interest they decided to leave it. Crystal withdrew her arm from the bin, which was now covered in a layer of chip fat with bits of rotten food stuck to it, and she recoiled. With nothing else to use, she took a few of the cleaner leaflets and wiped away the gunge as best she could.

'Great,' she said. 'So now I smell of rotten chips. I think we should call it a day, Ruby. I've had enough.'

'No way!' said Ruby, looking at the leaflet Crystal had passed to her. 'Look at this. There's another five shops to try yet so why stop at one?'

'But look at the state of me,' Crystal complained.

'No worries, there's some wipes in the car. And the nearest shop is only five minutes away in Rusholme so we're going, and that's that.'

34

'Eh, that's handy,' said Ruby as they cruised past the branch of Fries and Pies in Rusholme. 'There's a bus stop just over the road, and it's got a shelter. We'll easily be able to watch what's going on from there.'

'What, you mean…?'

'Yeah, we're going to sit outside and pretend to wait for a bus. Why not? We'll have a brilliant view.'

Crystal felt her heart thud as the nerves kicked in but she knew Ruby was right. Two minutes later they had parked the car and were approaching the bus stop. Ruby examined the list of buses displayed on the bus stop sign, taking her time to make it look convincing.

'There's a few buses running from this stop so it won't look too suspicious if we let a couple of them go by without getting on,' she said. 'I think that should give us about twenty minutes before anybody wonders why we're still here.'

Crystal nodded and attempted a smile before plonking herself on one of the cold, hard metal seats. Soon Ruby came to join her. Then they waited.

Within the space of ten minutes it was obvious that there was far more going on at this shop than the sale of greasy fish, chips and pies and this was borne out by the types of cars driven by some of the shop's customers. Crystal watched, amazed, as a third flash car pulled up outside the shop; this time it was a top-of-the-range Audi with new plates.

'Bloody hell! Here's another one,' she said.

'Shush,' said Ruby, staring avidly over the road. 'Let's watch what happens.'

As with the previous two vehicles, a man got out of the car and went inside the shop. Seconds later he came back out carrying a small package. It was obvious to both Crystal and Ruby that these packages weren't big enough to contain takeaway food and they surmised that there was definitely something else happening.

'Right, the next one that stops, we're going in there to see what we can find out,' said Ruby.

'You're joking!'

'Relax. We're only gonna watch. I'm not gonna say anything.'

'OK, I'll do it, I suppose,' said Crystal.

They didn't have to wait long before a flash BMW pulled up outside the shop and the driver emerged from the car.

'Quick!' whispered Ruby. 'We need to get in there before he comes back out again.'

They got out of the car and dashed across the road, with Ruby taking the lead while Crystal followed behind. As soon as they walked inside the shop Crystal could sense an antagonistic atmosphere. Three sets of eyes flitted warily across at them before the so-called customer pulled his hands away from the counter. The youth across from him quickly tucked something away out of view and then the customer spoke.

'I'll have salt and vinegar with that please, mate.'

Crystal couldn't tell what the youth had hidden but she just about managed to make out that it was some sort of small package. It was obvious to her that she and Ruby had walked in just as a deal was about to take place.

While the man was being served, a second youth nodded at them and asked, 'Yes?'

'Two lots of chips, please,' said Ruby.

They stood and waited at the back of the shop while their chips were wrapped, aware all the time of the atmosphere. The man who had walked in the shop was clearly pretending he didn't know the two youths but Crystal could sense that the three of them were just waiting for them to leave so that business could recommence.

At another nod from the youth Ruby went up to the counter again and handed over payment before they took their chips and left. Crystal was relieved to get out of the place. The man who entered before them was still standing at the counter waiting, but Crystal hadn't expected any different.

'Hold these chips a minute,' said Ruby. 'My lace has come undone.'

She passed the bag to Crystal then bent to the ground and tended to her shoes. Crystal was becoming nervous again, aware that Ruby was deliberately stalling. But she decided to make the most of the situation and casually glanced inside the shop. Just as she had expected, the youth behind the counter passed a package to the man then took a wad of notes from him. It was obviously too small to be a food order and far too expensive.

When the man came out of the shop he looked surprised

to see them still outside until he saw Ruby fastening her laces. She stood up and both girls watched while he got inside his car. The package was no longer visible but Crystal had seen him tuck it inside his jacket before he left the shop.

The girls carried on walking down the road till they reached Ruby's car. Crystal waited till she and Ruby were inside before saying anything.

'Did you see that?' she asked.

'No, I couldn't see from the ground but I hope you copped an eyeful.'

'Definitely. He took a package and put it inside his jacket before he left the shop. He gave a load of money to the lad too.'

'I thought he must have done. And he definitely wasn't carrying any chips,' said Ruby, smiling across at Crystal. 'It's made me bloody hungry going in there. It's been ages since I had any chips,' she added, opening one of the cartons and tucking in. 'Want some?' she asked between mouthfuls.

'You must be bloody joking,' said Crystal. 'After rooting through that rubbish bin I don't think I'll ever eat chips again. Just the smell of them is making me gag.'

'Alright,' said Ruby. 'I can take a hint. I suppose we'd better get going anyway.' Then she shoved a handful of chips into her mouth before putting the rest of them on the back seat and starting the engine.

'So,' said Crystal. 'Supposing that they are dealing drugs from the shop, and that's what it looks like to me, then I'm assuming Justin must know about it. The fact that he's connected with a bent copper and a known drug dealer makes it too much of a coincidence, not to mention the so-called drugs bust that Roger Purvis was involved in.'

'Yeah, I agree,' said Ruby.

'Then it means I was probably right about Dan Matthews too; he was just the fall guy. Which also means that Justin is probably importing drugs from overseas. It looks like this is a major operation, Ruby.'

'I know,' said Ruby but she didn't seem to want to be drawn into the conversation. It was as though she was troubled by the enormity of what they had discovered, which was a bad sign because Ruby didn't let many things faze her. But Crystal needed to know how Ruby felt about all of this.

'The question is,' she asked, 'What do we do now?'

35

Once Spud had resigned himself to the fact that he would have to hand Crystal to Justin, it had turned out much easier than he had anticipated to find out where she lived. Crystal was well known in the Rose and Crown so a few brief chats with regular customers enabled him to establish that she lived in Longsight – the newer part, apparently.

After that it was just a matter of turning up in Longsight, visiting a few shops and pubs and asking around on the pretext of being a relative who was trying to find Crystal to let her know about a family bereavement. In the second pub he visited, a sympathetic but very drunk old biddy was very helpful and even told him the street where Crystal lived.

Today was the second time he had visited Longsight in as many days but by now he had been given a house number. He wanted to make sure that the number and street he had been given were correct so he was currently sitting in a borrowed car across the road from the house where he thought Crystal lived. He hadn't seen any signs of life inside the house and it was currently early evening so he hoped that, wherever she was, she would soon be back for her evening meal.

Spud couldn't believe it when a car pulled up outside the house and Crystal got out; it had been so easy to find her.

She had a young girl with her, aged around eleven or twelve, presumably her daughter. Spud turned his head forward so his hoody would obscure his face from Crystal. He already had the driver's window inched open so he could hear part of what was being said. But nothing they said was of interest to him; the daughter seemed to be practising the days of the week in some foreign language from what he could make out.

He'd found out what he needed to know so he drove away from his vantage point before he was spotted. Then he re-parked the car a couple of streets away before ringing Justin.

Without preamble he said, 'I've found out where she lives.' He felt bad about what he was doing and just wanted it over with.

'Really? Are you sure you've got the right address?'

'Course I'm sure. I've just been sat outside the house in the car. I saw her come home with her daughter and go inside. They'd been to some after-school language club or summat.'

'You sure it's not a friend or relative's address?'

'No. It's definitely her house. Someone told me she lived there and I just went to double check.'

'Good,' said Justin. 'Well done.'

But Spud didn't feel as though it was a job well done; he felt like he'd just done a very bad thing.

'So, when do I get my money?' he asked.

'You'll get your fuckin' money when I'm good and ready, don't worry about that!'

Spud had a sinking feeling. Why was Justin stalling?

'You're not expecting me to bring her to you, are you? I've told you where she lives; that was the deal.'

'Relax, and stop whingeing. You're like a fuckin' old woman. You'll get your money but you'll have to come to me to collect it. And, don't worry; you won't have to bring her to me.' Then he laughed raucously before adding, 'I've thought of a much better idea.'

Crystal loved collecting Candice from her Spanish club. She was always so enthusiastic, avidly practising the numbers, days of the week or months of the year in Spanish, and loving the feeling of accomplishment at being able to speak some words in a foreign language.

She was such a bright girl, and Crystal felt a burst of pride at all her achievements, no matter how small. She was growing up fast and latching on avidly to her independence so Crystal knew that experiences like this wouldn't last forever.

Maybe in the future Candice would feel just as proud of her. If things went right then maybe she could take her to Spain one day and let her practise speaking the language for real. It was just one of the things she would love to do with Candice once she'd made enough money. But that was a long way off and at the moment she had other matters to deal with.

Later that evening while Candice was occupied in her bedroom, Crystal sat puzzling over the events of the previous night. She hadn't got much of a commitment from Ruby about what they were going to do next. All she had said was that she would have to think about it and that they'd have to be careful, whatever they decided. And Crystal was too worried to act alone.

But now she was growing impatient as well as fearful about the prospect of Justin or Roger catching up with her before she had a chance to stop them. For the second time that day she took out the letter she had retrieved from the fast food shop, and studied the words. They still didn't mean much to her and she was just about to put the letter away and do something to take her mind off things when something else caught her eye.

It wasn't the handwritten words on the letter that grabbed her attention but the small print at the bottom of the page. Why hadn't she noticed it before? It was the company's registered address. For some reason he had given the address on the Companies House website as one of his shops but that didn't appear to be the same as the registered address on the leaflet. Perhaps he had changed it for some reason.

The address shown here was in Poynton and she wondered if it could be where Justin lived. She tapped a few keys on her laptop and brought up a map of the address then she zoomed in to see a picture of the road. Well, it definitely looked residential but it was a far different world from hers. All the houses were huge, detached and set back from the road.

She checked the house numbers for the address on the letter, wondering whether it would be a house or whether there was some kind of office block further up the road. And there it was; not an office but a beautiful detached house set back from the road like the others, and with a flash Jaguar parked on the drive.

The building was what an estate agent would describe as characterful or desirable. It was fronted by a lengthy garden with a lush, well-tended lawn, a neat box hedge and mature trees. Lining the drive were several planters but these weren't the type you could buy from the local supermarket or DIY store for a few quid; they were huge stone ones filled with attractive shrubs. Even the gate at the opening to the drive appeared to be wrought iron and expensive-looking. The fast food chain must pay extremely well unless there was another reason for such a display of wealth, she thought sceptically.

She decided to ring Ruby. 'I think I've found out where Justin lives,' she said.

'You're joking! Where?'

'Some big fuck-off house in Poynton. There was an address at the bottom of that letter I took from the bin at the fast food shop. It says it's the registered address but when I put it in the Internet it was a house. You want to see it Ruby, it's massive! Check it out on the Internet. It's 320 Ormerod Avenue.'

'Really?'

'Yeah, and I tell you what, those fast food shops must be making a bloody fortune if that's the type of house he lives in.' She gave Ruby the address and said again, 'Check it out on the Internet. You won't believe the size of it.'

'That good, is it?'

'Oh yeah, it must be worth a fortune. It's a really posh one with a massive drive and he's got a flash Jaguar parked outside.'

'Sounds like drug money,' said Ruby.

'Definitely. You don't get a house like that with a few

poxy fast food shops. I mean, I don't know how much those places take but I don't think it's enough to afford something like that.'

'Yeah, and the other thing is, how did he afford to set them up in the first place? Even if he rents the shops, he'll still have had to pay upfront to kit them out.'

'So what are we gonna do?' asked Crystal.

'OK, I've been doing a lot of thinking since I was with you last night and I think we should make an anonymous call to the police about the Rusholme shop. Hopefully the police will raid it and find some fuckin' drugs on the premises. And if Justin ends up behind bars then hopefully your problems will be over.'

'Will it be enough though, Ruby? What about the house?'

'We can't do anything about the big posh house because there's no proof about how he got the money to buy it.'

'But what if the police think it's a prank caller and they take no notice, especially if Roger Purvis has anything to do with it?'

'Then we'll make double sure. Let's both ring. Surely they'll have to take notice of two calls from different people.'

'OK,' said Crystal. 'Let's do it. I'll let you know when I've done my bit.'

After saying goodbye to Ruby, Crystal mentally prepared herself for ringing the police. She knew it was what she had to do but the thought of it gave her a feeling of trepidation. She wasn't just worried that the police might ignore their calls. She was also worried about possible repercussions.

36

In a similar way to which Spud had sat outside Crystal's house in his car, Crystal was now outside Justin's. But the house and settings were far different. This was the sort of house Crystal had seen on the TV and hadn't even dared to dream about. And she'd never seen a road like this: lined with mature trees, devoid of litter and with hardly any cars on the street. The reason for that was because most of them were standing on wide driveways behind the pristine gates or tucked away in double garages. The cars that she did spot were all flash with nearly new number plates, and some of them with private plates.

The house itself was even better in reality than on the screen. It was bigger than she had thought but not in an overbearing, ostentatious way; no, it was far classier than that. Everything seemed well maintained to the point of perfection. Unlike the street where she lived, there was no sign of peeling paint, cracked windowpanes, rusty hinges or edgings full of weeds. A glance at the immaculate lawn told her it was probably tended regularly and she imagined that Justin must have staff to help with the upkeep.

Prior to visiting Justin's house, Crystal had been at home alone while Candice was sleeping over at a friend's. She had become restless, unable to settle while she waited to find out the outcome of the calls that she and Ruby had made to the police. Crystal hadn't arrived here with any real purpose in mind other than that she'd had to see it for herself: the expensive, upmarket family residence occupied by a vicious brute of a man.

Subconsciously perhaps she *was* looking for something – a visit by Roger Purvis or Spud or maybe even the police turning up to arrest Justin following the two tip-offs about drug dealing from his Rusholme fast food takeaway. She checked the drive and noticed that the Jaguar wasn't there, and she wondered if his wife was perhaps out in it. She could be at the police station now, waiting for him while he went through a gruelling interview. But then she caught sight of the double garage and realised that the Jag could be inside. And why would his wife be driving his Jag anyway? She probably had a car of her own.

During the ten minutes in which Crystal sat watching the house, she didn't see either the police or any other visitors. But what she did see, she wasn't expecting: Justin's Jaguar heading towards her and slowing down as it neared the gate. Crystal quickly ducked, knowing her car was incongruent with the surroundings and hoping Justin didn't check to see who was inside.

She listened as the car carried on, sounding slightly more distant but still in the vicinity, telling her he had turned into the drive rather than carrying on past the house. She waited until she heard the car doors slam three times in quick succession then she peeped through her driver's window.

Any hopes that he might have been arrested were shattered in that moment. Justin was standing at the boot of the car, two teenagers by his side, one male and the other female. He lifted some bags from the boot and passed them to the boy. Then he passed a bag to the girl who peeped inside then let out an excited squeal and hugged her father who grinned smugly.

A woman was just moving away from the car, towards the house, when Justin called her. 'Danielle, there's one here for you too.'

She turned back, a smile on her face, and walked towards him. He handed her a bag. 'Oh, Justin, you shouldn't have,' she said, her tone of voice revealing that she was delighted he had.

'You deserve it for putting up with me,' he said, taking hold of her tenderly and planting a chaste kiss on her lips.

His wife followed the children indoors while Justin grabbed the rest of the bags from the boot and locked the car then sauntered up to the house. To Crystal they presented a scene of blissful family life. She thought about what had happened to Holly and the contented scene sickened her.

Why did men like Justin get away with so much? It wasn't fair that he should be so happy when he caused other people so much misery. But she was no longer prepared to put up with it. Somehow she'd find a way to make him pay. Crystal had changed since her days with Gilly. She was beginning to realise what a fool she'd been with him and any guilty feelings over his death were gradually dissipating.

Roger watched the young man as he headed towards him via the outer office, a dated expanse of glass partitions, and textile screens in an insipid shade of beige. Roger's own office afforded no privacy; it was basically a glass box stuck in a corner of the vast space, and he knew the staff referred to it as the goldfish bowl.

Calum Draper, aged around twenty and new to the force only a year ago, irritated the hell out of him. Draper the Drip, as he liked to think of him, was one of those do-gooders, eager to save the world and keen to prove himself in the process. The young man reminded Roger a bit of himself when he was a newbie many years ago. But that was before he'd learnt how things worked in the real world, and developed a thick skin shrouded in cynicism. He could have told the lad he was wasting his time but he'd learn that himself eventually.

'We've had another of those calls, Sir,' said Calum as he bounced into Roger's office with an air of vomit-inducing exuberance.

'What calls?' asked Roger, fixing him with an inquisitive stare, even though he had a feeling he knew what the lad was about to say.

'About that fast food shop in Rusholme.'

Roger felt his stomach lurch, knowing this was the second call; his staff had already updated him about the call they had received yesterday. But he hid his unease behind a hostile retort.

'And is this something you should be troubling me with? I would have thought it a matter for your sergeant.'

'He wasn't there, Sir.'

As he spoke Calum looked across the office and stiffened uncomfortably when he noticed that the sergeant was now back at his desk. Roger eyed him through narrowed eyes, knowing that the lad had waited until the sergeant had left his desk before dashing across the office to tell him about the call. Well, if he thought he was going to earn any brownie points from him, he was well and truly mistaken.

'How long ago did you receive the call?' demanded Roger.

'Not long. Er, just now in fact, Sir.'

'You mean when you put the phone down ten minutes ago?'

The lad flushed and Roger could tell he had rumbled him even though he hadn't actually seen him on the phone. His intuition had furnished him with the likely scenario.

'I-I can go and speak to the sergeant now if you like, Sir.'

'Wait a minute. You can tell me more now you're here. Did the caller give a name?'

Calum's face lit up with a self-satisfied smirk now he was being given this new chance to prove himself. 'No, no name, Sir. It was another anonymous caller, like yesterday.'

'Male or female?'

'Female, Sir.'

'The same person?'

'No, this one sounded different… Sir.'

'OK. You can go back and report it to your sergeant now, like you should have done in the first place. But tell him to liaise with me as I'll be handling it from now on.'

'OK, Sir. Thank you, Sir.'

'Shit!' Roger cursed as soon as Calum had walked away from his office. 'This is all I bloody well need.'

He put his hand to his head and dragged it down slowly over his face. Then he got up and shut the door before sitting back down at his desk. Any minute now one of his subordinates would be here asking what action they were going to take about the situation, and he wanted to make an urgent phone call before that happened. He took his mobile out of his jacket pocket; there was no way he was risking making this call on the landline.

As soon as the phone was answered he came straight to the point. 'Justin, thank Christ I've got hold of you. We've got a problem.'

37

'What do you mean there's gonna be a fuckin' raid?' Justin hollered down the phone as soon as Roger explained the situation. 'I thought that's what I paid you for, to protect me from that sort of thing.'

'Justin, calm down,' said Roger, looking through his office window to make sure no one was hovering close by. 'I have to be seen to be doing my job when the public have reported a suspected drugs operation.'

'Surely there must be something you can do. You're a chief inspector, for fuck's sake!'

'Yes, and that's all the more reason why I have to be seen to be doing my job. How do you think my staff would react if I just sat back and did nothing? And what the hell would I tell them?'

'You can think of something, surely.'

'No, I can't, Justin. I mean, when it was just the one call, fair enough, I put it down to being a crank caller and told the staff we couldn't justify the manpower to send officers out to check. But two...'

'You didn't fuckin' tell me there'd been two calls!' snapped Justin. 'When was the first one and why wasn't I told?'

'One came in yesterday and the other only about fifteen minutes ago.'

'So you didn't bother telling me when you received the first call,' Justin reiterated, accusingly.

'I would have told you in passing but there was no point in ringing you especially. It was of no concern to you. Like I say, I instructed the officers not to investigate.'

He heard Justin sigh, but it came over more like a hiss. 'Who were the callers? Any ideas?' he then asked.

'No, but apparently they were both female.'

'It'll be that little tart of yours sticking her fuckin' nose in again.'

Roger was growing tired of Justin's aggressive tone so he barked back, 'She's not my tart! You had her too. Remember?'

Justin went quiet and Roger could tell he had obviously pricked his conscience, causing him to back down. 'Right, I'll tell you what I can do,' he said, hoping Justin would now be more responsive to his suggestion. 'I'll give you two days. That should give you time to shift the goods and any paperwork.'

'Two days? That's not much.'

'It's as much as I can manage. I have to be seen…'

Justin cut in with a note of fake boredom. 'To be doing your job. Yeah, I know, you said.'

'Two days I can justify, Justin. It will take that long to get things organised. But I can't give you any longer than that.'

'Yeah, OK. Leave it with me,' said Justin before cutting the call without even a thank you for tipping him off.

★

For days Crystal had been ardently watching news reports hoping to hear of a raid on Justin's Rusholme premises or, better still, his subsequent arrest. It was on the fourth day after her call to the police when she finally saw the news report.

'Shush,' she said to Candice as she flicked up the volume on the remote control and fixed her eyes on the screen.

The TV report showed several police officers flooding the same takeaway premises that Crystal and Ruby had visited a few days ago. The image then flashed back to a studio reporter who detailed the raid and described how two tip-offs from the public had prompted the police to take action.

Crystal grew excited, anticipating that he was then going to mention arrests in connection with the raid. But she was disappointed when the reporter then went on to say, *'Police found no trace of drugs on the premises, which has led to the belief that this is the result of hoax callers. Our reporter, Richard Salmon, spoke to Chief Inspector Roger Purvis about his concerns.'*

Crystal tensed as the image then flashed to Roger Purvis, all self-important and displaying mock concern. Dressed in full uniform he looked very official and responsible, and this was backed up by his words.

'We need to get the message across to the public that these crank calls waste a lot of valuable police resources, which could be utilised elsewhere.'

Crystal thought about the man he really was: base, vulgar and condescending, and she resisted the urge to spit. But her facial expression conveyed her scorn for the man who appeared on the screen.

'Are you OK, Mum?' asked Candice when she saw Crystal's reaction.

'Shush!' said Crystal again.

She was raging, knowing that Roger Purvis had somehow wangled it so that the calls from her and Ruby were not taken seriously. And why did the police not find anything on the premises when it was quite clear that there was drug dealing taking place there? Had they deliberately ignored it? But that would have meant that the officers visiting the place had been corrupt too, and Crystal thought that was unlikely.

The more likely explanation was that Roger Purvis had tipped off his friend Justin Foster, and given him time to get the drugs off the premises. And Roger Purvis would have instructed his officers not to check any further when there were no obvious signs of any drugs.

For a few moments Crystal watched the news report in silence until it had finished. Once her attention was no longer on the screen she noticed how her daughter was watching her.

'Are you OK, Mum?' Candice asked again, her face full of concern.

Crystal suddenly became aware of how her reaction must have appeared to her daughter and she did her best to backtrack.

'Yes, yes, I'm fine, love. I was just thinking about the news report. It's terrible what goes on these days.'

'Why? What did they mean, Mum?'

Crystal kissed her gently on the forehead. 'Grown-up stuff; nothing for you to worry about, sweetheart.'

Then she forced a fake smile and was rewarded by a look

of relief on her daughter's face. For a while longer she made small talk with Candice, trying to make up for her extreme reaction to the news report. But really she just wanted to ring Ruby to talk about what she had seen. Once she was satisfied that her daughter had bought her display of normality, she snuck off to her bedroom and made the call.

'Ruby, I've just seen a news report about the shop in Rusholme.'

'I know, I watched it too. I was going to ring you later.'

'Fuck! What do we do? I think Justin's onto me. And why the fuck didn't the cops find anything?'

'Chill, girl. Nobody's followed you since that one time, have they?'

'Well no, but...'

'And you haven't seen anything suspicious?'

'Not exactly but that doesn't mean they're not still looking for me.'

'But don't you think they'd have found you by now if they were still looking for you, Crystal?'

'OK, but what do we do about Justin in the meantime?'

'As long as he isn't bothering you, I'd leave it alone. We've tried to shop him but it hasn't worked so there's not much more we can do. Anyway, if the police are putting it down to crank callers then Justin might not even suspect you of reporting him.'

'Oh come on, Ruby. You don't really believe that, do you?'

Crystal could tell from Ruby's silent reaction that she was right; Ruby didn't believe the police story that it was probably crank callers who reported Justin's Rusholme shop. Like Crystal, she obviously knew that it was just a cover to explain why no drugs had been found on the premises.

Eventually Ruby spoke. 'Listen, Crystal, I know you're worried but try to take your mind off things. Like I say, if they were still looking for you, they'd have found you by now. I think it's best if you stay out of Justin's business as well. He sounds like a dangerous man and you don't want to fuckin' wind him up any more than you already have. With a bit of luck he'll have found something else to occupy him.'

Crystal rounded up the call but, despite Ruby's words of wisdom, she couldn't relax. She could feel the tension at the back of her neck and she rubbed it, trying to hold off the headache that she could feel coming. She knew what Justin was capable of and if that list of names was linked to anything corrupt then there was no way he would let things go until it was back in his hands. He was definitely planning something and she dreaded to think what that something might be.

38

Crystal was planning a special tea. It might not have seemed special to most people but bangers and mash with peas and onion gravy was one of Candice's favourites. Crystal had been so on edge lately and was concerned that Candice had picked up on it so she wanted to make it up to her.

She had defrosted the sausages, peeled and chopped the spuds and prepared the onion gravy in advance. Now all she had to do was wait for Candice to get home from school, as it was too soon to start cooking. Then she'd keep it a secret from her till the last minute when Candice could smell the sausages on the grill, and she would watch her lovely face light up with joy at her surprise tea.

While she was waiting for Candice she occupied herself with other things, trying to take her mind off the Justin situation as Ruby had suggested. *Typical,* she thought, looking at the clock as she ran the hoover through the lounge. *The day when I plan a special tea and Candice is late.*

Two minutes later she glanced at the clock again. Candice was only ten minutes late. Perhaps she and her friends had stopped off at the shop on their way home as they sometimes did. She tried ringing Candice on her mobile but there was no reply. Crystal supposed she'd have been that busy talking to her friends that she had missed the call. But when Candice was half an hour late and there was still no sign of her, Crystal became worried. She did a mental double check; was there an after-school activity today? *No, she thought. Not on a Wednesday.*

On the days when there were after-school activities Crystal would insist on bringing Candice home as there weren't as many people around at that time. But on the other days Crystal let Candice walk home with a friend. She hadn't been comfortable with it at first but she had to accept that Candice was getting older and it was all a part of her growing up. And, even though she was always there when Candice arrived home, she had let her have her own key as well; it was another nod to Candice's growing independence.

Crystal rang Candice's mobile again but there was still no reply. By now she was becoming anxious. She couldn't just stay here and wait; she had to be doing something. So she jumped in the car and drove to school, stopping at her neighbour's house beforehand to ask her to keep an eye out for Candice and to tell her she would be home soon. The neighbour agreed to let Candice stop with her until Crystal returned.

When she arrived at school Crystal could see that there was hardly anybody still there apart from a few teachers and cleaners, and her anxiety intensified. Thankfully Candice's teacher was still in the classroom stapling up displays of the children's work so Crystal dashed up to her, breathless.

'Hello, Miss Etchells, Candice hasn't stayed behind for any reason, has she?'

Even as she asked the question Crystal knew it sounded ridiculous. There was no obvious sign of Candice in the vicinity and Miss Etchells looked concerned.

'No. Why? Isn't she home?'

'No,' said Crystal. 'I'm a bit worried about her. Do you know who she left school with?'

The teacher adopted a grave expression. 'Sorry, I wasn't on yard duty when the children left the grounds but hang on a minute and I'll go and speak to one of my colleagues.'

The couple of minutes that Miss Etchells was out of the room seemed to last forever. It was clear to Crystal that something was badly amiss and she needed to find out what had happened to her daughter as soon as possible.

Crystal passed the time by admiring the wall displays, her mood lifting slightly when she spotted one of Candice's stories. But when she heard Miss Etchells returning down the corridor, her eyes automatically flitted to the classroom door. Miss Etchells didn't wait to reach Crystal before speaking. She must have been able to see the worry on her face.

'As far as anybody knows, she walked home with her friend Lucy Smeaton.'

'Thanks,' said Crystal, dashing past Miss Etchells and out of the door.

Crystal thought she heard Miss Etchells say something else after she'd left the room but she didn't go back to find out what it was. From what she heard it sounded like some sort of platitude and she was more interested in getting to Lucy Smeaton's house as quickly as possible.

Luckily she knew where it was as she'd picked Candice up from her friend Lucy's many times previously. Maybe that was where Candice was right now, spending some time with her friend. She tried to think whether Candice might have mentioned it. Had it perhaps slipped her mind while she'd been preoccupied with other things? But she didn't think so.

It wasn't long before she arrived at Lucy Smeaton's house. It was Lucy's mother who answered the door.

'Hi. Candice isn't here, is she?' asked Crystal.

'No, no she isn't,' said Lucy's mum, concerned.

'OK. Could I have a word with Lucy then please? She walked home with her apparently.'

'Sure, come in.'

'Lucy!' her mum called up the stairs. 'Candice's mum wants to have a word with you.'

'Did you walk home with Candice?' demanded Crystal as soon as she saw the child at the top of the stairs.

'Yeah,' said Lucy as she made her way down.

'Did you stop off anywhere along the way, sweetheart?' asked her mum, adopting a gentler tone, which made Crystal feel a bit guilty for speaking so sharply.

'No,' said the child who had now reached the bottom and was standing next to her mother. 'We just came straight home.'

'What about Candice? Where did she go after she left you?' asked Crystal.

'Home,' said Lucy with a puzzled expression on her face.

'Did you see her talk to anyone or was there anyone hanging about on the street?' asked Crystal with the same sense of urgency.

The child was beginning to look a bit startled now and

her mother chipped in, gently resting her hand on Lucy's shoulder as she spoke. 'We're just trying to find out if Candice went straight home or whether she got held up.'

'No, she went straight home.'

'And did she mention going anywhere else?' Crystal said.

'No, she was just going home.'

'OK, thanks,' said Crystal, making for the door.

'Hang on!' said Lucy's mum. 'Don't you want to wait here while we ring around some of her other friends? There's probably a good explanation.'

'No, no it's fine,' said Crystal, dashing out of the door.

On the drive home Crystal hoped that maybe Candice had just got talking to someone, and that she'd be there waiting for her when she got back. Her neighbour stepped out of her house as soon as Crystal parked up. She hoped she was going to tell her that Candice was inside but instead she asked, 'Any news?'

Her words had such an ominous air that Crystal had to bite back tears as she replied, 'No, nobody knows anything.'

'Aw, I'm sorry. Why don't you come inside and have a cuppa while we figure out what to do?' asked the neighbour.

But Crystal was beyond polite chit-chat. 'No, it's OK,' she said. 'I need to be in the house in case she comes back.'

She rushed indoors, half hoping that Candice might be waiting inside. Maybe the neighbour had missed her. But a quick scan of the house confirmed what she already knew in her heart. Candice was nowhere to be found.

Crystal felt a growing sense of unease, knowing deep down that this could have something to do with Justin. Her mind was in such turmoil, it was difficult to think rationally. Instead of ringing the police, she dashed from the house again. Her neighbour was outside, as though she had been on her way to see her.

'Any news?' she asked.

'No, and I need to go and find her,' said Crystal, heedless of the fact that she was contradicting her earlier statement about having to stay inside the house. 'Can you keep an eye out for her again please?'

Then Crystal was in the car again without waiting for her neighbour's response. She turned the key in the ignition and set off once more in a desperate search for her missing daughter. Her precious Candice.

39

Crystal's first stop was at Ruby's home. She didn't even bother ringing her beforehand as her instinct was to be doing something rather than sitting around in her house while she waited for people to respond to her calls. Apart from Spud, Ruby was the only other person she knew who was aware of Crystal's involvement with Justin and, hopefully, she would be able to offer some advice and support. There was a look of curiosity on Ruby's face when she found Crystal standing outside her door with no advance warning.

'Hi, Crystal. Is everything alright?' she asked.

'No, no it's not. It's…'

But Crystal couldn't get her words out before she burst into tears. Voicing what had happened brought home the reality of it and she was suddenly reduced to a quivering wreck.

'I told you,' she sobbed. 'I said Justin would do something. Didn't I? And now he's got Candice.'

Her sorrow and desperation gave her an aggressive edge and Ruby reacted defensively. 'I didn't fuckin' know he'd do that, did I? I hoped he'd have given up by now. What's happened? How do you know he's got her?'

Ignoring Ruby's question, Crystal yelled, 'You don't

know him like I do! He's a bad bastard. I wouldn't put anything past him and now he's got my little girl.'

Then Crystal broke down, sobbing uncontrollably again. Ruby looked lost, as though she wanted to help but didn't know what to do. It was Tiffany who ran over and put her arm around Crystal's shoulder.

'Come here,' she said, pulling Crystal towards her and cradling her in her arms while she cried out her anguish.

Meanwhile Ruby paced up and down the vast hallway of their detached Altrincham home, trying to deal with the situation in her own way.

'I'll pour us a brandy,' she said. 'I think we should all sit down and have a fuckin' drink, then we can decide what we're gonna do.'

Eventually, between the two of them, Ruby and Tiffany managed to calm Crystal down, but she refused the offer of a drink, knowing it was more important for her to be able to drive at the moment. Crystal surmised that although she had told Ruby her problems in confidence, she would have told Tiffany by now about everything that had happened. Ruby always confided in her girlfriend so Crystal wasn't surprised when Tiffany asked, 'Have you told the police what's been going on?'

'No, I can't. If I tell them about Justin they'll find out about me blackmailing him and I'll end up in the shit.'

'Well just tell them about Candice going missing then.'

'No, it'll be no use. If they don't know about me taking the list off Justin then they won't know where to start looking, will they?'

'Unless it isn't Justin who's got Candice,' said Tiffany.

Crystal didn't say anything for a moment, her tears threatening to erupt again as thoughts about what might have happened to her daughter whirled around in her mind. Ruby flashed a look of reproach at Tiffany for her lack of subtlety and she hung her head, chastened.

Then Crystal looked directly at Ruby. 'We all know it's him who's got her,' she said. 'It's just too much of a coincidence. I want you to help me find her, Ruby. Please.'

'Yeah, course I will,' said Ruby. 'But where the fuck do we start?'

'With Spud,' said Crystal, knowing Justin was unlikely to be keeping Candice at his own home; he wouldn't risk his family finding out what he was really like. Besides, she was still nervous about meeting him, feeling that he might dispose of her once he'd got his hands on the list. 'I'm convinced there's something Spud's not telling me,' she continued. 'He might even know where Justin has taken Candice. Will you come with me to the Rose and Crown? Maybe he'll tell us.'

Before Ruby had chance to respond, Tiffany asked, 'Does Candice have a mobile?'

'Yeah. I've tried ringing her a few times but there's no reply.'

'Why don't you try again before you go?'

'OK,' said Crystal.

She did as Tiffany suggested but when there was still no reply, she stood up, put her mobile in her handbag, then turned to Ruby and said, 'Come on. Let's go.'

*

When they arrived at the Rose and Crown, Crystal and Ruby didn't waste any time in scouting round the pub looking for Spud. Unfortunately there was no sign of him.

Ignoring the queuing customers, Ruby went straight up to the bar. 'Has Spud been in lately?' she asked Moira who was busy serving.

'Not for a while,' said Moira. 'Why, what's the matter?'

'Nothing,' said Ruby. 'We just want a word with him, that's all.'

They left the bar area, passing their friends Amber and Sapphire who they had walked straight past on the way in.

'Are you two alright?' asked Amber, picking up on the sense of urgency with which Crystal and Ruby had entered the pub.

'Yes, fine,' said Crystal, following Ruby who was heading for the door. Then she stopped and asked, 'Have you seen anything of Spud?'

'No, he's not been in here for a few days from what I know,' said Amber. Crystal had turned towards the door again, and Amber quickly asked, 'You not staying for a drink then?'

Crystal failed to hide the feeling of despondency that surrounded her. 'Not today,' she said.

Amber stood up, leaning over the table towards Crystal who had carried on making her way to the door.

'What the hell's wrong, Crystal?' she asked.

'I'll tell you another time.'

It wasn't till they reached the street that Ruby stopped and turned around.

'Amber says he's not been in the pub for days,' said Crystal. 'It seems funny.'

'Yeah, if you ask me, I think he's staying out of sight for a reason,' said Ruby.

'Then we need to find him,' said Crystal. 'Let's go back in, see if anyone might know where else he hangs out. They might even know where he lives.'

'None of his usual crowd are in,' said Ruby. Then she sighed. 'I think the best thing you can do is go home and ring the police, Crystal. It's obvious we're not going to find Candice ourselves.'

'But what do I tell them?' asked Crystal. 'They won't find her unless they know about Justin and the list.'

'It's up to you how much you want to tell them; whether you just tell them about Candice not coming home from school or whether you tell them about all the other stuff too. Only you can decide that, Crystal. Maybe you could just tell them about the money and the list you took from Justin but leave all the other stuff out. What's a bit of petty theft compared to your daughter's safety? Hopefully the police will see it that way too.'

Crystal shrugged. 'Come on,' she said. 'I want to get home in case Candice turns up.'

'OK,' said Ruby, forcing a smile. 'Let me know how you get on with the police.'

Crystal had driven into Manchester but she didn't really want to drive Ruby all the way back to Altrincham, feeling that she would be wasting valuable time.

'Rubes, would you mind if I dropped you at the taxi rank?' she asked. 'I'll pay for the taxi if you want but I really need to get home.'

'No worries,' said Ruby. 'I understand, girl, and don't worry about the fare. Just you let me know how you go on. Eh, and drive carefully.'

Once she had left Ruby in Piccadilly, Crystal could feel the tears spring to her eyes again as she thought about her missing daughter and how helpful and understanding Ruby and Tiffany had been. But she brushed her tears aside; they were obscuring her view of the road and she needed to get home safely.

It wasn't long before she arrived at her home in Longsight. Even though she had intended to arrive safely, she couldn't help rushing. During the journey she had resigned herself to making that call to the police once she was inside. Perhaps it was her only hope now.

She parked the car and raced across the pavement. Managing to avoid her neighbour she put the key inside the lock and opened the front door, her heart racing as she acknowledged to herself that she was unlikely to find her daughter inside. Despite her resignation, she still dashed down the hallway and pushed open the living room door. But what she saw inside there made her stop and stare in shock.

40

Crystal couldn't quite believe the sight that met her as she walked into her living room. The place had been ransacked. Drawers had been pulled out from the wall unit, their contents tipped onto the floor. Cushions had been dragged from the three-piece suite and slung across the room. The rug had been tugged away and left in a crumpled heap, and the contents of the bin had been dumped everywhere.

As the shock registered she rushed through the house calling out Candice's name. Her mind was in a muddle; still focused on finding her daughter but also trying to make sense of these latest events. She raced upstairs where the scene was similar, with clothes dragged from the wardrobes and strewn across the beds, the drawers upended and the pillows and cushions strewn across the room.

Crystal carried on running through the house, searching, but it soon became apparent that Candice still wasn't home. Finally, she reached the kitchen, which was in an even bigger mess than the other rooms. All the drawers had been emptied and the floor was a muddled mass of cutlery, broken crockery, tea towels and various kitchen utensils.

She crossed the room, carefully, taking in the mess and destruction as she made her way to the work surface. Like everywhere else it was littered with smashed pots and other debris. But there was something else that made the breath catch in her throat.

There amongst the chaos was a plate with half a dozen uncooked sausages. On the hob were a pan of chopped-up potatoes waiting to be cooked and a pan of onion gravy ready to reheat. It was the meal she had lovingly prepared for Candice when she had still been expecting her to return from school just like any other normal day. But Candice wasn't coming home today. And as she stared around at the devastation Crystal succumbed to tears once more.

As soon as she was calm enough, Crystal rang Ruby.

'Any news?' asked her friend.

'No, still no sign of Candice but someone's wrecked the house. It's a fuckin' mess. They've been right through and tipped out all the drawers and wardrobes, and chucked everything all over the place. It's a fuckin' mess, Ruby,' she repeated. 'I think it's Justin. He's after that list of names; I just know he is.'

'Shit, Crystal. I'm so sorry! Do you think he found what he was looking for?'

'No, the list is still in my purse.'

'How did they get in?'

Crystal had been so shocked that she hadn't even thought to check if any of the doors or windows had been smashed. She quickly checked them out while Ruby waited on the other end of the line.

'I don't know. It's strange. I can't see *how* they got in.' Then a thought occurred to her and her heart plummeted. 'Oh shit!'

'What? What is it?' asked Ruby.

'They used a fuckin' key, didn't they?'

'A key? What do you mean?'

'I mean they must have used Candice's key,' said Crystal, her own words striking fear into her.

'Oh my God!' yelled Ruby. 'You've got to ring the police, Crystal. You can't afford to piss about any more. This is serious!'

'Do you think I don't fuckin' know that?' shouted Crystal, her tone bordering on hysteria. 'I'm not ringing the police though. Justin wants that list so I'll contact him and offer to give it back provided he lets me have Candice.'

'No! Don't be so fuckin' stupid, Crystal. If he's as dangerous as we think, do you really think he'd let you walk away just like that, knowing you could have copied the list? You've got to get the police involved now.'

When Crystal didn't say anything more, Ruby said, 'Right, I'll let you go so you can call them. But let me know how you get on and, once they've been, you're welcome to come and stay here.'

'No. Thanks but I can't,' said Crystal. 'Candice might still come home. I need to be here for her.'

She finally finished the call, ready to ring the police. But, before she redialled, the irony of her own words hit her. Candice wasn't coming home. Not if Justin had her. She just hoped to God that he didn't harm her little girl. She tried not to let her thoughts run away with her as she keyed 999 into her phone with trembling hands.

It was an hour later and two police officers were in Crystal's living room, sitting across from her. Crystal had managed to tidy up enough for them to find a seat but there was still a hell of a lot of work to do before everything was back as it should be. The eldest of the officers was a woman; she reminded Crystal of a teacher at school who the kids used to call Miss Frosty Knickers. But she was very professional and didn't seem to want to miss anything. Crystal presumed she must be the more experienced of the two officers as she was doing the speaking while her colleague, a young male, was taking notes.

When they first came round, Crystal rushed to tell them what had happened, eager to let them know as soon as possible so that they could start the hunt for Candice. But it soon became apparent to Crystal that Miss Frosty Knickers didn't work like that.

'OK,' she said. 'I want you to tell us everything you know. Let's start with your daughter's name and age, shall we?'

'Candice. Eleven.'

'And what was she wearing when she disappeared?'

'Her school uniform.' The two officers looked keenly at Crystal and she realised they wanted her to elucidate. 'A royal blue sweatshirt and grey trousers. Oh, and she would have had her coat on, a black waterproof anorak.'

'And what time was it when she disappeared?'

Crystal was becoming exasperated. 'I don't know! I've told you, she didn't come home from school.'

'OK, so what time does she usually get home?'

'About quarter to four. Her friend, Lucy Smeaton, was the last one to see her when they walked home together. Candice got as far as Lucy's house, and then she just disappeared.' Crystal's voice became shaky as she said the last few words.

'Can you give us Lucy's address please?' asked the female police officer. 'And could you also explain why it has taken you several hours to report her missing?'

The female police officer's words immediately put Crystal on her guard, knowing that the real reason she hadn't reported Candice missing straightaway was because she suspected Justin was involved, and to report him would mean she would have to tell them about the items she had stolen. She hesitated a moment before responding to the police officer's question.

'I tried to look for her myself, first at the school and then at her friend's house.'

'That would still mean that several hours have elapsed between you looking for her and reporting her missing. As she spoke the officer looked around at the chaos in Crystal's home, and Crystal guessed she knew there was something else amiss.

Crystal sighed. 'OK,' she said. 'There's a reason I didn't report it straightaway. It's because I think I know who's taken her.'

The two officers sat up straighter in their seats, their full attention now on Crystal as she took a deep breath and went on to tell them about Justin Foster and the list of names she had stolen along with the money. But she didn't tell them about the credit card or the blackmail, deciding that she would only reveal what was absolutely necessary in the hunt for Candice. She would already be in trouble as it was.

She told them she no longer had the list, claiming she had thrown it away as she didn't realise how important it was to Justin Foster. Some sixth sense told her to hold on to it for now in case it might come in useful. Crystal didn't tell them about Spud or Roger Purvis either. She didn't yet know the full extent of Spud's involvement so she didn't want to implicate him if she could avoid it. And as for Roger Purvis, if she mentioned his name she might alert the police to her own criminal activities.

Crystal was correct in her assumption that she would be in trouble. As soon as she divulged the fact that she had stolen money from Justin Foster, the tone of the interview changed.

The officers looked at her disapprovingly then Miss Frosty Knickers spoke, 'I'm afraid that, in view of what you have told us, you've left me with no alternative but to place you under arrest.'

Then she read Crystal her rights, adding, 'We'll have to continue this interview at the station.'

Crystal held her head in her hands. This was all she needed!

Once they had arrived at the station, Crystal was led into an interview room and offered a cup of tea. She had only just begun drinking it when the two officers filed back into the room and continued the interview, firstly asking her for further information on Justin. Trying to avoid their contemptuous stares, she told them his address, the mobile phone number he had contacted her on, and everything else she knew about him.

Once the officers had taken notes about Justin and asked any relevant questions, they then moved on to the break-in. On and on the questions went. Crystal was becoming frustrated with the time it was taking, and a little distressed, but she supposed they were just doing their job and, as far as they were concerned, the more information they had, the easier it would be to find Candice. She therefore made sure she pointed out that Candice was carrying a key to her home so there was a possibility that whoever had taken her could also have used the key.

She was glad when the police finally left the interview room, hoping they would now set to work on finding Candice but also aware that her theft of Justin's money would not be ignored by them. It was getting late by now and Crystal was tired but she hung on patiently for the officers to return.

It was a few hours later when they finally did and unfortunately they didn't bring any good news. Instead Crystal was charged with theft then released pending a court appearance.

41

It was obvious to Justin as soon as he answered Roger's call that his associate wasn't happy.

'Just what the hell is going on, Justin?'

'What do you mean?'

'Kidnapping. That's what I fuckin' mean. I've just had one of my inspectors report it to me. They're coming to take you in for questioning any minute now.'

'And what makes you think it's me?'

'Because that little tart reported you last night. And, if it hadn't been for the fact that the two officers she spoke to were finishing their shift, someone would already have been along to see you by now.'

'You're joking! I can't believe she'd do that.'

'Well she fuckin' has. And never mind her; just what the fuck do you think you're playing at? I mean, turning a blind eye to your drugs operation and giving you the odd tip-off, that's one thing. And you wouldn't have been getting that from me if you hadn't found something on me and threatened to tell my wife. But kidnapping a fuckin' child? That's a whole other matter! Just what the hell possessed you to do that?'

'I thought she'd cooperate and let me have the list if I agreed to let her have her kid back.'

'Oh, did you? So now I'm supposed to fuckin' cover that up too! And just when did you decide on this ridiculous course of action?'

Justin didn't bother admitting that he already had the kidnap in mind last time they spoke but he'd been too preoccupied with the drugs raid on his takeaway shop to do anything about it. Instead he just said, 'Does it matter? Look, I need to find out exactly what your lot know so I can be ready for them when they arrive.'

Roger appeared to take a more reasoned approach then, saying, 'Just that she took some cash and a list of names from you and she thinks that's why you've snatched her child. Oh, and she thinks you're responsible for ransacking her home too. Are you?'

'Well, what do you expect? I need to find that fuckin' list! Anyway, it wasn't there. And keeping hold of her kid seems like my only chance of getting her to give it back.'

'Well, there's fat chance of that now she's got us involved, is there?' asked Roger, referring to the police.

'Oh, I don't know. It's her word against mine. You don't think I'm gonna admit it to your lot, do you? So, it's back to plan A – I'll make fuckin' sure she gives me the list once I've been released from questioning. And don't forget that while this tart is pissing us about, it's ballsed everything else up. I've got the supply due to arrive in a couple of weeks and we need to be ready to take stock. We can't put the Lithuanians off. I need to have my distribution chain set up and ready by the time the drugs arrive.'

'Shush!' said Roger at the mention of the word 'drugs'.

But Justin had heard enough so he cut the call. By this time he was just as angry as Roger had been. He resented the way Roger spoke to him. Oh how he'd love to dispose of him just like he did with all his problems. But he couldn't do that with Roger because he needed him onside. Corrupt DCIs were hard to come by.

It was the early hours of the morning when Crystal finally got home and after snatching only a couple of hours' sleep she woke up. As soon as she came to, she had that feeling of dread in the pit of her stomach as she recalled what had happened yesterday. And as she thought about her missing daughter, she couldn't help but shed more tears. The lack of sleep, combined with her persistent tearfulness, meant that her eyes were now red-rimmed with dark circles underneath them.

She tumbled out of bed and walked slowly down the stairs, her leaden feet reflecting her dire frame of mind. The state of her home made her feel even more downhearted and she resolved to carry on putting it back in order some time later that day. In the kitchen, she flicked on the kettle and brewed herself a coffee, her stomach too unsettled to manage anything else.

Crystal sat watching TV while she decided what her next step should be. She was reluctant to rely solely on the police, knowing that Justin had a senior officer, Roger Purvis, working for him from inside the police force. There was every chance that between them they might try to discredit her story. Crystal was therefore deliberating over whether to go round to Justin's herself, despite her reluctance to meet him, and offer the list in return for her daughter, or whether to wait till the Rose and Crown opened and have another attempt at locating Spud so she could find out if he knew anything.

In the end she decided to go to Justin's house and offer him the list. Sod the consequences! She needed to have her daughter back home and she wasn't prepared to sit around waiting for the police to take action, knowing that Roger Purvis would probably be doing everything in his power to stall the investigation.

It wasn't long before she was ready to go. She hadn't bothered ringing Ruby. What was the point? She would only try to talk her out of it and at the moment she didn't need that. Whatever Ruby said, it wouldn't change her mind so why waste time? She took a last look around her ravaged home before she left. To hell with the mess! That could wait; she had more important things to think about at the moment.

Half an hour later Crystal was sitting in her car outside Justin's luxury home in Poynton. Something about the affluent area made her feel suddenly self-conscious and she checked her appearance in the car mirror before taking a deep, calming breath and stepping out of the car. This time she had pulled up right outside Justin's home, determined not to hide from him anymore.

She crossed the pavement and peered through the wrought-iron gate, noticing the Jaguar parked on the drive. *That must mean Justin is in,* she thought, and her heartbeat speeded up. She pushed the heavy iron gates open and stepped tentatively on to the drive. Its sheer size made her feel inadequate, her mind automatically comparing the surroundings with her modest rented home. Those feelings of inadequacy were heightened when she looked around at the immaculate lawn and perfectly manicured shrubs.

Crystal pushed her negative thoughts aside and approached the front door where she reached up and pressed the bell. It took a while for someone to answer but when they did it wasn't Justin she saw but an attractive blonde who she recognised as his wife. She looked about ten years younger than him but, on closer inspection, Crystal concluded that she was probably also in her forties although very well maintained.

The woman was stunning: slim with long, straight blonde hair, and perfect makeup and features. A swift glance at her casual but classy clothing told Crystal that it didn't come cheap. Yet, despite her stunning appearance, the woman's face was strained, her eyebrows slightly drawn and a couple of fine, tell-tale lines around her lips.

She surveyed Crystal through narrowed eyes. 'Yes!' she snapped, her tone conveying to Crystal that she wasn't welcome on these premises.

For want of a better way of opening the conversation, Crystal said, 'I'm looking for Justin, Justin Foster. Is he in?'

'No, he isn't,' said the woman, her tone hostile.

'You must be his wife,' said Crystal. 'Have you any idea where he is? I need to speak to him, urgently.'

'What do you need to speak to him about?' The woman's tone was still unfriendly and an air of suspicion surrounded her.

Crystal took another deep breath as she prepared to say the line, which would probably shatter this woman's world. 'I think he's got my daughter.'

Her reaction was just as Crystal had expected and for a moment she stood there speechless, her mouth dropping wide open. She quickly grabbed on to the doorframe as if she needed to steady herself. Then she spoke, her hostility now suffused with an element of confusion.

'It's you, isn't it? You're the one who reported him to the police. Why? Why would you do that? Justin would *never* do something like that.'

'I wouldn't be so sure of that if I was you,' Crystal replied, unable to help herself. 'He's capable of a lot of things you probably don't know about.'

'How dare you!' said the woman, but even as she protested, Crystal could spot the bemused expression on her face, and she surmised that Justin's wife didn't place as much faith in her husband as she claimed. But she still kept up the act. 'Go away!' she shrieked. 'I don't want malicious people like you near my home. Have you any idea how much upset this has caused for me and the children?'

'Have you any idea how upset I was when my eleven-year-old daughter didn't come home from school?' Crystal countered, her voice cracking.

Her obvious distress seemed to play to the woman's empathetic nature and she moderated her tone as she said, 'I'm very sorry for you, I really am. But I can't have you throwing accusations at my husband.'

'But it *is* him,' Crystal insisted.

'How do you know it is? How do you even know him? Why should I believe a word you say? I don't even know who you are!'

For a moment Crystal deliberated over how much to tell Justin's wife. There was obviously a whole area of his life that she knew nothing about. The woman was already upset by Crystal's accusation and the fact that the police were taking it seriously enough to get involved. But there was also an air of uncertainty about her. Maybe Justin's wife had suspicions about his extra-marital activities, and perhaps she could use that uncertainty to her advantage.

For a moment she was tempted to tell her everything, including his use of prostitutes and his sadistic tendencies, assuming she wasn't already aware. But she didn't really want to cause the woman any more distress and, besides, she needed to get to Candice as soon as possible. 'Is Justin with the police now?' she asked.

'Yes, thanks to you.'

Crystal could sense her battling with her emotions. 'Look, I know this is difficult for you,' she said. 'But is there anything at all you can tell me that would help? Is there anywhere you can think of where he might have taken her?'

Justin's wife glared at Crystal, her expression one of incredulity; whether genuine or contrived, Crystal wasn't sure. Either way, it made no difference to her response. 'I've already told you, my husband would never do a thing like that. Now get off my premises before I bring the police back to deal with you.'

Then she slammed the door shut, denying Crystal any opportunity to persuade her to answer her questions.

'Damn!' Crystal cursed, convinced that she had come close to getting some information out of Justin's wife. It was obvious she suspected something even if she was loath to admit it.

Undeterred, Crystal decided that she would tell his wife

everything if she had to, and to hell with her hurt feelings. It was more important that she should find Candice. Maybe something she said would trigger some recognition in his wife's mind of occasions when Justin had behaved suspiciously.

For several minutes she hammered on the door but there was no reply. Crystal thought she saw a curtain twitch, and she became aware of a man in the house next door pretending to busy himself in his garden while he observed her. In the end she realised that it was pointless and she returned to her car, dejected.

Her only hope now was that Roger Purvis had washed his hands of Justin and was no longer trying to protect him. If that was the case then maybe the police would get a result and she'd soon have her daughter with her.

But even as the thought passed through her mind she knew that there wasn't much chance of that. A ruthless operator like Justin wasn't likely to confess all to the police; the more likely scenario would be that he'd be doing all he could to wrangle his way out of it.

42

It was the following day and Crystal had heard nothing further from the police. She had made an attempt at tidying up but there was still a lot to do. While she was putting things back in place she had discovered that a frame holding a photo of Candice had been damaged during the attack on her home, and this had reduced her to tears yet again. But she quickly quashed her tears. Crying wouldn't get her anywhere; she needed to be strong for Candice.

In a similar way to the previous day she had fixed herself a coffee when she got up then plonked herself down on the living room sofa while she thought about her predicament. Since Candice had disappeared she hadn't had much to eat; just a couple of slices of toast and a banana yesterday. She decided to ring the police to see if there were any updates since Justin had been taken in for questioning.

When she took the phone out of her handbag she did a quick check for any messages but there was nothing. She was just about to make her call to the police when the phone rang. She was so preoccupied as well as overwrought about Candice that it made her jump. She rushed to answer it expecting it might be the police with some news for her. But the number that flashed up on the screen made her breath judder in her throat. It was Candice!

In her rush to answer the call, she imagined her daughter, stuck alone somewhere and anxious to get hold of her, and she expected to hear her voice at the other end of the line. When it was Justin who spoke, she let out a squeal of alarm. That could only mean one thing; he definitely had her daughter. She was also devastated on realising that, if he was phoning her on Candice's phone, then the police must have released him.

'Oh my God! What have you done to her?' she screeched. 'I hope you've not harmed her or I swear to God…'

'She's fine. Shut the fuck up while you hear what I've got to say, will yer?' When Crystal remained silent, he continued. 'Right, now I want you to listen carefully. I want you to meet me later today. Shall we say one o'clock? If you bring the list with you I'll let you have your daughter back. OK?'

'Yeah,' said Crystal, her voice shaky.

'Right, well get a pen and paper. I want you to write down the location.' Crystal did as he said but before she'd got chance to get all the details down, he spoke again. 'I want no fuckin' police involved this time. You're lucky you're getting your daughter back after that stunt you pulled. Did you really think that would work? You must be sick in the head. They'll get fuck all out of me!' Crystal again kept quiet so he carried on with his instructions. 'I want you to come on your own, and don't tell a soul about this. Do you understand?'

Again, the only word Crystal could muster was, 'Yes.'

'Good. Because if I find out you've told anyone then I'll see to it that your daughter suffers.'

Then he cut the call, leaving Crystal rushing to write down the rest of the details before she forgot them. She stared at her own writing. The whole of her body was now trembling at the thought of what might happen to Candice if she didn't cooperate.

Crystal wondered where Justin might be holding her daughter and she keyed the details he had given her into the map on her phone. Then she pulled up an image. From what she could make out the nearest main town was Poynton, which made sense seeing as how that was where he lived but, other than that, she couldn't tell where he was leading her to as there were no properties listed anywhere near that location. In fact, it wasn't even a proper address, just the intersection of two rural roads.

She looked at the clock. It was still only eight thirty in the morning and she knew the hours until one o'clock would drag. Crystal wondered why Justin hadn't chosen an earlier time but maybe that was all part of his nasty plan: to make her wait and therefore prolong her suffering.

As she sat there trembling, her mind coming up with all sorts of shocking scenarios relating to her daughter, Crystal was tempted to ring Ruby for advice. But she resisted, too fearful of the repercussions if Justin found out.

By the time it reached ten o'clock, Crystal's anxiety was rocketing. She'd tried pacing round the room, doing some tidying up and taking a refreshing shower, but nothing had calmed her. If ever there was a time when she was tempted to drink and drug herself into oblivion then that time was now. Crystal had reached the point where she couldn't cope with the pressure any longer. She needed to do something.

Crystal knew she daren't involve the police again after what Justin had said. So she changed her mind about ringing Ruby, and dialled her number. Surely there was no way he would find out about that! And she desperately needed to confide in someone.

'Ruby, I've had a call from Justin. The bastard's got her.'

'What? When was this?'

'This morning, first thing. The police took him in for questioning yesterday but now they've released him. According to him he just denied everything.'

'Bastard! What else did he say?'

'He wants me to meet him. If I take the list, he'll hand Candice back.'

'No! Don't do it, Crystal. I've told you before, you'd be endangering yourself.'

'What choice have I got? The police are doing fuck all, and this is the only chance I've got of getting Candice back. But you mustn't tell anyone what I'm doing. Justin has warned me to come alone and he's threatened to make Candice suffer if I tell anyone.'

'Shit!' said Ruby. 'Where does he want you to meet him, anyway?'

'It's a country lane near Poynton.'

'Can't you see?' said Ruby. 'He's deliberately getting you to meet him somewhere secluded. That's so nobody can see what he's up to. I'm warning you, Crystal, don't go. It's too dangerous!'

'It's also near to where he lives so that might be the

reason,' said Crystal. 'Mind you, I doubt he's got her at his house otherwise his wife would have known about it, and it didn't seem to me as though she'd be involved in something like that.'

'What do you mean? You haven't been to see his wife, have you?'

In her distressed state, Crystal had overlooked the fact that she hadn't told Ruby about her visit to Justin's wife the previous day. For a moment she felt a pang of guilt but then she had a swift change of heart. It was up to her what she did, and if Ruby had been in her position then she had no doubt that she would have done the same.

'Course I have,' she replied. 'You didn't think I would just sit around and do nothing, did you? Candice is my daughter, Ruby, and I'll do everything I can to get her back.'

For several minutes Ruby carried on trying to talk Crystal out of meeting Justin but eventually she gave up. Crystal was relieved when the call came to an end. It had made her feel even more dejected and she wondered why she had bothered ringing Ruby in the first place. She supposed that she had been looking for some kind of reassurance but, instead, Ruby had just faced her with the brutal truth: that Justin would stop at nothing to get his hands on that list and to stop her from divulging its contents.

For a while Crystal pondered over what to do. Maybe she should wait and see if the police managed to find Candice or some kind of evidence that tied Justin to her daughter's disappearance so that he was forced to confess. But a big part of her doubted that that would happen, especially given Roger Purvis's involvement.

Every minute that she waited for the police to act was a

minute in which her daughter was away from her. Candice had already been missing for two days and Crystal didn't know how much longer she could stand not knowing where her little girl was. She wished she hadn't deliberated so much yesterday. Otherwise, she might have arrived at Justin's home before the police took him in for questioning, and persuaded him to hand her daughter back in exchange for the poxy list of names.

She knew that Candice would be missing her mother just as much as Crystal was missing her; they shared a close loving bond and each of them hated to be apart from the other. Crystal pictured her daughter, lonely and scared, perhaps tired and hungry too. Then her mind drifted to thoughts of other abuses Candice might be suffering at this moment.

She couldn't bear it! She was Candice's mother and she owed it to her to do everything in her power to go to her rescue. So, even though she would be placing herself in danger, Crystal decided that she would meet Justin as arranged. She just hoped that it ended well.

43

Candice was crouched in the corner of an abandoned barn, trembling from cold and fear, her hands and feet bound with rope. Around her was draped an old musty blanket, which was insufficient against the cold wind that rustled in the rafters and whistled through a small hole further along the roof. She was sitting to one side of a large mound of foul-smelling hay, an empty sandwich wrapper and drained bottle of water to her other side.

She hadn't known where the men were taking her when they'd bundled her into a car on her way home from school two days earlier. At first she had screamed and struggled to break free but then the men had gagged her and put a blindfold on.

Eventually, they'd arrived at their destination and Candice had been pulled from the car. She walked across what seemed like some kind of a yard, the ground feeling like stone beneath her feet. Candice guessed she was no longer in the city. It smelt similar to the farm she had visited on a school trip: a mix of fresh air and cowpats.

Then she was ordered to wait while the men opened the door to some sort of building. She heard the creaking of rusty old hinges and then she was led inside. The stench hit her as soon as they opened the doors but became stronger with each step she took. It smelt of animals and dankness. But it was more than that; it was a dirty, cloying smell that made her want to retch.

It seemed to take forever to traverse the inside of the building and she guessed that it must have been large. Then the men stopped her abruptly and told her to sit down on the floor. She bent and put her hands out to the back of her, recoiling as her fingers touched on something slightly damp and straw-like.

She heard a snigger. 'It's only bloody hay. What's wrong with you?' asked the man.

So that was why it smelt of the countryside and dirty animals. She must have been in a farmhouse or a barn or something. Once she was sitting down, she felt one of the men kneel towards her, and she flinched as she felt his hot breath on her cheek. Then he grabbed her legs, placing her ankles together as he wrapped something round them. She was being tied up.

Candice had stopped struggling by now. What was the use? If she tried to run she wouldn't get very far wearing a blindfold. So she sat while the man bound first her feet and then her hands.

'I'm tying your hands in front of you,' he said, matter-of-factly. 'So you can eat and drink, and do whatever else you've got to do. But don't think that means you can untie your legs. If I find you've messed with the ropes when I come tomorrow then you'll get a fuckin' good smacking, and I don't just mean a slap either.'

And then he removed the blindfold and gag. The sight of him struck fear into her. He was big with a tough-looking face and a sneer. She didn't like him or the language he used. It reminded her of how her mother had occasionally spoken when she used to get drunk a lot, but she didn't do that anymore. His friend was standing to one side of him. He didn't seem very friendly either and he was looking at her intently and grinning. He was holding the blanket, and he threw it at her.

'There, that should keep you warm,' he said. 'And there's a drink and some grub there. We'll be back tomorrow so you behave and don't even think about trying to escape or you know what you'll get.'

As he spoke, he pulled out an evil-looking knife then bent forward and waved it in front of her face. Candice drew back into the wall of the barn, pulling herself tightly into a ball, and whimpering at the sight of the blade. But the man put it back inside his jacket then nodded to his friend and left her there crying for her mother. Candice didn't even scream; she was too afraid the men would hear her and return to do what they'd threatened. Instead, she sat there trembling and sobbing for some time.

When she had calmed down a little, she looked around the building. From the smell, the damp hay next to her and the damaged wooden structures, she guessed that it was a barn, which was as huge as she had imagined. It was chilly inside and dark, the only light coming from a small hole in the roof, which caused a puddle of water on the ground below. Although there was a window near to her and some others further along, they had been boarded up from the outside so that the only view through the glass panes was of wooden slats.

As she looked more closely, Candice noticed spiders'

webs under the sills of the boarded-up windows and she shuddered at the thought of spiders crawling on her in the night. About halfway along the barn was an old plough. It was now rusted and broken and Candice guessed that nobody used it anymore. There was a cartwheel leaning up against the barn wall but that was also broken and splintered.

At first Candice refused to eat the food or drink the water, not trusting the men and afraid that they might be poisoned. But as day started to draw into night she gave in to her thirst and hunger; she hadn't had anything since lunch. It also helped to alleviate some of the boredom that had now beset her after several hours inside the barn.

After she had finished drinking and eating she noticed that inside the barn it was becoming darker. Even the shaft of light from the hole in the roof was diminishing, and her fear intensified at the prospect of staying there on her own all night. It was spooky. The insects, the dark, the evil men brandishing daggers – they all presented a persistent threat. It was also becoming colder and, even though she had wrapped the rough blanket tightly around her, she found herself shivering and her teeth chattering.

Candice snuggled up beneath the foul-smelling hay, drawing some comfort from its warmth. Despite her fear and abhorrence at the thought of having to stay here alone, she was glad that the floor was at least dry in this area of the barn and the hay offered some shelter against the cold night air. It also acted like a flimsy barrier of protection against all the perceived horrors of the oncoming night.

She was so terrified that she fought sleep for as long as she could, but eventually, exhausted, she drifted off only to be awoken by the sound of scampering across the barn floor. The sight of two enormous rats made her squeal and she drew even more tightly into herself, unable to relax until they had scuttled off to the far side of the barn.

The following day Candice woke up with a full bladder. She peered around the barn for a bucket or something else she could use. But there was nothing. She therefore crawled along the rough, grubby barn floor as best she could and found a spot away from the relatively dry hay and behind the old plough where she could relieve herself.

With her arms bound in front of her, she struggled to undo her clothing and felt ashamed of what she was doing. The ankle binds made it difficult to balance and when she toppled over her clothes became covered in urine as well as the hay, dust and animal droppings off the barn floor. She crawled back to her spot in the corner and tried to forget it had happened.

During the day Candice's thoughts turned to escape. She looked around the barn but the only outlet to the outside world seemed to be the hole in the roof. Unfortunately, it was far too high to reach. She could try smashing the windows and forcing the wooden slats open but she had nothing with which to smash them and she doubted she would be strong enough to force the slats.

The door was at the far side of the barn and Candice was so exhausted that she didn't think she'd make it across the barn floor with her hands and feet bound. It had been a big enough struggle crawling to the area that she used as a toilet. Candice knew the men had locked the barn door anyway; she'd heard the slam of the heavy bolt after they had left her. She was also afraid of crawling across the barn to the far side in case the men should return and guess that she was trying to escape. The consequences were too horrifying to contemplate.

It was late that day when the men returned, and Candice hadn't eaten or drunk anything all day. By now she was hungry and extremely thirsty. Despite her fear of the men, she was relieved just to see another human being and welcomed the prospect of food and drink. The first man was carrying a pack of sandwiches and a bottle of water. While he walked towards her, his friend wandered around the barn examining the windows and any other possible escape routes. Candice reached out to grab the food and drink, and the man slapped her hand away.

'Fuckin' wait!' he growled. 'We wanna make sure you've been behaving yourself first.'

Candice withdrew her stinging hand, feeling a rush of tears. When the other man confirmed that everything seemed to be intact, the first man threw the sandwiches and water at her, forcing her to scramble across the grimy floor in order to retrieve them.

The men didn't say much else to her that evening other than to ridicule her because she had soiled the ground on the other side of the barn. They also issued another austere warning to her not to try to escape. And then they were gone, leaving Candice alone once more.

For some time after the men had left Candice couldn't stop shivering. She had been so glad of the food and water but, at the same time, she had been petrified of what they would do to her. She'd heard stories of what evil men did to young girls and she dreaded what might happen, knowing that there must be a reason why they were holding her in this barn.

That night was similar to the previous one and by the third day Candice was exhausted, having slept very little for the past two nights, as well as being hungry and thirsty. Once the morning arrived, her fear began abating and boredom set in. But each time she heard an alien sound, the intense fear would return, her senses on full alert as she dreaded what would await her.

By now Candice was becoming grubby, not having washed since her capture. Her school uniform was dirty from scrambling along the barn floor and was ripped where she had caught it on a sharp piece of metal protruding from the old plough. She hadn't brushed her teeth or hair since the day before last, leaving her hair looking bedraggled and a stale taste in her mouth. And her dried-up tears formed furrows through the dust that smeared each of her cheeks.

Candice's weakened state was affecting her state of mind and her brain ran through all sorts of terrifying scenarios. She had just had a particularly terrifying half hour when she heard the unmistakable sound of a car pulling up and someone approaching the barn for the third time. Candice tensed. The men were back.

44

Spud had thought his involvement was over when he'd given Crystal's address to Justin. But he should have known better where Justin was concerned. Not happy with knowing where Crystal lived, he'd then got him to find out what school her daughter went to. Spud didn't really want to comply; he felt bad enough giving him Crystal's address but to involve the child was just too much. Then Justin had grabbed him by the throat and issued another of his threats, forcing Spud to give in to him.

When Spud heard news of the child going missing, she had already been away from home for two days. It confirmed what Spud had been dreading: that Justin had snatched the child to get at Crystal. Spud felt sick in the pit of his stomach when he thought about what he had been a party to. He needed to get away; he couldn't do this anymore. And he vowed to himself that as soon as he sorted out somewhere else to live he would leave Manchester for good because, as long as he stayed, he would always be under Justin's control.

But he had to put some arrangements in place first. As well as a place to stay he would need a new supplier because his drug habit was so bad that he couldn't bear the thought of going without his fix while he looked for another supplier in a strange area.

So Spud scanned through his list of contacts and made a few calls. It was after several that he finally struck lucky and found an old acquaintance in Liverpool who was willing to let him sleep on his sofa for a few nights. Spud didn't like to broach the topic of drug supplies yet; although his friend had been heavily into the drugs scene when he had lived in Manchester years ago, he might have moved on from that now and Spud didn't want to risk losing the offer of his friend's sofa for a few nights if he didn't approve of his habit.

He decided the best thing to do would be to take his own supply with him – just enough to keep him going until he found somewhere to score in Liverpool. But to do that he needed money, which meant he would have to call Justin to get the money he owed him for the last job.

Justin had told him over the phone to collect the money from his house and Spud was full of trepidation when he arrived there. But he tried to keep calm by reassuring himself that this would be the last of his dealings with Justin and, after that, he'd be rid of him.

'Come in,' said Justin when he answered the door, puffing on a cigar with an air of nonchalance about him.

Spud stepped into the vast hallway, noticing the enormous chandelier and Justin's attractive wife hovering at the other end of the hall.

'It's alright, he's come to see me,' Justin said to his wife dismissively as he led Spud through to his spacious home office.

Those few seconds were enough to tell Spud that the body language of Justin's wife was the exact opposite of his.

Her attractive features were strained and she was fiddling nervously with a tea towel. As soon as Justin spoke to her, she had scuttled away as though relieved that Justin seemed to have things in hand. Spud couldn't help but wonder how much she knew.

'Sit down!' ordered Justin as he marched across the office and sat himself down on a leather captain's chair behind a vast mahogany desk.

Spud took the relatively ordinary-looking chair at the other side of Justin's desk and sat facing him, waiting for Justin to hand him the money he owed.

Justin reached into a desk drawer and pulled out an envelope. 'Here's your money,' he said, holding it out on the desk in front of him. Spud reached to grab it but Justin withdrew it just as his fingers grazed the envelope. 'Wait your fuckin' sweat!' he said. 'There's something else I want you to do first.'

'B-but you said that last job was the end of it…'

Justin cut in, 'I know what I fuckin' said. But something's cropped up.'

Spud looked across the desk at him, confused. 'What?'

'Well, let's just say I've had a few staffing problems and the people I had lined up for a job today have been called away to tend to something else. So that means you'll have to do it instead.'

Spud felt his heart quicken, and his hands go clammy, dreading what Justin was going to say next. His worst thoughts were confirmed when Justin continued, 'It's to do with the girl.'

'No, no, I won't do it,' Spud shouted, becoming more anxious at the thought of what Justin had in store for him.

Before he could react further, Justin crossed the desk and had him by the throat. 'Keep your fuckin' noise down!' he demanded. 'Do you really think I want my wife and kids hearing you?'

Spud was stuck for words as he stared back at Justin with terror in his eyes. Seeming satisfied with his cowed reaction, Justin continued, 'You'll do exactly as I tell you, otherwise you'll lose more than your fuckin' money.'

As he issued his threat, Justin squeezed harder on Spud's throat, leaving him gasping for breath and in no doubt that Justin wouldn't hesitate to do him harm if he didn't obey. When he finally released his grip, Justin said, 'Right, are we understood?'

Spud nodded, fingering the tender area of his neck and desperately trying to control his sudden urge to urinate.

Justin returned to his seat, adopting his calm demeanour once more, and took another huge drag on his cigar while Spud waited nervously for his orders.

'You probably realise by now that I've got her,' he said.

Spud nodded, his eyes wide with fear.

'I had no choice!' Justin quickly added in defence of his action. 'That cheating little tart has forced me to this. She stole my cash and a list of people I do business with and it's the only chance I'll have of getting the list back. But don't worry, she'll get her comeuppance. Anyway, this is where you come into it.'

Spud gulped, and carried on staring at Justin in silence as he outlined in vivid detail exactly what he wanted him to do.

45

As Spud approached the barn, clutching the key Justin had given him, he was afraid of what he might find, knowing that the child had now been there for two days. He had toyed with the idea of going to the police but ruled it out. While he was still in Manchester, there was a chance that, even if Justin was arrested, he would put someone on to him who would take him out before he got a chance to leave the city. So he'd reluctantly decided to do as Justin ordered, promising himself that this time it really was his last job.

He slid the huge bolt on the barn door then, using the key Justin had given him, he unlocked it and heard the squeaking of rusty old hinges as he pushed it open. The place was vast and it stank – a mix of animal smells, decay and human waste. He couldn't see the girl at first but he guessed she would be in a corner of the building, behind the dilapidated old plough. He locked the door and crossed the barn.

As he passed the plough he noticed the stench of human waste become stronger and he tried to avert his eyes from the sight of two days' worth of human excrement and urine. *Poor little cow!* he thought. *What a way to have to live!*

He continued past the plough until he spotted her,

cowering in the corner, and clinging to a ragged old blanket for comfort. Her hair looked matted and her clothes were soiled and creased. As he edged nearer she seemed to shrink into herself, drawing her legs up and backing into the large bale of rotting hay to one side of her.

'It's OK,' he said. 'I've just come to give you some food.'

He held out a pack of sandwiches and a bottle of water but the girl didn't reach out for the food. Instead, she stared at him, her pupils enlarged with fear. Spud stepped closer still and she let out a squeal, recoiling as though expecting a slap.

'Here,' he said, dropping the sandwiches onto her lap and placing the bottle of water on the ground nearby.

Despite her initial reluctance she clawed at the pack of sandwiches until the cellophane wrapping came apart then she grabbed at the first sandwich and rammed it into her mouth, ravenous. As she raised her hand to eat Spud noticed the red marks on her wrist where the rope binding had chaffed. He glanced down and noticed that her feet were also bound.

The sight of her was distressing and for a few moments he looked away while she ate, taking in the surroundings. There was another empty sandwich pack and water bottle not far from her and he guessed that was all she had eaten since she had been taken captive nearly two days ago. Spud wished he'd had the foresight to bring more food but then he'd cursed himself for being so soft. Justin had sent him to do a job and it didn't pay to get too emotionally involved.

He backed away, ready to leave the barn and lock the door behind him but as he turned around he heard a tiny, trembling voice. 'Are those other men coming back?' she asked.

He turned and looked at her. The wide eyes, drawn

eyebrows and hunched shoulders painted a picture of intense dread and he felt for her. 'Did they hurt you?' he asked instinctively and although she clammed up again, her body language gave him the answer. Bastards! He knew that he'd done some bad things in his time, mostly because of his drug addiction. But he would never hurt a child.

His mind was in torment. He hated what he was doing; hated seeing a young child so terrified and desperate. But he consoled himself with the thought that at least he was the one to visit her today rather than Justin's bully boys who had scared her so much. For a moment he was tempted to help her but then he thought about the consequences and couldn't do it. He walked away, reluctantly, leaving the child in misery in his attempt to save his own skin.

At least it hadn't been as bad as he had thought. When Justin first mentioned a job in connection with the child, he had envisioned him asking him to dispose of her. And Spud knew that, whatever punishment Justin threatened him with, he wouldn't have done that. At least by feeding her he was helping her in a way.

Despite trying to reassure himself that he was doing the right thing, guilt ate away at him as he turned the key in the lock. He was leaving a child on her own inside a disgusting old barn with none of her home comforts. No bed to sleep on, hardly anything to eat or drink all day and only a scruffy blanket to keep her warm at night. And, apart from the physical discomforts, the poor kid was petrified, and that would only get worse as night fell.

He tried to dismiss his concerns, and carried on to his car. He couldn't afford to let sentiment get in the way, not when he was dealing with someone as ruthless as Justin.

*

Spud knocked on the front door of Justin's lavish home for the second time that morning. Justin answered the door and led him through to his office again before plonking himself in his captain's chair and ordering Spud to take the seat opposite.

'So, you've done it then?'

'Yes.'

'And did you drive around for a while before coming here like I told you to?'

'Yes.'

'OK, you can have your money then.'

Spud couldn't believe that Justin was so callous as to not even ask how the girl was. But he wasn't daft enough to say anything before the money was tucked inside his coat. Only then did he voice what was on his mind.

'The poor kid's terrified, y'know.'

Justin glared at him. 'Did I ask for your fuckin' opinion?'

'I just thought you might want to know. I don't know what those guys did to her but she's terrified in case they might come back.'

'They know not to touch the kid,' Justin snapped. 'Anyway, she needed to be frightened. I don't want the little fucker thinking she can escape the minute no one's there. Hopefully she'll be too shit-scared to even think about it.'

'How long will she be there?' Spud couldn't help asking.

'Not long. It's not her I'm after; it's her mother. The little scrubber that ripped me off.' Justin then made a show of looking at his watch before adding, smugly, 'It shouldn't be too long now.'

'What will you do with the kid then?' asked Spud.

'You ask too many fuckin' questions! But don't worry, the kid'll be fine.'

'And her mother?'

'Like I say, you ask too many questions. Now, you've got your money so why don't you just fuck off? And not a word to anyone...' Justin then put his finger to the side of his neck and mimed slitting his throat, adding, 'Or you know what'll happen.'

46

Crystal's heart was hammering as she drove to the meeting point near Poynton. When she drew nearer she was gripped by a terrifying sense of foreboding. But, despite her fear, she was early for the meeting, eager to be reunited with her daughter as soon as possible. Inside her purse the list was tucked away. Crystal hadn't bothered taking a copy. She was no longer interested in revenge. It was more important to bring Candice home safely and then put this whole episode behind her.

She parked up her car where Justin had instructed, at the intersection of two rural roads, and instinctively checked her watch. Twelve fifty – she still had ten minutes to go. Crystal took a good look round but couldn't see much. She spotted the vague outline of a building in the distance but, other than that, nothing. This place was certainly deserted and she shuddered as she recalled Ruby's words: *He's deliberately getting you to meet him somewhere secluded. That's so nobody can see what he's up to.*

But Crystal couldn't let her fear stand in the way. As far as she was concerned it was the only chance she had of getting her daughter back. And if that meant risking her own life then that was what she would have to do. So she waited, tapping nervously on the dashboard while she listened for approaching cars and glanced repeatedly in her rear-view mirror.

It was less than a minute before she heard the sound of a car in the distance. Although she tried to tell herself that Justin wouldn't be here yet, and it was probably just a passer-by, nevertheless her fear intensified. She could feel her senses on full alert, as the adrenalin pulsed through her body leaving her mouth dry and her limbs twitchy.

Through her rear-view mirror she spotted a red car approaching and the driver seemed to be in a hurry. As it sped closer, she could see that it was a small car rather than the fancy Jaguar she had been expecting. At first she thought it was perhaps Justin's hired hands who were inside the car but as it drew even closer she realised that the car was an old one and she assumed that organised villains would be driving something more flash. There was also only one person behind the wheel. Crystal was ready to dismiss the car as a passer-by. But then she caught a more detailed look at the driver and realised she knew him.

It was Spud!

For a few seconds she was immobilised by shock. But then anger set in. The bastard! No wonder he had refused to tell her anything and then gone AWOL. He'd been working for Justin all the time and now he'd sent him to do his dirty work for him.

But her desire to get her daughter back overrode all other feelings. Expecting Spud to have fetched Candice in return for the list, she strained her neck to see if she could spot

Candice in the back seat. But she couldn't see her daughter. Maybe the bastard had her in the foot well of the back seats or maybe even in the boot.

She saw the left indicator light up on Spud's car and expected him to pull up alongside her car so they could do the exchange. She took a deep breath and squared her shoulders, preparing herself for the meeting. But then something strange happened. Spud carried on past her and took a left turn.

Why? Hadn't he seen her? Or was he deliberately ignoring her? Had Justin sent him ahead for some reason? Was it a trap? Her frantic thoughts were filling her mind with confusion and indecision. But then she thought about her poor daughter perhaps stuck in the cramped boot of that poxy little car waiting to be rescued and concern for Candice galvanised her into action.

Crystal started the engine, stamped down hard on the accelerator and turned left. She took Spud by surprise as she tailed him into the country lane and then drew level with him. He obviously hadn't realised it was her sitting inside the Fiesta. The lane was narrow and for several seconds her car bumped alongside Spud's as she tried to squeeze into the gap between Spud's car and the thicket on her right. Spud glanced over at her with an expression of alarm as he tried to keep control of his car.

Crystal heard the branches of a bush scrape the side of her car and she pulled down hard on the steering wheel, swerving to the left. The impact sent Spud's car crashing into the ditch on the other side of the lane. The car turned onto its side until it was forced to a halt, the wheels on the right of the car spinning in mid-air.

Crystal pulled up in front of Spud, parking side-on and blocking the lane, so he couldn't go any further even if he could have retrieved his car from the ditch. Then she slammed on the brakes, cut the engine and fled from her car, turning back and rushing towards Spud's vehicle. She struggled to open the driver's door slightly, which had been dented by the impact with her car and the lock seemed to have partially jammed. Eventually she prised it away and found Spud staring up at her in bewilderment.

'You fuckin' backstabbing, drugged-up bastard!' she yelled. 'What have you done with my fuckin' daughter?'

'Nothing. I'm helping her. I'm going to get her. Now!'

'What do you mean? What the fuck's going on? Are you getting her for Justin so he can bring her to me?'

'No! I'm rescuing her.'

'I don't believe you. You've got her in the back of that fuckin' car, haven't you? Justin's gonna be here any minute. He's supposed to be bringing her to me. It's a trick, isn't it? Justin isn't bringing her at all. You've got her, haven't you?'

'No! I'm not supposed to be here,' shouted Spud, exasperated. 'But I've come to get her.'

'Tell me where she is. I'll get her my fuckin' self!'

'No! It's too dangerous on your own. Like you say, Justin will be here any minute. And once he's got the list you stole from him, I think he's gonna fuckin' take you out.'

'Fuck!' said Crystal as a ripple of fear shot through her.

'Let me help you. Get me out of this car. We'll go in yours. I can explain everything later.'

'Why should I trust you?' demanded Crystal.

'Because you haven't got a fuckin' choice!' shouted Spud,

attempting to heave himself out of the car, which was lying precariously on its side.

Crystal glanced around her. The sense of urgency was overwhelming and she could feel her heart pounding as she anticipated Justin's arrival at any moment. She had to act now if she was to have any chance of both she and her daughter surviving, and she'd already wasted enough time.

She reached into the car to help lift Spud from the wrecked vehicle. It was a tight squeeze at first as the dinted door wouldn't open fully. After several minutes they managed to get Spud out of the car and he sprang to his feet.

'Quick, let's go!' he gasped, racing towards Crystal's car and jumping into the passenger side. Once Crystal was in the car alongside him and was turning the key to the engine, he pointed ahead. 'It's that way. She's in an old barn, tied up. We need to get to her before Justin gets here. You don't know how dangerous he is!'

'Oh, I think I do,' said Crystal, as she turned the car around till it was facing forward then hit the accelerator. 'It was him who had Holly killed, wasn't it?'

'Yes,' muttered Spud. 'And Phil.'

'Phil?'

'Yeah, the guy he hired to follow you home from the pub. Only, he messed up when he lost you. After that Justin didn't trust him, said he was too much of a liability as he knew too much.'

'Shit!' said Crystal.

The car was dragging as she tried to speed up the bumpy country lane, and her ears were pounding as her adrenalin pumped fiercely, sending the blood gushing around her body. But she attempted to stay focused, concentrating on the barn ahead of her and wanting to make it there as quickly as possible, unaware of what she would find but praying that Candice would be alright.

47

R uby couldn't settle after she finished the call with Crystal. Knowing how impulsive her friend could be, she was worried she'd go against her advice and meet Justin anyway, especially because he was holding her daughter. For several minutes she paced her living room trying to decide what to do for the best. In the end she rang her again, concerned when there was no reply.

'What's the matter?' asked Tiffany.

Although Tiffany knew what had happened, including the kidnap of Candice, she wasn't aware of the thoughts that were running through Ruby's mind.

'It's Crystal,' Ruby replied. 'I'm worried she won't take my advice and will go to meet that bloody Justin anyway. I'm tempted to show up there myself. I might be able to help her.'

'No chance!' said Tiffany, surprising Ruby with her abrupt manner. 'You're already involved enough, Ruby, but I'm not having you putting your life at risk. I know Crystal's a friend, and all that, but it's not your mess to sort out.'

For a moment Ruby stood and stared at her girlfriend, still puzzling things over in her head. 'There must be some way I can help her,' she said. 'I can't just leave it. I wouldn't be able to live with myself if something happened to her. And what about Candice? What if something happens to her?'

'Why don't you ring the police? If you tell them the meeting place they can send someone.'

'No, it's no use, not with a dodgy copper in charge. If he gets a message back to this Justin that Crystal has told someone then she'll be in even more danger.'

Then something occurred to her. Her client, Ray! He was a DI on the drugs squad so, if anybody could help, he could. But she didn't really want to get him involved. As she'd told Crystal previously, her business relied on client confidentiality and he wouldn't want people to find out about his association with her. But what did his reputation matter when the lives of a close friend and her daughter were in danger?

Ruby was still clutching her mobile so she quickly scanned through the contacts till she found Ray's number.

'You ringing Crystal again?' asked Tiffany.

'No, I'm ringing Ray, that DI who comes to see me.'

Tiffany frowned and pursed her lips but stayed silent as she waited for Ruby to speak.

'Ray, I need a favour,' said Ruby.

'What kind of favour?' asked Ray.

Ruby went through recent events concerning Crystal, keeping it as brief as possible but, at the same time, trying to stress the urgency of the situation.

She was disappointed with his reply. 'No, Ruby, I'm afraid I can't do that. You need to ring the police direct and they'll deal with it.'

'I can't,' she said. 'We think one of the senior policemen

is involved with Justin Foster and I can't risk him warning Justin. It might put Crystal in more danger.'

'Who is this officer?' asked Ray.

Ruby deliberated for a moment, unsure whether to give Ray his name, but she couldn't think of any reason why she shouldn't. 'Roger Purvis,' she said.

'Roger P... Roger? No, impossible! Roger would never do such a thing. He's one of our best.'

'Yeah, and he's also been suspected of corruption in the past.'

'Nothing was proven. Do you realise how easy it is to damage a policeman's career once he's suspected of doing something untoward?'

The implication was obvious, and Ruby knew that he was also referring to any damage to his own reputation if he became involved. But his haughty tone put her back up. Sod his reputation! He didn't have to divulge who had given him the information; he could say it was an anonymous call. Despite her thoughts, she decided to tread lightly for now because she needed Ray onside.

'Ray, can you really afford to take the chance of not getting involved? There might be lives at stake here and how would you feel if someone died because you didn't step in?'

'Please, don't try your emotional blackmail with me, Ruby. I've told you, Roger's a good guy and there's no need for me to get involved. Now, I suggest you call the police direct like I've told you to, and stop trying to bypass the official channels by pulling in favours.'

Ruby stared at her phone, livid at his attitude and upset

about Crystal, but desperately trying to hold it together. It was obvious that Ray was being completely intractable and she was growing desperate. Her close friend Crystal was probably careering into danger right at this very moment and she was at a loss as to what she could do to save her and her daughter.

'Thank Christ you're here!' said Justin, stepping out onto his drive and meeting the two men as they emerged from their car, a light blue Range Rover. He had been standing at his front window for the last ten minutes waiting for them to arrive and was annoyed that when they finally drove up to the house there was hardly any time to spare. 'Get back in the car. We're going straight there. I don't wanna be late. The meeting's at one.'

He turned back, remembering he'd not shut the front door, but found his wife standing in the doorway.

'Where are you going, Justin?' she asked. 'You didn't tell me you were going out.'

'Business meeting,' he muttered before dashing over to the waiting car. As he clambered inside he glanced over at his wife who was still standing in the doorway wearing a confused expression so he added, 'It's about the new development.' Then he slammed the car door shut before she could quiz him any further.

'Step on it, Dennis!' he yelled at the driver as he swung out of his drive and into the road. Justin turned and spoke to the man sitting in the back. 'What took you two so fuckin' long anyway?'

'We've only just finished that other job you sent us on,' said Dennis.

'Really? That should have been finished fuckin' ages ago. I've had to send Spud to feed the kid this morning.'

'There were complications,' said the man on the back seat.

They were the same two men who had snatched Candice two days prior and then visited her at the barn yesterday. Both were big and mean-looking but Dennis was muscular where the other man, although muscular in places, was also carrying a lot of weight around his middle.

'You can tell me about it later,' said Justin. 'We've got other things to concentrate on at the moment. Are you both clear on what you've got to do when we get there?'

Dennis nodded while the man on the back seat mumbled a 'yes'.

'It's in there,' said Dennis, nodding his head towards the glove compartment.

Justin opened it up and took out a gun, holding it between his legs, out of view, while he examined it. 'Good,' he said. 'And when we've sorted the tart out there's another problem we need to take care of.'

'What's that, boss?'

'Spud. I don't fuckin' trust him! He's been asking too many questions.'

'What sort of questions?'

'Oh, about what I'm gonna do with the kid when I've finished with the tart; that sort of thing. He was going on about the kid being scared too, as though it was really bothering him. I'm worried he might fuckin' grass.'

'OK. We'll sort it.'

Dennis carried on driving and they soon arrived at the meeting point but there was no sign of Crystal. Justin peered at his watch. Two minutes past one. He couldn't understand why Crystal was late when she'd been so keen to get her daughter back.

He glanced across at Dennis who asked, 'What's happening, boss?'

'Dunno, hang on a minute,' said Justin as he looked at the side mirror to see if there was any sign of an approaching car. Then he glanced towards the barn. 'What the fuck?'

'What? What's wrong?' asked Dennis, straining to see through the passenger window.

'It's Spud's car. In a fuckin' ditch! What the hell is he doing here? I told you we couldn't trust him. I didn't like the way he was going on about the kid and how frightened she was. I bet the dickhead's gone back for her.'

'Let's get him,' said Dennis.

Justin gazed ahead of Spud's car while he considered his next move: whether to go after Spud or whether to wait here for Crystal to arrive. But then he spotted something else. 'There's another car there!' he yelled. 'Look, in the distance.'

'Who the fuck can that be?' asked the man on the back seat.

'Well, there's only one person I can think of who'd be going to the barn at this time. It'll be that little tart. I bet the two of them are in it together. Quick, Dennis, get after them. We've got to stop them before they get to the kid.'

48

Ruby was currently sitting in the passenger seat of a Silver Merc while the driver sped through the streets of Manchester. They'd left her home in Altrincham around twenty minutes ago and were now on the A555 approaching Poynton. Tiffany hadn't been happy about her going but Ruby wouldn't let that stop her. And as she dashed out of her Altrincham home she had heard Tiffany warning her to be careful and make sure she had backup.

She pointed at the sat nav on the dashboard. 'Next left!' she ordered.

'I know, I know!' said the man in the driver's seat who had been fractious all the way there.

Ruby was aware of the time ticking away. She checked her watch again. Five to one. 'Shit! We're gonna miss them,' she said.

'I'm going as fast as I bloody can,' said Ray, 'and I wouldn't have been here at all if you hadn't bloody blackmailed me.'

'Look,' she said. 'It's not as if I haven't helped you out plenty of times. Besides, this is really important; my friend's life could be in danger, not to mention her daughter's.'

Ray puffed out a breath of air but didn't say anything more. Ruby still felt a pang of guilt though, knowing it was her threat to expose Ray's penchant for hard porn that had finally persuaded him to set out with her on their rescue mission. But, although he'd reluctantly agreed to go with her, up to now he'd refused to get anyone else on the force involved, insisting that they'd see how the land lay first.

It wasn't long before Ruby saw the road they were looking for: Ormerod Avenue. 'This is it,' she said. 'Number 320 we want.'

She had deliberately written down Justin's address when Crystal had given it to her, knowing that it might come in handy. Now she was glad she had. Crystal's description of the meeting point had been vague but she guessed that it probably wasn't very far from where Justin lived. As she stared at her watch, though, she was beginning to despair, knowing that he would already have left for the meeting with Crystal.

But she had to start somewhere so she told Ray to swing into the drive as soon as she spotted number 320. Then they both emerged from his car and ran up to the front door. Ruby pressed hard on the doorbell, letting it ring for several seconds.

'Leave the talking to me,' said Ray, and when a glamorous blonde answered the door he held out his ID and asked, 'Is Mr Foster at home please, Mr Justin Foster?'

'No, he's out,' she answered. Her features were strained as though she was worried about something, but she was doing her best to disguise her anxiety by putting on an act of cool composure.

'Are you Mrs Foster?'

'Yes.'

'Would you mind telling us where he's gone to?'

'I don't know,' said the blonde, glancing nervously over her shoulder at the two teenagers who hovered in the background.

'Have you any idea at all where he might be?' Ray asked.

'No. Why? What's this about?'

'It's a very serious matter I'm afraid and it would help us a great deal if you could give us an idea of where he might be.'

'I've told you, I don't know.'

Ruby was becoming exasperated so she butted in, despite Ray's instructions. 'We think he's involved in a kidnap.'

She had been ready to continue until Ray glared at her, obviously unhappy that she should come straight out with it when nothing had been proven.

'No he isn't!' said Justin's wife. 'Justin would never be involved in anything like that! And the police have already released him because they know he's innocent.'

'I'm afraid we've received further information since then,' said Ray. He was obviously trying to play it down, mindful of making false accusations. 'And it would be really helpful if you could tell us anything, anything at all, that might lead us to his whereabouts.'

'What information? I don't know where he is,' said Justin's wife who still sounded affronted but there were also signs of nervousness as her words were rushed, the sentences clipped. 'He left with two business associates. They were going to a meeting. And that's all I know.'

Ray persisted for a little longer until it became obvious that they weren't going to get any further information from her. They walked back to the car and Ruby slammed the door shut, angry with Ray for butting in on her. But Ray was also annoyed.

'I thought I told you to leave things to me,' he raged. 'You can't go around hurling accusations like that. It could lead to all sorts of problems for the police. I wouldn't mind but I'm not even here in an official capacity.'

'Well what the hell was I supposed to do? She wasn't telling you owt, was she? And I'm bloody sure she knows more than she's letting on.'

'But we still have to tread carefully, Ruby.'

'Yeah, and in the meantime something could have happened to my friend!'

Ruby could feel herself becoming emotional so she didn't say anything else and for a few seconds they both remained silent, the car immobile, while Ruby tried to choke back her tears.

Eventually Ray glanced over at her. 'It might not come to that,' he said, his tone now more measured.

'But what if it does?' demanded Ruby.

When he didn't reply, Ruby turned her head till she was staring into his eyes. 'Right, well if you're the one making all the decisions,' she said, 'then maybe you can tell me what the fuck we're supposed to do now!'

49

Crystal skidded to a halt outside the barn and jumped from the car. Anxious to get inside, she slid the bolt on the door but found it still wouldn't open. 'It's locked,' she shouted, turning to Spud who was holding a key. 'Give it here!'

'No, I'll do it. The lock's a bit iffy. It'll be quicker.'

She stood aside and waited impatiently for him to unlock the door then she helped him to push it back and dashed inside the vast, gloomy interior. Despite her haste, she soon noticed the state of the place: the rank odour, the filthy floor, and the sound of rainwater dripping from a hole in the roof.

'Jesus!' she said, disturbed that her daughter was being kept in a place like this and desperately searching around for her. 'Where is she?'

'At the back. Behind that old plough.'

Crystal sprinted across the barn following the sound of a low whimpering coming from the far side. She ran past the plough. Then she spotted her.

'Shit!' she muttered as she ran closer to her daughter and took in her appearance.

Her beautiful Candice! Except she didn't look like her Candice. She had all the same features, instantly identifying her as Crystal's daughter. But she was more like a zombified version. Her hair was matted, her skin pale and lifeless. She was slumped lethargically against a mound of rotting hay and looked thin and gaunt, her clothes crumpled and soiled.

'Candice!' Crystal yelled, her eyes filling with tears.

Despite the state of Candice she dashed towards her and picked her up off the putrid hay, pulling her close for precious seconds. 'Oh my God. Candice! Are you OK, love?' She cradled Candice's head in her bosom, kissing her tenderly on the top of her head.

Candice felt frail in her arms, clinging desperately to her and sobbing, 'Mummy, Mummy,' and Crystal couldn't help but let out an anguished wail. In the space of two days her eleven-year-old daughter had regressed into a helpless toddler.

Crystal didn't know how long they remained like that but after a while she sensed movement to the side of her and she turned to see Spud shifting anxiously from foot to foot. Her fleeting thought was that he needed a fix but then his words alerted her to their situation.

'We need to rush, Crystal. They could be here any minute!'

She heard Candice whimper again then she clung to her even more tightly at the thought of the men returning. Crystal was gripped by anger. What had those bastards done to her little girl?

'OK,' said Crystal, trying to stay calm. 'I need to let go of you for a minute, Candice, so that we can get you out of here.'

She laid her back down on the hay and prised her tiny hands away. Candice reluctantly let go and stared up at her with tear-filled, frightened eyes.

'We need to get these ropes off her,' Crystal said to Spud as she picked at the knots.

'Here, let me do it,' said Spud, stepping forward with a blade in his outstretched hand.

Crystal saw Candice recoil, and she yelled, 'No!' more loudly than she had intended. She reached out for the knife. 'She's obviously scared. Give it to me. I'll do it.'

Even though it was Crystal who was now holding the knife, Candice still drew away from her. The sight of her daughter so timid and petrified brought more tears to Crystal's eyes and, despite her anger at what had happened to Candice, she spoke tenderly.

'I just need to cut the ropes, love, so we can get you out of here. I promise it won't hurt. Will you let me do that?'

She waited for Candice's reply, aware all the time of Spud's frantic movements as his anxiety spiralled. Candice nodded slowly and Crystal set to work with the knife. It wasn't easy trying to release her daughter from the binds as quickly as possible while also taking care not to be too rough. Eventually she cut her hands free and, when she saw the fleeting expression of relief on Candice's face, she set about the ankle binds more swiftly.

'Come on, love, let's get you up,' said Crystal once the ropes had been cut.

She took hold of her daughter's hand and helped her off the floor once more. Crystal could sense how weak she was and, mindful of the fact that she hadn't been able to walk properly for the past two days, she let Candice stand still for a few seconds until the blood started to flow back into her cramped limbs and she regained her balance.

She noticed Spud in the background, letting out

exasperated puffing sounds while he waited for them to flee the barn.

'We've got the car waiting outside. Are you ready to make a run for it?' she said to Candice. When her daughter nodded, Crystal added, 'Come on then,' and, keeping a tight hold of Candice's hand, they fled towards the barn door.

Although Crystal knew they needed to escape as soon as possible, she paused next to the plough.

'What is it?' asked Spud.

'I think I can hear something outside.'

'Like what?'

'Dunno, maybe a car.'

She felt her daughter flinch and Spud muttered, 'Shit!'

As Spud carried on towards the barn door, Crystal looked around her for something that could be of use. She noticed a metal bar that was loosely attached to the old plough and she took hold of it, twisting it in every direction until she wrenched it free. It dropped to the floor with a clatter and Crystal bent to pick it up patting the pocket of her jeans first of all to make sure her car keys were still inside. Then she continued to the doorway, with one hand gripping her daughter's once more and the other clutching the metal bar.

She thought she heard a banging noise but dismissed it as the sound of Spud heaving open the barn door. By the time they reached him, he had it open, and Crystal stepped out into the daylight with her daughter. Only then did it become apparent that the sound she had heard was the slamming of a car door. And as her eyes adjusted to the sunlight she saw Justin and his cohorts all heading towards them.

50

Ruby was looking to Ray for answers but all she received were a lot of platitudes and warnings about the need to follow protocol. The more she listened to him the more irate she was becoming. Crystal and Candice were in extreme danger and all he could do was waffle on about a load of crap instead of doing something about it. In the end she could take no more.

'Fuck this!' she yelled. 'If you're not prepared to do anything then I am. And to hell with the consequences! My friend could be fuckin' dead while you're piss-arsing around.'

Before Ray could stop her she stormed out of the car and rushed straight up to Justin's front door where she began hammering with her fist. Ray dashed after her trying to calm her down and coax her back to the car. When verbal persuasion didn't have any effect he grabbed her from behind and tried to drag her away.

That was a big mistake! By this time Ruby was so fired up that nothing was going to stand in her way. She wanted answers. In her fury all she could think of was fighting Ray off so she could get at Justin's wife. She swung round, her arm raised, until it smacked Ray to the side of his face, impacting his eardrum and leaving him disorientated. Then she raised her knee and brought it up to his genitals with full force.

Ray yelled and reached for his groin, the sudden movement on top of his buzzing ears, sending him dizzy. He tumbled to the ground clutching his throbbing testicles.

Ruby was unconcerned. The prospect of saving Crystal and Candice was the only thing occupying her thoughts. She continued to hammer on the door. When there was no response, apart from a twitching curtain, Ruby began to yell.

'Answer the fuckin' door. Now! Otherwise all your neighbours will find out just what your arsehole of a husband gets up to in his spare time.'

She assumed Justin's wife must have had her suspicions because, as soon as Ruby made the threat, she answered the door straightaway.

'Just what the fuck are you hiding?' asked Ruby.

'Nothing! I've told you, Justin hasn't done anything wrong.'

But when the woman refused to make eye contact, it confirmed Ruby's suspicions that she knew more than she was letting on. She grabbed the front of the woman's immaculate blouse, twisting and scrunching it between her fingers till Justin's wife was pulled forwards and forced to look up into Ruby's angry eyes. Ruby stood at almost six feet tall and was broad and honed. She knew straightaway that the woman felt threatened by her imposing physique as well as her fury.

'Right, you might claim not to know anything but I know you've got your suspicions. That's fuckin' obvious otherwise you wouldn't be scared shitless about your kids and your neighbours finding out what he gets up to.'

'I don't know…' the woman began to protest.

'Yes you fuckin' do!' yelled Ruby as Ray continued to lie on the ground, writhing in agony. 'Do you realise a child's life is in danger because of your fuckin' husband? You could save her if you told me where I can find him. But if you won't tell me anything then you could have that child's death on your conscience for the rest of your fuckin' life! And, believe me, if that happens I'll fuckin' hunt you down till I get justice.'

'Ruby, Ruby!' called Ray who was now struggling to get up.

'Shut the fuck up!' said Ruby, waving her free hand towards where Ray lay, indicating that he should stay put.

Before he had chance to intervene, the woman spoke. 'OK, let go of me and I'll tell you what I know.'

Ruby released the woman's blouse but stayed where she was, invading the woman's personal space with a scowl on her face to signal her ongoing threat.

'Yes, you're right. I do have my suspicions but I still don't really know much except that he's been hanging around with some dodgy characters.' She glanced to the back of her, presumably making sure the children weren't listening. Then a teenage girl appeared behind her.

'What's the matter, Mum?' she asked. 'Is it something to do with Dad?'

The woman turned her head to the side. 'No, it's nothing,' she snapped. 'Go inside. I'll tell you later.'

She waited for the girl to walk away then pulled the door to. When she swivelled her head round to face them again, Ruby could see that her eyes had misted over. But she didn't sympathise. To hell with the woman's feelings! The only thing Ruby was interested in was saving Crystal and Candice.

'Carry on,' she urged.

Ray was now up off the ground and Ruby could sense him behind her. But he hung back, perhaps realising they were on to something.

Justin's wife continued. 'There's a barn not far from here. He bought it for a business venture – something to do with redevelopment for houses or offices or something. Only, he doesn't seem to have done much with it. Anyway, I think that's where he's gone with two of his associates.' Then she sighed and there was a tremor in her voice when she added, 'They don't look like businessmen to me, more like crooks.'

'Where is this barn?' demanded Ruby.

Justin's wife gave her directions and Ruby turned to Ray to make sure he had taken a mental note. He nodded.

'How long will it take to get there?' she asked.

'Not long. About five minutes.'

Ruby walked away without thanking her. 'Come on!' she shouted to Ray who hobbled after her.

'OK,' Ray grumbled. 'You take the driving seat. I need to make a call.'

Ruby started the engine while Ray struggled into the passenger seat and took out his phone. He quickly keyed in some digits then pulled his seat belt round him while he waited for someone to answer his call. Ruby had already set off down the road at full speed, anxious to get to her friend before it was too late.

She was only vaguely aware of his spiel about name, rank

et cetera as she was concentrating on the road ahead and making it to the location as quickly as possible. But when she heard him call for backup and an armed response team, it drew her full attention to what he was saying. At last he was taking her seriously!

Then she heard him say, 'Things could turn nasty,' and she plunged down even harder on the accelerator, her focus on the road ahead once more.

51

Crystal became aware of Candice clinging to her even more tightly than she had done inside the barn. She also saw the expression of scorn on Justin's face as his two bully boys flanked him on either side, awaiting his instructions. The one nearest to Spud was carrying a gun and the other one had his eye on Crystal.

'Did you really think you could get away?' asked Justin with a smirk on his face.

Crystal didn't reply. She was too busy thinking of a way out of this. Her first concern was for Candice who she told to stand behind her. She could feel her heart pounding. But she wasn't prepared to let fear get in the way. She glanced across at Spud and could see him clutching the knife and eying the man with the gun.

'Shoot him!' ordered Justin.

'No!' shouted Crystal, stepping forward with her fingers gripping the metal bar tightly. She thought of how Spud had come to rescue Candice, and knew she owed him. 'If you kill him, you can forget the list.'

The guy who wasn't armed made a move towards her and she raised the bar into the air, waving it menacingly at him till he backed off. Then she spoke, feeling a tremble in her voice but hoping the enemy hadn't noticed.

'I want us all in the car first then I'll let you have the list. I'll put it on the ground outside the driver's door and you can pick it up after we've driven off.'

Justin nodded and Crystal took hold of Candice, guiding her towards her Fiesta. Spud followed after them, a few steps behind. When she reached the vehicle, Crystal encouraged Candice to get in the back. She was about to get inside too when the unarmed man dashed towards her. Crystal lunged at him with the metal bar. It struck him hard on his arm and he let out a yell, clutching his throbbing elbow and backing off once more. Justin ran to the man, checking he was alright.

At the same time, Crystal became aware of Spud yelling at her to go without him. Perhaps he realised that the men would get to him before he reached the car and he charged at the man carrying the gun, his arm fully outstretched and wielding the knife. Crystal dashed back to the Fiesta and jumped inside. Chucking the metal bar into the foot well of the passenger seat she then shoved the key inside the ignition. For a moment she hesitated, not wanting to leave Spud after he'd tried to help her. But before she could start the engine, a shot rang out and Spud dropped to the ground.

With shaking hands she turned the key to start the engine. It was all about saving her and Candice now. She felt guilty; Spud had been loyal to her and now she was leaving him for dead. But she had no choice. She either saved herself and Candice or risked all three of them getting killed.

While Justin and his men were trying to recover themselves, she had started the car up and was just moving into first gear. Justin, realising he was at risk of them getting away, ran to his own car with his goons. Crystal needed to turn her car around before she could get out of there. She cursed the fact that she hadn't done it previously, ready for a quick exit. But she had been too eager to get to Candice.

By the time she was facing the lane Justin's driver had set off and the Range Rover carrying the three of them was tearing towards her. She tried to get away but he was too fast. Before she could make her escape the Range Rover had hit her side-on. She felt her car judder and Candice let out a terrified yelp. Thank God she and Candice were both sitting on the other side of the car. She didn't even try to examine the damage from inside; it was more important to get away.

'It's OK, sweetheart, we'll soon be out of here,' she said and, once she had recovered herself, she put her foot back down on the accelerator.

But Justin's men weren't finished. The Range Rover reversed then headed for her again. Before she could get very far she felt another smash as the Range Rover slammed into her car. Then the driver did it again and again, inflicting more damage each time and making it increasingly difficult to get away as her damaged car struggled to set off.

Her little Fiesta didn't stand much chance against the mighty Range Rover. As Crystal took in the damage she was worried that she and Candice would become badly injured or that her car might even catch fire. The impact could easily cause a rupture in the fuel system.

Despite her reassuring words to her daughter, Crystal was beginning to despair about them ever getting out of here alive.

*

'For Christ's sake, Ray!' yelled Ruby. 'Shouldn't we be there by now? She said it was a narrow country lane off this road but I've seen nothing.'

'Me neither,' muttered Ray with a note of dejection in his voice.

'Well, haven't you been watching the fuckin' road?' asked Ruby.

'You forget, Ruby. I'm not the only one in this car.'

'But I'm busy driving,' said Ruby who was still travelling rapidly along the country road. 'You should be doing the fuckin' navigating!'

'I've been busy myself, making calls. The speed you're going at we could easily have missed it. And would you mind not using that sort of tone with me? I've dropped everything to come here and help save your friend and her daughter when all's said and done.'

'Yeah, against your fuckin' will,' she snapped. 'Anyway, where's the fuckin' cavalry? I ain't seen nothing yet.'

'I'll give them another call,' he said.

She tried to remain patient while he took out his phone, dialled the number of someone in the force and spoke to the person on the other end of the line.

'Well?' she asked after he had cut the call.

'They're on their way and getting close apparently. They've spotted a barn where there's some activity taking place, and they're making their way towards it now.'

'How come we haven't fuckin' seen them then?'

'I don't know. I think it's us that's come too far, Ruby. Turn the car around!'

She did as he ordered, and Ray peered intensely through the windscreen while Ruby carried on speeding along the road, heading back the way they'd come. As she drove Ruby desperately hoped that one of them would soon spot the barn before it was too late.

52

It was becoming clear to Crystal that she and Candice needed to make a run for it. Their best chance would be to head for the bushes on the perimeter of the barnyard. They were almost two metres in height so they should offer them some cover while they tried to make it to the shorter hedgerow that bordered the lane.

Trying to make herself heard over the sound of gunning engines, screeching tyres and Candice's wailing, she said, 'Right, Candice, when I say go, I want you to get out of the car and run for those bushes as quickly as you can.' With her hands holding tightly onto the steering wheel, she nodded towards the perimeter bushes to show Candice which way she should run. When Candice carried on whimpering but didn't speak, Crystal yelled, 'Can you hear me?'

'Yes,' said Candice, her voice sounding tearful.

Crystal knew the best chance of escape would be if she timed it just right. Knowing the damage to her car was getting worse with each smash, she waited for the next impact. It was so forceful that the side of the Fiesta caved in and she felt it rock as it tipped slightly on one side.

As soon as her car steadied she shouted to Candice, 'Quick, run. Now!'

Making sure Candice was out first, Crystal opened her car door and dashed after her. Glancing momentarily across, she noticed that the Range Rover seemed to be stuck in the side of her car. She could tell by the sound of its engine revving that the driver was having difficulty backing out.

'Quick as you can, Candice, and don't stop!' she shouted.

When she heard a volley of shots and saw one of the bullets skim the ground within a metre of her, she was glad she had let Candice run in front. 'Head for the bushes, Candice!' she shouted.

As she and Candice ran for cover, she spotted several vehicles heading up the lane towards them. Fixated on getting to the bushes, she didn't take in more than a vague outline. For a second she was worried that even more of Justin's men were on their way.

But then she heard the sirens and picked out the detail of the cars. Thank God! The police had arrived. She didn't know how they'd found out where Candice was being held but she didn't care. Crystal was relieved that at least they were here. Now she just needed to avoid the bullets till she and Candice could reach safety.

As soon as they reached the bushes, Crystal crouched down low and told Candice to do the same. She draped one arm protectively across her daughter's shoulders and pulled her head into the shelter of her bosom. Then, releasing her daughter, she said, 'Come on, quick. We've got to keep moving.'

After a few seconds Crystal could still hear shots but they weren't coming as close now. She glanced through a gap in the bushes and was surprised to see that Justin was now in charge of the gun while his gunman was taking care of the driving.

As Justin leant out of the window of the Range Rover and fired at the police, she could see shots being fired back. She heard the police drawing closer but she couldn't see them from where she was hidden. Despite the police presence, she was still too near to Justin to feel safe so she decided to head for the hedgerow close by.

'We're going to run for those bushes over there, Candice,' she said, 'but you need to keep crouched low.'

'But they're not as high,' cried Candice.

'I know, love, but we need to get away from here,' she said. 'Those men are getting closer and we need to be nearer to the police. And, don't worry; they won't be able to see us as long as we keep low.'

'But… ' said Candice, her eyes beseeching, and Crystal could see she was scared.

Then a bullet skimmed the ground close to them. Justin was now becoming desperate, firing indiscriminately at her and Candice as well as the police. She couldn't afford to cajole her daughter anymore; they needed to act now. Trying to ignore Candice's cry of alarm, Crystal grabbed her hand and pulled her along.

'Quick as you can, love. We need to get away. Keep low.'

Thankfully, she didn't feel any resistance from her daughter. Candice had obviously picked up on her sense of urgency and was trying to hurry while crouching low and letting out desperate little cries of alarm as sharp twigs pulled on her clothing and her feet negotiated the uneven ground.

Justin must have seen movement in the hedgerow because the bullets were now coming closer. Crystal kept going forward, hoping to avoid the gunshots. Each time a bullet shot past her, she tensed, full of dread in case one of them struck her or Candice.

As they made their getaway she could feel her adrenalin pumping, making her heart beat rapidly and pushing her on. She was moving so fast that twigs grazed her exposed flesh and she knew Candice must be feeling the same. Maybe that was the reason for her tiny squeals, she thought. Crystal felt like squealing herself but she knew she had to be strong for her daughter.

They kept moving and it seemed like an age before they spotted a police car getting closer. Crystal felt a small surge of relief. She was beginning to think they might actually make it. But she didn't want to get complacent yet. They continued along the path of the hedgerow, still keeping their heads low until Crystal saw another two police cars approaching. Then she noticed something else – the bullets were now further away.

Crystal stopped and turned, facing the old barn. The Range Rover was now retreating with the police cars pursuing it. But there was nowhere for Justin to go. The lane was the only way into the barnyard. The sides and the back of it were surrounded by bushes and fields and would therefore be hazardous for a car to drive through.

She watched the Range Rover speeding away from the police and was amazed when Justin's driver set off across the fields, the vehicle's progress slow and arduous. The first police vehicle was now in the barnyard and was gaining ground. Then she saw the rear tyre of the Range Rover burst as a bullet hit it and she squealed in triumph as the police vehicle almost drew level with the Range Rover.

Crystal was so busy watching the pursuit of Justin and his mob that she didn't realise the last of the police cars had now passed them apart from one. A silver Mercedes drew up in the lane beside her and it wasn't until she heard the door slam shut that she noticed. An official-looking man had got out of the passenger side of the vehicle and he was now approaching them.

'Are you alright?' he asked.

Crystal thought she recognised the man but she wasn't sure where from. She was about to respond to his question when she spotted the driver of the car.

'Ruby!' she shouted as her friend emerged from the driver's side.

Then Crystal realised who the man was; he was the DI who was one of Ruby's clients. Regardless of the sound of gunshot in the barnyard and the enormous bang of colliding vehicles, she and Candice clambered out of the hedgerow, and Ruby dashed towards them, hugging both Crystal and Candice at the same time.

'Thank God you're alright!' she said.

The tears that Crystal had suppressed for most of the morning now erupted and for a while she and Candice both clung to Ruby, sobbing. By now Candice's frail little body was trembling. But, despite that, it was good for Crystal to feel safe and in the comforting arms of her strong and loyal friend. Crystal was surprised to see that even Ruby's eyes had clouded with tears.

The moment was broken when the DI spoke. 'They've got them,' he announced as his gaze led them to the scene at the side of the barn.

The three police cars were now surrounding the Range Rover, which was badly damaged. Both of the rear tyres had ruptured, the rear bumper was hanging off and the right side of the vehicle was dented. Crystal couldn't see the front of the car but she assumed that it must be dented too considering how violently it had hammered into the side of her Fiesta.

Armed officers were approaching the Range Rover on all sides and, as the girls watched, Justin and his cohorts emerged from the vehicle. The officers frisked them, took the gun from Justin, then lined them up at the side of the car and clapped them in handcuffs. In the foreground another two officers were walking across the barnyard towards the prone body of Spud.

'Oh, shit. Spud!' yelled Crystal. 'I need to see if he's OK.'

She took a few steps towards the barnyard but the DI, Ray, stepped in front of her, blocking her way. 'I can't let you go there,' he said. 'It's a crime scene. Don't worry; my men will take care of things.'

She turned to Ruby who said, 'He's right. You need to let the police deal with it, Crystal.'

Then Crystal heard another siren and watched as an ambulance made its way up the lane. The DI instructed Ruby to pull the car over so the ambulance could get through. Then he looked at Crystal, and spoke in a tone that brooked no argument, 'I need you two to stay here, and don't move until I tell you.'

Crystal had no choice but to watch, helpless, as the DI made his way towards the ambulance and spoke to the driver before the vehicle carried on along the path. She felt bereft as she watched the ambulance head towards the prone body on the ground: Spud, the man who had risked his own life to save her daughter. And now, she couldn't even check if he was still alive.

53

Crystal and Ruby were both at the hospital, sitting in the waiting room while a team of health professionals tended to Candice and carried out various checks. Back at the barn, they hadn't had much time to talk before a second ambulance had arrived and Ray had insisted that Crystal should go with her daughter to hospital.

Ruby had followed them in Ray's car while he went to join his officers so that he could organise the crime scene. Although Crystal was glad she had got her daughter back safely, she was concerned about any lasting emotional effects. She was also upset about Spud and kept thinking about him dropping to the ground when the bullet hit and then lying there lifeless.

When they had set off for the hospital, the other ambulance was still in the barnyard. Crystal had strained her neck to see what was happening with Spud but it was difficult because he was surrounded by paramedics and police officers.

Now, as her thoughts turned to her daughter, she said, 'I hope Candice will be OK.'

Ruby squeezed her hand. 'Don't worry; she's in the right hands.'

'No, I mean, how will this affect her mentally? We don't know what those bastards did to her.' Then her eyes filled with tears again when she pictured the scene in the barn. 'You should have seen the state of her, Ruby.'

'I know. Try not to think about it. She'll be OK.'

Ruby didn't say anything further. There was no point offering any more assurances because they just didn't know how Candice would be affected as a result of the time she had spent in captivity.

Crystal's mind drifted to other matters. 'How did you know where I'd gone?' she asked.

Ruby smiled. 'I knew you'd go to meet Justin, especially when I found out you'd already been to his house. I was bloody worried sick. You can be a stubborn cow at times, girl.'

'Sorry,' said Crystal, 'But I had to do something.'

'Don't worry, I'd have probably done the same thing in your position,' said Ruby.

'How did you know where to find me?'

Ruby smiled again. 'Remember when you gave me Justin's address? It was on the leaflet from that takeaway shop.' Crystal nodded in acknowledgement. 'I knew it would probably come in handy so I'm fuckin' glad I kept hold of it.'

'But, surely, Justin's wife didn't tell you where I was meeting him?'

'No, she didn't know. But, after a bit of persuasion, she told us about the barn.'

Despite her worries, Crystal laughed. 'I know your type of persuasion, Ruby.'

'Yeah, that bloody Ray took some persuasion too.'

'I'm amazed you got him involved. You seemed dead against it before. How did you manage to persuade him?'

'Well, let's just say he wanted his secrets to be kept secret.'

'Shit!' said Crystal. 'I bet that didn't go down well.'

'Not really. But, just like you, I had to do something, didn't I?'

Crystal felt a twinge of guilt knowing that Ruby might have lost a good client. 'I'm sorry I put you in that position, Ruby, but thanks for everything you've done.'

Ruby shrugged. 'You're a mate, aren't you? And I know you'd do it for me.' Then her eyes flitted to the doorway, and Crystal looked up to see what she was looking at. 'Talking of the police,' said Ruby as two plain-clothes officers strode into the room.

Crystal and Ruby could tell they were police even though they weren't wearing uniform. Their formal dress, and the way they purposefully approached them, confirmed it.

'Laura Sharples?' asked one of the officers.

'Yes,' said Crystal, nodding.

'We'd like to interview your daughter about what happened. You're welcome to stay with her.'

'The doctors are still with her,' said Crystal.

'OK, well, in that case, we'd also like to have a word with you,' said the same officer, a tall bald man, aged about sixty. 'Do you mind if we do it here?'

'No, that's fine,' said Crystal.

'I'll leave you to it,' said Ruby, getting up from her seat. 'I can go and see if the doctors have finished attending to Candice if you like.'

'Yes, that would be good,' said the police officer before Crystal had a chance to speak.

The officers began to question Crystal, trying to fill in the gaps from the point where she reported Candice missing up to the point where she had ended up rescuing her from the barn. Crystal wasn't really in the mood for this, especially as there was so much she hadn't told the police and she knew she had to be careful not to slip up. But she also knew they were only doing their jobs.

There was no point telling the officers how she had pursued Justin through her discovery of his fast food outlets. It would only complicate matters and might even point the finger of suspicion in her direction, especially as she had remained anonymous when reporting the drug dealing at one of Justin's fast food premises.

In the end she decided it was best to stick to the truth as far as possible but just leave some of it out. So she confessed that she had kept the list after all because she knew it was of value to Justin and might come in handy. Then she told them about Justin arranging to meet her in order to exchange the list for her daughter.

The rest was just as it had happened; she had arrived early, seen Spud's car and followed him to the barn where they had tried to escape with Candice when Justin and his men had turned up. She had almost reached the part where one of Justin's men had shot Spud when the door to the waiting room opened again, and Ruby rushed in.

'I'm so sorry to interrupt,' she said to the officers, 'but there's something my friend needs to know.'

Crystal's heart began to race, suspecting it was something connected to Candice. But then Ruby switched her attention to her, ignoring any protestations from the two police officers, as she said, 'It's Spud, he's just been brought in. He's still alive!'

54

When Crystal arrived at hospital the following day, she noticed the sterile smell straightaway, which highlighted the stark reality of the place. She hadn't given it much thought the previous day as she'd been so preoccupied about Candice and Spud. But now it hit her. There was something unique about the inside of a hospital – all neutral tones and bare walls and floors. It made the place feel cold even though the temperature was on high.

As she drew nearer to the ward she couldn't help but relive Candice's police interview. Her daughter's words had chilled her and made her realise just how terrifying the experience of being abducted had been for a child of eleven.

'So, what happened when you saw the car?' the officer had asked.

'They dragged me inside it and when I screamed they put something in my mouth and blindfolded me. It was dark and I couldn't see where I was going.' Then Candice had turned to her mother and, with trembling lips, had said, 'I was really scared, Mum.'

'What happened next?' asked the officer.

'They took me somewhere. I couldn't see anything but it

smelt like a farm. I kept tripping up and then when we got inside the stink was really bad. It made me feel sick.'

'Did the men hurt you?' asked the officer.

Crystal tensed as her daughter replied, 'A bit when they tied me up, and when one of them slapped me.'

'And what did they look like?'

'They were scary,' said Candice, her voice now cracking, 'And they said they'd hurt me badly if I tried to escape.'

'What happened next?'

By this point Crystal could see her daughter was fighting back tears.

'Can she have a break?' she asked but it seemed that Candice wanted to confide in someone about her ordeal.

'It was scary, Mummy,' she repeated. 'The man had a knife and when they left me I was really frightened. It was dark and full of spiders and rats.'

Seeing her daughter so traumatised made Crystal angry and she felt like crying with her. She noticed the way Candice had called her 'Mummy' instead of 'Mum' and she was worried that this experience would make her regress and could badly affect her for a long time to come.

Eventually she managed to calm Candice down enough to answer the officers' questions but she was glad when they'd finished. Although she knew it was necessary for the police to gather evidence against Justin and his men, it couldn't have been easy for Candice having to relive her ordeal and it certainly wasn't easy for her having to witness it.

She tried to put those thoughts aside. It would do Candice no good to see her stressed; she had to hold it together for her daughter. The hospital had kept Candice in overnight and Crystal was hoping she would be able to take her home today. Once she could get Candice back into a normal routine then maybe her daughter would become more relaxed and start to recover.

Crystal soon reached the side ward where Candice was being kept and she popped her head round the door. Her daughter was fast asleep but Crystal was pleased to see that she was already looking a lot better now that she was clean and fed. A nurse must have seen Crystal going into the ward because she appeared behind her, eager to have a word. The nurse was portly and middle-aged and she seemed to have a friendly, easy-going manner when she spoke.

'She's been sleeping a lot since they brought her in,' she said.

'Yes, she was asleep when I left her last night,' said Crystal.

'It's no wonder. She probably didn't get much sleep in that barn. The poor little thing must have been frightened to death.' Although the nurse was being sympathetic, Crystal could have done without such a harsh reminder of what her daughter had been through. She seemed to pick up on Crystal's discomfort as she quickly changed the conversation. 'She was awake late last night though, feeling hungry, and again this morning. She's eaten well.'

'Good,' said Crystal, forcing a smile.

'You've just missed the consultant, I'm afraid. But there's a junior doctor on the ward. I can get him to have a word with you if you like.'

'Yes, please.'

The nurse left the side ward and Crystal plonked herself down on the chair next to her daughter's bed. She was tempted to grasp Candice's hand in hers but resisted, wary of waking her up. Instead she sat and watched as Candice slept, her chest rising and falling gently and a soft purring sound coming from her mouth each time she exhaled. Seeing her like that, looking so peaceful, brought a tear to Crystal's eye.

The door to the side ward swung open and the junior doctor walked in accompanied by the same friendly nurse as earlier. He looked so young, suddenly making Crystal feel old even though she was still only in her early thirties. She was about to doubt his competence because of his youth but he soon put her mind at ease.

The doctor strode across the room, confidently introducing himself and holding out his hand. 'I'm Doctor Collins.' He pulled up a chair opposite Crystal, his manner friendly without being intrusive, then he said, 'I believe you want to chat about Candice.'

Crystal nodded, afraid to speak in case her voice shook as she was so consumed with worry. The doctor seemed to pick up on her discomfort as he allayed her concerns straightaway.

'OK, we've been able to establish that she hasn't been harmed physically, but obviously it's left her shaken as well as tired and hungry. Doctor Myers would like to keep her in for a further night, purely as a precaution. We're also going to refer her to a psychologist once we've discharged her but it's nothing to worry about. A psychologist will know the best way to help her talk through what happened so that she can come to terms with it.'

He smiled at Crystal and then asked, 'Is there anything you would like to ask?'

'No, I-I think you've covered everything, well, the things I was worried about anyway.'

'Good, glad to hear it,' said the doctor. 'I know an experience like this can be traumatic for the parents as well as the child but hopefully I've put your mind at ease.'

'Yes, yes you have,' said Crystal, smiling back.

When the hospital staff left the ward she heaved a sigh of relief. Thank God it hadn't been as bad as she was dreading. She might not be able to take her home today but at least she knew that she was safe now and that she hadn't come to any physical harm.

For a while longer Crystal sat watching her daughter, feeling overwhelmed with love for this beautiful child of hers. Eventually, when she realised that Candice was likely to be asleep for a while longer she decided to go and see how Spud was getting along.

55

Unlike Candice, Spud was lying in bed, fully awake. When he saw Crystal approach, he looked a little sheepish. But he needn't have; although it was obvious that he had played some part in Candice's abduction, he had also risked his life to save her, so Crystal's initial feeling towards him was one of gratitude. She was still anxious to find out what had happened beforehand though as well as the extent of Spud's involvement.

'How are you?' she asked when she reached his bed.

'Not too bad,' said Spud, his eyes flickering towards the heavy bandaging that reached diagonally across from one of his shoulders to his underarm.

'Where were you hit?' she asked.

'In my chest,' said Spud, pointing to an area where the bandages were slightly stained. Crystal noticed some blood had seeped through.

'Shit!' she said. 'You were lucky.'

'Yeah, it just missed my heart apparently.'

'Shit,' she repeated. 'I thought you were a goner.'

'No. I was awake but I pretended to be dead. I was shit-scared they might shoot me again if I got up.'

'I don't blame you – they probably would have,' Crystal uttered, managing a tight smile.

Then Spud adopted an awkward expression and seemed pensive as though he was deciding on his next words. Finally he spoke. 'I just want to say I'm sorry for everything. And that, well, I haven't been straight with you. When I warned you off Justin it was because I knew he was looking for you.'

Crystal shook her head, not wanting to believe what she was hearing. 'How?'

'Because he told me to find out where you lived. He rang me after you'd been talking to me in the pub that night, but I didn't tell him you were there. It was me who told him where you lived though. Sorry.'

'What?' Crystal shouted, becoming annoyed at this revelation. 'Surely you knew what would happen when you gave him my address!'

'Yeah, well, kind of. I didn't think he'd grab your kid though. And... and... I didn't want to do it, honest. But he made me. Trust me, you don't know what he's like.'

'Oh, I think I do,' said Crystal.

She had a sense of déjà vu, feeling they'd had this conversation before. Then her mind switched to that hotel room and what Justin had done to her, and she shuddered.

'Sorry,' Spud repeated. 'He threatened I'd end up the same way as Holly and Phil.'

'I still can't understand why he had to have Holly killed,' she said.

'She knew too much, same as Phil Thomas did, and Justin doesn't like loose cannons. She was the one who was giving Phil information about you because he paid her. And then Phil let Justin down when he lost you while he was trying to follow you home. Justin thought he was just pissing him about and playing for time while he was on the payroll.'

Crystal recollected Amber's concerns when she revealed that a man had followed her home, and the words of Moira the barmaid who had also been worried. 'Jesus Christ!' she said. 'I can't believe Holly would do that. I mean, I know she was pretty badly hooked on drugs but I wouldn't have thought she'd have sold information about me. And Justin really is a bad bastard, isn't he?' When Spud nodded and frowned, Crystal asked, 'Have the police been to see you yet?'

'No, they left me alone last night while the doctors were patching me up. They're bound to be back today though.'

Crystal's annoyance turned to concern; after all, Spud had done what he had done under threat of extreme violence so she couldn't blame him in a way. 'What will you do? You're gonna be well in the shit, aren't you?'

Spud attempted a shrug but then his face contorted with pain. 'Steady,' said Crystal.

'I dunno,' said Spud, replying to Crystal's first question. 'I was ready to leave Manchester before all this happened. I knew Justin would never leave me alone; it was always just one more job and I'd had enough of it. But now... I don't know.'

Seeing him like that, Crystal actually felt sorry for him. He'd been on the receiving end of Justin's brutality just as she had. 'Look, I should have said thanks. I don't blame you for what you did; not now I know what you were up against. And, at the end of the day, you did save Candice and you put your life on the line to help me and Candice escape.'

Spud looked embarrassed. She guessed he wasn't used to being thanked and for a few moments they both remained silent, the atmosphere between them now awkward. Then a thought occurred to her and she knew she had to voice it before the police arrived.

'Spud,' she said, 'have you thought about turning Queen's evidence?'

'Maybe. I dunno. I'll have to talk to my brief. Anyway, what are you gonna do? You've been charged with theft, haven't you?'

Crystal was amazed at how the news had travelled so fast. 'How do you know?' she asked.

'Justin told me.'

Crystal nodded. It made sense; with Justin's contact in the force he was bound to find out.

She wished Spud hadn't reminded her. She had been thinking that things might improve once Candice was home but with a court appearance hanging over her, she had more problems still to come. If she had to serve time for theft then how would she explain that to her daughter? And how the hell could she look after her from inside prison?

56

Candice had now been home from hospital for a few weeks and she was settling back into life, having just had her twelfth birthday. The visits to the child psychologist were helping and, recently, she'd seemed as though she was getting back to her old self. Crystal wished she could draw comfort from that but she had too many other worries kicking around inside her head.

The date for her appearance at the magistrates' court was drawing closer and she was worried sick. There was a good chance she would serve time, especially in view of her previous convictions for soliciting. Despite her criminal record, she hadn't been in prison before and the idea of it was terrifying. In the past, the most she had received in the way of punishment was a fine.

The prospect of prison was bad enough but the thought of spending time away from Candice was even worse. For weeks she'd fretted over what she would do if that happened until she'd finally reached the conclusion that she would have to make provisions for Candice's care if she was sent down. But that meant having to ask her mother and stepfather to take care of her, which was why she was currently sitting in their living room filled with trepidation.

'There's summat on your mind, isn't there?' asked her mother, Kath.

Crystal gazed across from her seat on the sofa to where Kath was sitting on one of the two matching armchairs. On the other armchair sat her stepfather, Gary, who, despite his kind-heartedness, also had a temper; he did his best to suppress it but there were times when it got the better of him. Crystal had only seen him lose it once or twice but the thought of it made her dread what she had to tell them even more.

'There is actually,' said Crystal.

They both looked keenly at her, their faces expectant, and Crystal felt terrible at the prospect of what she was about to say. She rushed to get it out of the way, skipping the detail while she awaited their reaction.

'I've got to go to court.'

'Court. What the bloody hell for?' asked her stepfather.

'Theft.' She watched her mother's alarmed reaction then said, 'Sorry.' She immediately realised how half-hearted and inadequate her apology sounded.

'What do you mean theft, love? Is it that nightclub you work in? You've not been dipping the till have you?' asked her mother, her tone conveying her need for an explanation that might justify her daughter's actions or at least lessen their impact.

'I don't work in a nightclub, Mum,' said Crystal.

Her voice had become quiet and timid, her head bowed and shoulders slumped, and she was finding it difficult to maintain eye contact.

'What the bloody hell are you on about?' asked Gary.

Again Crystal rushed to get her words out, wanting to unburden herself now she'd finally plucked up the courage to confront them with the truth. 'I've been working as a prostitute. I have been ever since I left home.'

'Prostitute! What the fuck?' asked Gary.

Crystal nodded.

'Are you fuckin' serious?' he yelled.

Crystal nodded again, looking down at the surface of the coffee table, her eyes nervously tracing the outline of a small drop of tea that had spilt when her mother had brought the drinks in.

'Look at me when I'm fuckin' talking to you!' shouted her stepfather, leaning forward in his chair.

'Alright, Gary,' said her mother, reaching across to him and placing her hand gently on his arm. 'Let her speak.'

Crystal dared to look up and carried on speaking. 'I used to be on the game, a street girl.' Her eyes filled with tears as she watched the expressions that traversed her mother's pretty features. Disbelief. Then revulsion. And, finally, disappointment.

'What, you mean…?' asked her mother, but she couldn't finish her sentence.

Crystal said the words for her. 'On the streets, yeah. Aytoun Street; the red light district. Getting in cars with strange men and having sex with them for money.'

'Why the fuck would you want to do that?' demanded Gary. 'You've got a daughter for God's sake! And what about your mother? Is that any way to repay her for everything she's done for you?'

Crystal turned to face him. 'It wasn't always like it is now. When my mum was with Bill it was really bad so I left home.'

'So, is that any reason to fuckin' sell yourself?' he asked, outraged.

'What was I supposed to do?' asked Crystal. 'I was living on the streets. I had no money and nowhere to stay.'

'You could have come home to your mother,' said Gary.

'What? And risk having Bill beat me up again?'

Gary's gaze drifted from Crystal to her mother, the stern expression on his face demanding answers. Crystal followed his gaze. She would never forget the look on her mother's face, the disappointment now replaced by guilt. Neither would Crystal forget that feeling of having let her down.

For a while nobody spoke but then Gary said, 'I think you'd better go, Crystal. Your mother's upset, and we don't need this at our time of life.'

Crystal noticed that, despite his words, his tone had now softened, as though he was acknowledging the part Kath had played in all of this by allowing a monster into her home.

'No, it's OK,' said Kath.

Her voice was shaky and Crystal felt awful. She had never wanted to bring her mother to this, never wanted to make her feel bad because she had lived with a violent man who had struck terror into all of them. Crystal knew her mother had always had a weakness for men but she didn't blame her. All Kath had wanted all along was someone like Gary who would cherish and protect her. She didn't deserve to be reminded of the past because, despite everything, Crystal now realised that she'd always tried her best.

'Laura, I don't want you to go,' she continued. Then she turned to Gary, 'We'll just have to accept it,' she said. 'Laura did what she had to do. I'm sure she didn't want to end up as a...'

Again she couldn't say the word.

'What about the bloody theft, anyway?' asked Gary. 'What's that got to do with any of this? Why did you need to go thieving? Don't those fuckin' tarts earn enough as it is?'

'Gary!' shouted her mother. 'Don't use that sort of language, and let Laura finish what she's saying.'

Crystal could see the compassion in her mother's eyes and she had to hold herself together while she continued her story. 'I turned to drugs but, before you say anything, I'm not on drugs anymore. I went to rehab. I'm not on the game anymore either. I stole the money when I was still on the game from a client who...' she was about to reveal Justin's abuse but then she took in her mother's hurt expression again and knew she couldn't do it '...who wasn't very nice to me,' she continued.

Then she got up from the sofa, knelt on the floor next to her mother's chair and took hold of her hands. In a tear-filled plea, she begged her mother to help her. By now the words were gushing from her. 'I don't know what to do, Mum. If they put me away I might lose Candice. And I'm trying to make things right for her. I've come off the game and got myself clean and now I just want to give her a better life.'

Her mother leant over her, releasing her hands from Crystal's grip. Then she took her in her arms and wept. Sensing her mother's bitterness for the past and remorse for what it had led to, Crystal too lost control and sobbed. While they stayed locked in an emotional embrace full of sadness and regret, Gary slipped from the room and left them to it.

57

A few weeks later, Crystal was standing in the witness box inside Manchester Magistrates' Court. Her friend, Ruby, was in the public gallery but her mother and stepfather hadn't attended as they were looking after Candice. This place had become familiar to her during her years as a working girl but this time she hoped it would be her last. She had sworn to herself that, no matter what the outcome, she would get her life together.

Because she had already admitted to the police that she had stolen Justin's money, Crystal had felt she had no choice but to enter a guilty plea. Otherwise, she knew that the magistrates were bound to believe the police account of events rather than her own.

The prosecution had also brought forward Justin as a witness. The sight of him sickened her. She'd had to watch while he acted outraged; claiming that she had taken his money after they'd met in a bar and agreed to a one-night stand. But she wasn't bothered that he'd glossed over the fact that he had spent the night with a prostitute. She knew it wouldn't be too long before he was facing the Crown Court as the accused for far more serious crimes than hers.

Amazingly, Justin hadn't mentioned the theft of his credit

card or the fact that she had tried to blackmail him. She put the credit card down to the fact that he was using one with a false ID but she wasn't sure about the blackmail. Maybe it was all part of him trying to convince the world that he didn't sleep with prostitutes or perhaps he had more pressing matters on his mind.

Finally, when all the evidence had been heard and the witnesses interviewed, the magistrates retired to make a decision. She tried to wait patiently in the side room but her mind was wandering, preoccupied with everything that had happened in the weeks leading up to her court appearance.

Candice didn't even know that her mother was attending court. How could she tell her daughter that she had stolen money from a client while working as a prostitute? But her confession to her mother had been fruitful as well as painful. They'd spoken for over an hour with Crystal disclosing to her mother most of what had happened since she had left home and Kath apologising for all she had been through, which she attributed to her ex-partner Bill's treatment of them.

After a long and emotional discussion Kath had reassured Crystal that no matter what happened she would make sure Candice was taken care of and that she would talk to Gary about it. Thankfully, even though Crystal's stepfather had gone ballistic when he'd found out she was a prostitute, he did eventually come round.

Crystal didn't know what her mother had said to Gary but since that day he had never spoken to her in that way again. Instead he had reassured her that he and Kath would take care of Candice and they had also agreed not to tell

Candice anything unless absolutely necessary so, unless Crystal was sent down, her daughter would never know.

One thing she was glad about was that Spud had turned Queen's evidence as she had suggested. Currently, the case against Justin and his cohorts was awaiting trial at the Crown Court but, from what Crystal had learnt via Ruby and her friend on the force, Spud had told the police everything he knew.

Crystal had also handed the list of names to the police, which would serve as evidence. From what Crystal had been told, the police were confident that they had enough to nail Justin and the rest of his gang including the corrupt police officer, Roger Purvis.

Eventually Crystal was called back into court and told to stand in the dock while the magistrates announced their verdict. The chairman of the magistrates, a beady-eyed man in his late thirties stared across at her and announced the guilty verdict. Although it didn't come as a surprise in view of her guilty plea, the word still struck terror into her. The prospect of spending time in prison was now becoming more real.

The chairman then asked her to make a statement of mitigation. Crystal was ready for this as her solicitor had talked her through it but she still felt a shudder of fear at the thought of having to speak in front of the court again. This time it would be worse, because she wasn't just answering questions about what had happened; she was, in effect, begging the court for leniency. She cleared her throat and, trying to ignore her shaking legs, began to speak.

'I'm trying to turn my life around. I know the prosecution

have told you about me being on the game and addicted to drink and drugs but that was all in the past. I went to rehab at the end of last year and I haven't taken any drugs since.'

She paused, trying to steady her nerves, and giving the magistrates a chance to take in what she had said. Then she continued. 'I've got a twelve-year-old daughter. She's just started secondary school and I want to make a good life for her. That's why I came off the game. We're living on benefits at the moment but I've got big plans for the future. I want to start my own business and...'

The chairman cut in, 'OK, thank you. That will be all.'

Then he turned to the magistrates on either side of him, each one in turn, and whispered something. The lady to the left of him whispered something back then, for a few moments, the three of them sat huddled, whispering to each other while the court awaited their decision.

Crystal could feel her palms sweating and her heart was beating frantically. Around her people were also whispering, their tones gradually becoming louder as they waited for the magistrates. Crystal wished they'd hurry up and speak. She just wanted it over now, whatever they decided, and she'd resigned herself to facing the consequences of her crime.

Eventually the chairman asked for order in the court and Crystal held her breath, waiting to hear what he would say. But then he referred back to the prosecution and Crystal let out a big puff of disappointment as the prosecutor read out a list of her previous convictions. Apart from her frustration, it was embarrassing hearing her life of crime aired in open court.

She was almost relieved when it was the chairman's turn to speak again. At least she was a step nearer to finding out her fate. But she had to wait a while yet.

'Ladies and gentleman,' said the chairman. 'You have heard the evidence presented before you today. You have heard from the prosecution and defence and also from the various witnesses involved in the case, and the defendant has been pronounced guilty. We have also heard from the defendant herself who admits to her crime but tells us that she has since made attempts to turn her life around.'

He then shuffled some papers in front of him, pulled one out of the pile and referred to it. 'The defendant attended a rehabilitation programme in December 2011 and since that date she has been free from drugs. The defendant has voluntarily submitted herself for drugs testing and that test has come back negative.'

He then pulled another piece of paper from the pile and quoted from it. 'She has also been attending a business management course for several weeks and her probation officer reports that she is committed to the course and has received good feedback from her tutors.'

Crystal thought he would waffle on forever but then he suddenly announced the sentence: six months. Six months! How could she be away from Candice for all that time? Crystal swallowed but before the despair sank in, he carried on his speech.

'However, in view of the fact that the defendant seems to be turning her life around and is committed to improving the quality of life for her daughter, I don't think a custodial sentence would be beneficial for either the defendant or her daughter. It is far more important that they continue to rebuild their lives as a family and I am therefore prepared to suspend the sentence for two years.'

Crystal was overjoyed and her eyes felt steamy with unshed tears. The chairman then went on to list the conditions attached to the suspended sentence but Crystal didn't take in everything he was saying. She was too busy rejoicing in her imminent release as she listened to the mutterings in the public gallery and heard her friend, Ruby, let out a loud cheer.

By the time she left the court Crystal was crying tears of joy. She couldn't wait to ring her parents with the good news. Then she would rush back to their home to pick up Candice. But before she could begin to rebuild her life there was one last thing she needed to do, and she knew she wouldn't settle until she had done it.

58

Crystal felt an extreme sadness as she watched the mourners gathered round the grave of Tim O'Brien, the man who Gilly had killed for abusing her. She had chosen her vantage point carefully under the guise of visiting the grave of a loved one. She was near enough to view the proceedings but not too close that she was being intrusive.

Attending the funeral was a frail, elderly couple who looked to be well into their seventies. She guessed they were possibly his parents, and she assumed that the two other couples in their forties or fifties were his siblings and their spouses.

Tim O'Brien didn't appear to have had any friends, and the fact that his absence had been reported by a neighbour led her to believe that his relationship with his family was probably a distant one too. Apart from the half a dozen people, there were no other mourners. But at least he had more family in attendance than Gilly had had at his funeral.

She watched as the coffin was lowered into the ground, and flinched as the elderly lady let out a piercing screech then buried her head into her husband's chest. He put his arm round her awkwardly, fighting back tears himself.

The rest of the mourners remained stoic. To Crystal it was upsetting to think there were so few people who actually cared about Tim O'Brien. She dreaded the thought of being so unloved that hardly anybody came to her funeral.

As she observed the scene before her Crystal couldn't help but recall the events leading up to Tim O'Brien's death. The hours Gilly had spent in the red light district searching for the man who had abused her. Gilly's rage at what the man had done. His obsession with getting revenge. And the part she had played.

Crystal had gone along with it all; too obsessively in love with Gilly to question his actions and too drugged up to think rationally. She had even passed him the knife that killed Tim O'Brien and later helped him cover up the murder.

While she had been addicted to drugs she hadn't focused too much on what had happened. But in her new sober state the guilt was tearing away at her. Crystal also felt bad about what had happened to Gilly, knowing she shouldn't have fled the scene. But she had tried to put that guilt behind her. He had been part of a bad phase of her life that she refused to revisit. She couldn't be held responsible for Gilly's self-destruction and at least she had turned things around so that she wouldn't end up the same way.

Crystal knew Tim O'Brien had done a bad thing and she hated to think that he might have abused countless other women as well as her. A part of her had wanted to expose him for what he was, perhaps through a letter to the press from an incognito prostitute who had suffered at his hands. He deserved to have his memory tarnished. But she didn't think his family deserved that.

Witnessing their sorrow, after waiting for so many years to bury him, made her realise that the family had suffered enough and she felt terrible for her part in their suffering. His crime wasn't their crime and yet they had been punished for it.

Crystal no longer felt the need for vengeance. It had taken her a long time to realise that revenge wasn't always the way forward.

Before long it was time to go. The mourners were leaving the graveside and Crystal felt a degree of atonement for finally reporting his death and the location of the body through an anonymous call to the police. Although she would always carry the guilt of his death, at least she had now made sure he had had the chance of a proper burial.

Epilogue – Three Years Later

It was almost three years since Justin Foster, Roger Purvis and all their cohorts had made court appearances for a number of offences ranging from drug trafficking to murder and perverting the course of justice. Thanks to the evidence that Laura and Spud had given in court, as well as a lot of police work, all of the men were now serving lengthy sentences, and Laura was finally able to put it all behind her.

She gazed around the upmarket fashion shop where she was browsing through outfits with her fifteen-year-old daughter, Candice.

'What about this one, Mum?' asked Candice.

Laura looked at the dress, low-cut and short. No, she couldn't possibly wear that. She'd be sending out all the wrong signals. The irony made her smile to herself. Just a few years ago that would have been exactly the sort of outfit she would have chosen. In fact, it would have been a big improvement on the sort of clothing she used to wear, which was generally cheap and tacky.

Maybe that's what Candice had in mind when she picked it out for her or maybe she was seeing it through the eyes of a teenage girl. Laura thought it sad how youngsters all felt the need to go out wearing next to nothing these days. But that was no longer Laura's style.

'No, love, I don't think it's right for me,' she said, fingering the high-quality garments.

She continued working her way along the rail, finally settling on a pair of tailored trousers and a matching top. Made from chiffon and lined with silk, the top was elegant and dressy without being too over the top. She glanced at the price tag; ninety-five pounds for a top, but it was worth it for quality, she thought.

Laura cast her mind back to the journalist who had made such an impression on her all those years ago: Maddy, the woman who Gilly, Laura's former pimp and lover, had fallen for. She was classy as well as attractive, and her stylish, tailored clothing formed a part of that image.

It was the sort of image Laura was trying to cultivate for herself now that she had moved away from her life of prostitution and drug addiction. She was amazed at how people could form a certain opinion of you just by looking at your clothing, makeup and hairstyle, and she was enjoying the way she was now perceived.

And the image she had chosen was in keeping with her new status in life. Thanks to Ruby and her offer of a loan, Laura had been able to fulfil her dream of setting up a business without the need to carry on blackmailing people. She'd almost paid the loan off already, and it had been far less stressful than dealing with the fallout from blackmail and extortion.

As Laura made her way to the changing rooms with the trousers and top, and another two alternative outfits that she wasn't quite as keen on, she became carried away with her thoughts. Yes, all in all she was quite pleased with the way her life had turned out. And it was the perfect choice of business for Laura and her new persona.

She loved the classy range of clothing she had stocked in both this shop and the other branch that she had recently opened in Wilmslow. Her only association with her former life was in the name she had chosen for the shops: Crystals of Manchester and Crystals of Wilmslow.

She'd amused herself by stealing the idea for the names from the irritating former client, Nigel Swithen, who had made such a show of having two upmarket restaurants: Swithen's, Deansgate and Swithen's, Alderley Edge. For a shop, the name Crystals actually sounded elegant and chic and, rather than reminding her of her days on the street, it made her reflect on how far she had come and how grateful she was for all her achievements.

Laura was finally ready to move on, which was why she had joined a dating site and was now choosing an outfit to wear on her first date. For the past three years she had concentrated on rebuilding other areas of her life but now she felt ready to meet someone special, with the blessing of Candice.

When she thought about the prospect of going on a date, Laura felt strangely nervous. It was weird to think that meeting strange men used to be an everyday occurrence and yet the prospect of it now filled her with trepidation. But then, she supposed that it was different somehow. She was no longer looking for a quick earner; now she was looking to meet someone who would both love and respect her, and that was far more important.

When she got inside the changing room she tried on

her first choice of outfit straightaway. If it suited her then she'd have it; she couldn't see any point in wasting time on second choices.

Laura was pleased when she saw her reflection in the mirror. The outfit was the perfect accompaniment to her chic hairstyle and subtle, high-end makeup. Even to her own eyes she appeared attractive in a sophisticated way. But she'd see what Candice's reaction was before she made the final decision.

'Well, what do you think?' she asked as she stepped outside the changing cubicle and twirled around in the outfit.

'You look lovely, Mum,' said Candice and Laura could tell from her tone of voice and enthusiastic smile that she wasn't just humouring her.

'Thanks, love,' she said, planting a kiss on the top of her head.

'No, thank you,' said Candice.

Laura stood back and looked into her face, puzzled. 'Why?' she asked.

'For being the best mum in the world. I'm so proud of you,' said Candice.

Laura smiled then turned away. She didn't want her daughter to see the tears of joy that clouded her eyes. At last, she'd achieved the very thing that she had wanted most of all from life; she had made her daughter proud.

Acknowledgements

Out of the three books to date in The Working Girls series Crystal has been the easiest and most pleasurable to write. I'm really excited about this one and it feels great to be reaching publication date especially following the success of the first two books.

I have so many people to thank for their help in getting this book out there and for all their support along the way. The staff at Aria Fiction have been brilliant as usual. In particular I would like to mention Hannah Smith, my developmental editor who, once again, has made some excellent suggestions on how to improve the novel. My copy editor, Helena Newton, has also done a top class job in ensuring that no mistakes or inconsistencies escape her keen eye.

All of the staff at Aria are wonderful at marketing and promotion and they support their authors in so many ways. As well as Hannah, I'd like to add a few more names to the list: Vicky Joss, Nikky Ward, Laura Palmer and Rhea Kurien.

Thanks to my agent Jo Bell of Bell Lomax Moreton for all her help and sound advice and to all the staff at Bell Lomax Moreton for their support. I am also grateful to my fellow authors for their support and camaraderie.

I am taking this opportunity to thank the Writers Bureau once again for their excellent creative writing course and for featuring me in last years' advertising campaign as one of their success stories. I recently had the pleasure of meeting their principal, Susie Busby, who kindly attended one of my book launch parties.

Big thanks to all my dedicated readers who have purchased copies of The Working Girls series of novels and any of my previous books. I hope this latest one will give you hours of reading pleasure. Thanks also to the book blogging and reviewing community who are a valuable asset for both authors and readers.

I would like to extend my gratitude to everyone who has assisted me with the research for this and other books, namely the Manchester Magistrates' Court for help with this book, and MASH and Lifeshare for help with the forthcoming two books in the series, Amber and Sapphire.

Lastly, I would like to thank my children, family and friends for your continued support. I am lucky to be surrounded by so many wonderfully loyal and caring people.

About the Author

HEATHER BURNSIDE started her writing career more than twenty years ago when she began to work as a freelance writer while studying for a writing diploma. As part of her studies Heather wrote the first chapters of her debut novel, *Slur*. She later ran a writing services business before returning to *Slur*, which became the first book in the Riverhill Trilogy. Heather followed the Riverhill Trilogy with the Manchester Trilogy then her current series, The Working Girls.

You can find out more about the author by signing up to the Heather Burnside mailing list for the latest updates including details of new releases and book bargains, or by following any of the links below.

Sign up to my mailing list
www.eepurl.com/CP6YP

Find me on Twitter
twitter.com/heatherbwriter

Find me on Facebook
www.facebook.com/HeatherBurnsideAuthor/

Visit my website
www.heatherburnside.com